CRUEL FORTUNE

CRUEL FORTUNE

CRUEL BOOK TWO

K.A. LINDE

Visit my website at
www.kalinde.com

Join my newsletter for free books and exclusive content!
www.kalinde.com/subscribe

Cover Designer: Sarah Hansen, Okay Creations., www.okaycreations.com
Photography: Lauren Perry, www.perrywinklephotography.com
Editor: Jovana Shirley, Unforeseen Editing, www.unforeseenediting.com

ISBN-13: 978-1948427258

ALSO BY K. A. LINDE

CRUEL

One Cruel Night

Cruel Money ✦ Cruel Fortune

WRIGHTS

The Wright Brother ✦ The Wright Boss ✦ The Wright Mistake

The Wright Secret ✦ The Wright Love ✦ The Wright One

AVOIDING SERIES

Avoiding Commitment ✦ Avoiding Responsibility

Avoiding Temptation ✦ Avoiding Intimacy ✦ Avoiding Decisions

RECORD SERIES

Off the Record ✦ On the Record

For the Record ✦ Struck from the Record

ALL THAT GLITTERS SERIES

Diamonds ✦ Gold ✦ Emeralds ✦ Platinum ✦ Silver

TAKE ME DUET

Take Me for Granted ✦ Take Me with You

BLOOD TYPE SERIES

Blood Type ✦ Blood Match ✦ Blood Cure

ASCENSION SERIES

The Affiliate ✦ The Bound ✦ The Consort ✦ The Society

Following Me

To 'The Devil Wears Prada'
Sometimes, you forget who you were
to become what you're meant to be.

PROLOGUE

PENN — ONE YEAR EARLIER

I rushed out of the small Charleston airport and straight to the empty taxi line. I jerked open the door to the first cab, tossed my bag inside, and then followed in a hurry.

"Where to?" the cab driver leisurely asked. As if he had all day.

But I didn't.

"Montgomery Gallery on King Street."

"Oh, you know the Montgomerys?" he asked with a cheery smile as he slowly merged into the nonexistent traffic. "They're good people."

"We're acquainted," I told him.

Though I wanted to tell him to put his foot through the pedal. I'd just flown almost a thousand miles, I hadn't slept in three days, and I was in an almost-manic state of urgency. I didn't want to wait another half hour to get into the city and finally see Natalie.

It was bad enough that I'd let her walk out of my life after she found out about the bet. Three days had been long enough for her to go on thinking that I didn't care for her.

1

That she was only a bet. That I wasn't going to man up and make this right.

She was probably face-first into a container of icing. And I hated—*hated*—being the one who had brought her that pain. I should have told her about the bet long ago. Long before she had to eavesdrop on the information and come to her own conclusions about the whole thing.

Because none of this had been a lie for me. I'd only entered the bet as a joke. I wanted to spend time with Natalie, and I wanted my friends to stay out of it. Then, when Katherine had gotten serious about the whole thing, it was too late. It never should have gotten this far.

Now, here I was, in her quaint, seaside Southern town, desperate to make amends. I couldn't let Natalie slip through my fingers. And I wouldn't go down without a fight.

I tapped my foot impatiently as we drove down King Street. It was beautiful in a completely different way than New York, but I could hardly appreciate it. Not now. Not like this.

"All right," the cabbie finally said, pulling over. "That's Montgomery Gallery right there."

"Thank you." I handed him money for the fare with a generous tip and all but vaulted out of the car.

I saw the Open sign in the large floor-to-ceiling window to the gallery and burst through the white door. The space had a generous display of artwork on large pillars and lining the room. Thankfully, it was empty of people. Only one woman stood at the back. She turned to greet me and then stopped.

"Penn?" Amy Montgomery, Natalie's best friend, asked in surprise.

"Where is she?"

"What are you doing here?"

"I'm here to win her back."

"Penn...no," she said with a shake of her head. "You shouldn't be here. You shouldn't do this."

"Where is she, Amy?"

Her body went rigid, and she crossed her arms over her chest. "Are you even listening to what I'm saying? Natalie doesn't want to see you. You should go home and live a life of abject misery, like you deserve."

"You're right. I should, but I can't. She has to know how I feel."

"Does she?" Amy asked. "Or do you just want to force your feelings on her? Have you even thought about what she's going through right now?"

"Of course I have. That's why I'm here. We need to talk. We need to clear the air. I can't let her go on like this, thinking that she means nothing to me. When she means *everything* to me."

Amy's eyes were like fire. "You *bet* on her, Penn. I told her to have some fun with you and not let her heart get broken. And, now, she's back here because you did exactly that. I warned her from *day one* that you were trouble. I know exactly the kind of guy that you are, Penn Kensington. I'm not going to stand back and let you fuck with her heart some more. Get the fuck out of my gallery and *stay away from her.*"

"Amy, that's enough," a soft voice said from a back door that I hadn't even noticed. "I'll talk to him."

"Nat, no. Let me handle this," Amy said.

"It's okay." Natalie patted Amy's arm. "He came all this way. I can at least hear what he has to say."

"Don't believe a word of it," Amy hissed low.

She stepped past Amy and finally moved into my line of vision. She was dressed in jeans and a white T-shirt. Her feet were bare, and her hair was tucked back into a slick ponytail. I'd never seen her dressed like this before. Normally, she was completely boho or dressed to the nines. This was...subdued.

3

She wore no makeup, not that she needed it. But I could tell there were circles under her eyes, and they looked puffy, like she'd been crying recently.

"I'll be in the back," Amy said with a sigh and then disappeared through the back door.

Natalie crossed her arms. "What do you want, Penn?"

"I want you back, Natalie."

"Well, that's not going to happen."

I took a step forward. "I know I made a mistake. I know I should have never made that bet. But I have never felt this way about anyone in my entire life."

"But you *did* make that bet," she said tightly.

"I know. And I can apologize until I'm blue in the face if that will make it right with you. I just can't envision a world in which this ruins us. In which you walk away and don't see that we're perfect for each other."

"All I see is someone who flew out here, thinking a grand gesture would fix everything," she said crisply.

"You know that's not true. I'm not just telling you what I want you to hear. If it were all a lie, why would I even be here, Natalie?"

"Because you get everything you want in your life, and I'm the only thing that walked away of my own volition."

"I'm standing here because I want to make this work. I want us to work. You might delude yourself into thinking this was all a bet, but it was real. Every night we spent together in that house was real. How I feel for you is real. We have perfect chemistry. We work so well together." I took another step forward and grasped her hand. "Natalie, I've fallen in love with you."

She wrenched her hand back and glared at me. I could see the emotions warring through her. "How can you even say that to me?"

"Because it's the truth."

"What is the truth?" she snapped at me. "The truth means nothing to you. All you ever do is lie and manipulate to get your way. You have no idea what is true, and you have no idea what love is."

"You know that's not true. You feel it, too."

"Maybe I did," she said, her voice cracking. "Maybe I fell in love with you. But what does that matter now after what you did to me? How can you ever make that right?"

"I'll do anything to make it right, Natalie. Just give me the opportunity."

Her face crumpled, and she sniffled. "God, I can't believe you're really here."

"Of course I'm here. I couldn't let you walk away, thinking that I didn't feel the same way. We can make this work. We can."

"How?" she asked, brushing away a stray tear. "Tell me how this works. In what reality does an Upper East Side playboy and the help work out? Because I don't see it."

"Because none of that matters. The only thing that matters is how you and I feel."

"But it does matter." Her brilliant blue eyes lifted to mine. "Love isn't enough."

"Natalie…"

"If it were just us—right here, right now—maybe it would be different," she said. "Maybe it would be happily ever after. But it's not like that. It's not that at all. How we feel is not the only issue here."

"I know it's not, but we can conquer anything together. I know we can."

She paced away from me, shaking her head. She was clearly conflicted, but I knew that I could get through to her. I could reach her. Have her see that we could work because I knew we could. I'd never been more certain about anything.

"The first time we met, you said that your deepest,

darkest secret was that you hated your family and their expectations. You said you wanted to live a different life. Well, it's six years later, Penn, and as much as you think you've gotten out, you're still living that life. You still live on the Upper East Side. You still hang out with the same crew. You're still making bets, seducing women, and ruining lives. There is nothing different about your life."

"You're different."

She laughed hollowly. "But, if we were together, I'd have to live that life, too."

I paused, hearing what she was saying. I was a full package. I didn't just come with me and my puppy, Totle. It was so much more. And she was finally seeing how horrible it was. Something I'd known for so long.

"So, if it were just me and you," she whispered, "then... maybe. But it's not. And it never will be. You will always have to deal with your mother and friends and the Upper East Side. You'll always be in the public eye. You'll always have to deal with secrets and drama and skeletons in the closet and all of this stuff that I can't even comprehend."

"We don't have to deal with any of that," I tried to assure her.

"You're right. We don't. But you do."

"Natalie, please, listen to me. I don't need any of that. I only need you."

"I wish I could believe you," she said, taking a step backward. "But I don't. You can't escape the Upper East Side, Penn. You tried and failed. So, how the hell would I be able to get away?"

I froze in place and stared at this beautiful woman who I had completely fallen for. And I realized...she was right.

I hated my life. I hated the obligations and drama and expectations. I wanted out. I'd wanted out for a very long time. But I hadn't gotten away.

"We both know the answer," she said softly.

"But I love you," I said one more time in desperation.

She nodded as a tear trickled down her cheek. "That's not enough. Not after what we went through and what you did. There's no future in which I come back to New York with you. Your mother hates me. Your friends hate me. I don't belong in that world…and you do."

I opened my mouth to contradict her, but I couldn't seem to do it. I wanted her in my world. I wanted her there desperately. But, if I hated my life and didn't want to live in it, then how could I blame her?

"So, please, just go." She brushed more tears from her cheeks. "Don't call or write or try to see me again. I can't handle being near you."

Gallantly, I swept her hand into my own and placed a tender kiss on it. Just as I had done the very first time we met. "I wish it were different."

She choked back tears. "Just…go."

I didn't want to go. I wanted to wrap her up in my arms and shut the rest of the world out. To make her see that this was all that mattered.

But never once in my entire life had *love* mattered. Not with my drill-sergeant mother or alcoholic father or train-wreck brother. Not with any women in my life or even the crew. We were bound by loyalty and secrets, not love. Not really. Why had I thought Natalie would be any different?

PART I
IT ALL STARTED IN A BOARD
ROOM IN MANHATTAN

NATALIE

1

Natalie,

I spoke with Gillian last week and confirmed the remaining details for your New York trip. We're both so excited to see you and celebrate the release of *BET ON IT*. It's been a year in the making. Hard to believe that it's finally here.

I've attached the itinerary that Gillian sent over and penciled in our lunch to discuss your next book. I am interested to hear all your brilliant ideas.

If you need anything or have questions, I'm always a phone call away. Congratulations, Natalie! I'm so proud of you!

Regards,

Caroline Liebermann

Whitten, Jones, & Liebermann Literary

Fwd:

Caroline,

Here is the finalized itinerary for Natalie. I hope to see you at the party as well.

Best,

Gillian Kent

Senior Editor

Warren Publishing

Itinerary

Sunday

1:20 p.m. Flight—ticket attached

Monday

10:30 a.m. Warren tour

11:00 a.m. Warren meeting

7:30 p.m. Warren dinner @ Twig

Tuesday

12:00 p.m. Lunch w/Caroline @ Norma's (You'll love it!)

6:00 p.m. *BET ON IT* release party @ Club 360

Wednesday

12:00–4:00 p.m. Signing @ The Strand on Broadway

8:00 p.m. *Hamilton*

Thursday

7:30 a.m. Flight—ticket attached

I stared down at my phone, then back up at the Warren Publishing building on Fifth Avenue, then back at my phone, and then back up to the building.

"Would you chill out, Nat?" Amy muttered next to me. "This is clearly the right place."

Of course it was. With its distinct, flourishing W that

looked like two crossed Vs with a loop off of the last one. I'd dreamed about this moment my whole life, and now that it was here, I didn't feel excited or relieved or giddy. I felt sick mostly. Really sick. Like, at any moment, the stress and anxiety of knowing that I was going to release a book tomorrow might overwhelm me.

"I know it is. I just can't believe this is happening," I finally said.

"Your dreams are all coming true. What's wrong with that?"

"Nothing. Except for the fact that all I've done since I finished the edits on *BET ON IT* is write a few paragraphs and delete them. Rinse and repeat. Now, my agent, my editor, and the entire publishing team at Warren are going to want to know what I'm writing next. And I haven't written anything."

Amy rolled her big brown eyes. "Just be a diva about it and tell them that genius only strikes when it's ready. You aren't beholden to them. God knows I've worked with enough artists to know that. Your publisher should, too."

Amy was probably right. But it didn't lessen my nerves an ounce.

Not the least of all because I was back in this city.

My eyes scanned the skyscrapers, dirty sidewalks, crush of taxis, and jittery, frazzled pedestrians rushing to and fro. A year ago, I'd thought that this would be my home. That, despite getting fired from my job as a vacation home watcher for the mayor of New York City, I'd still land on my feet here in this beautiful, crazy city.

But, now, when I looked around at all the hustle and bustle, all the glamour of the city that never sleeps, all I saw was *him*.

Penn Kensington.

My heart lurched uncomfortably in my chest. I didn't like

to think about him. Or what he'd done to me. Or how he'd used me. Again.

But being here...it was hard not to see him on every street corner.

Those all-knowing blue eyes. The dark hair that he'd constantly mussed as he furiously wrote philosophical musings into his leather-bound notebook. The shape of his muscular body. The habit of slipping his hands into his pockets and staring straight into my soul. His smile, his laugh, the way he'd insisted on teaching me how to sail, how to think, how to learn. Not to mention, his tiny Italian grey-hound puppy, Totle. Every little thing about him that had made me fall head over heels, madly in love with him.

And how it had all shattered into pieces a year ago.

"You're thinking about him again," Amy said quietly. She touched my shoulder as if she were trying to reel in a kicked dog.

"I'll be fine." I cleared my blurred vision and shook away the stray scraps of him from my imagination. "Anyway, I guess I should probably head inside."

Amy gave me one last concerned look before nodding. "Damn straight. You're going to rock this."

"You're sure you don't want to take the tour with me?"

"And give up shopping on Fifth Avenue? Are you crazy?"

I chuckled. "You are an enigma."

"I'll look for something nice for you. Maybe some Louboutins of your own." She winked.

"Don't you dare!"

Amy cackled. "That'll be the day."

"You're ridiculous."

"And you love me."

"I do."

"Remember that you're a star, this book is going to blow up, and they should be wooing you. Not the other way around." Amy smacked my ass. "Now, get on in there and be the rock star you already are."

"I'll meet you for lunch," I called out to her as she sashayed down Fifth Avenue toward Bergdorf Goodman.

Amy waved her hand in response.

With a deep breath, I yanked on the large gold handle, heaved open the glass door, and entered Warren Publishing. My heels clicked on the white marble floor as I stared, awestruck at the massive entrance. It looked more like a ballroom in a European palace than the foyer of a publishing house. Marble columns lined the room with decorative molding festooned around the perimeter. An enormous domed ceiling was on display high above, painted with a life-sized mural of cherubs enjoying a summer's day. The entire effect was stunning, if not a bit overwhelming.

"Natalie!"

I startled out of my trance and found my editor, Gillian, striding confidently toward me. She was in her mid-thirties with short, dark hair that swept across her forehead, square black glasses, and bright red lipstick. She was tall and wiry in a straight black pantsuit.

She vigorously shook my hand. "It's so good to finally meet you! I recognized you right away with that silver hair. I love it. I keep telling my wife to dye her hair that color."

I reflexively fingered my silvery-white signature locks. I'd dyed it that color in college, and it had stuck. I'd thought about chopping it all off last fall when I got home, but I couldn't do it.

"Thanks, Gillian. I'm so glad to finally meet you."

"I feel like we've known each other for years," Gillian said. She gestured for me to follow her out of the main entrance, and we walked toward an array of elevators. "I'm glad we were able to get this to work out."

"Me too."

"How are you feeling about tomorrow?" she asked as we stepped into an empty elevator. She pressed a button, and the doors slid closed.

"Nervous," I admitted.

"Me, too. Always am on release days. Even ones I know are going to go crazy, like yours. The preorder numbers are through the roof, and the early reviews are spectacular. But still…nerves!"

I laughed at Gillian's effusive manner. We'd had a few calls leading up to this point, and she had always seemed over the top then, too, but she was practically larger than life in person.

"Okay. We don't have a ton of time for a tour. But I want you to see my favorite things and then meet the team. Sound good?"

I nodded. And as Gillian took me around the various divisions of Warren Publishing, I wondered why I had ever been nervous about it. She was lively and eager to introduce me to everyone. In person, we were as close as we had been on the phone. Everyone seemed excited to meet me. It actually felt like coming home. Like I could just open up my laptop and get to work.

"And this is the Bookshelf," she said as we stepped up to a small bookshelf lined with forward-facing books. "This is where all the new releases are held."

And there at the center was *BET ON IT* with its intense blue cover and cleverly placed white letters with a little tagline that read, *Based on a true story.* At the bottom was the pen name I'd chosen: Olivia Davies.

I'd wanted to use Natalie Bishop. I'd always envisioned my own name on the book, but *this* book, this one right here, it wasn't possible. Not when Penn or his mother or any of his friends could pick it up and see it had pieces of what had happened woven into the pages.

So, I'd used my middle name and my mother's maiden name. It didn't feel like *me* quite yet. Even as Gillian introduced me as Olivia to the rest of the team. *She* knew me as Natalie because we'd worked together for a year, but it wasn't widely known, and I wanted to keep it that way.

It was why I wasn't going out on a book tour for this book, to my publisher's chagrin. I'd agreed to one book party and one signing—no pictures allowed—while I was in the city. Lord help us all that they didn't ruin everything.

"Would you mind signing it?" Gillian asked, holding out a Sharpie.

I took it reverently and then signed my name on the inside. I'd practiced signing as Olivia, so I wouldn't mess it up, and seeing it there like that made me glad that I had.

"Magic," I whispered.

"It's perfect! Now, let's head up to our meeting, and then you'll be free until dinner."

I placed the book back on the Bookshelf and then followed Gillian upstairs to the meeting room. I braced myself for questions about what I was working on and the lies I was surely going to tell. I had other books that I'd tried to work on. Plus, I had my road-trip book that I had started writing last year. I'd put it aside to work on *BET ON IT* and was glad I'd done so. Now, I didn't know how to tell them that I had nothing else. That my muse had vanished as swiftly as I'd finished this story.

I hoped that I wouldn't have to admit that today.

"The lady of the hour," Gillian called excitedly as she entered the room, "Olivia Davies."

I laughed and stepped into the conference room. My heart was in my throat at the splatter of applause from everyone at Warren. They all stood up from their seats and came over to say hello to me. I was just moving up to the head of the room with Gillian to take my seat when a side door opened, and a figure ducked his head into the conference room.

"Sorry I'm late. Traffic was hell."

My eyes lifted to meet his as I realized that I recognized that voice. I took in the black suit that molded to his body, the award-winning smile, smooth brown skin, and dark chocolate-brown eyes that I'd been certain I wouldn't see here. Because he didn't work for Warren Publishing. He worked with hedge funds. *Not* the publishing company that was his namesake.

"Lewis?" I gasped.

When he took in my shock, he smirked. "Hey, gorgeous."

NATALIE

2

*M*y stomach dropped out of my body. It was the same sensation as getting to the top of a roller coaster and free-falling into oblivion. Sudden and total paralyzing fear ripped through me.

Because this wasn't supposed to happen.

No one from last year was supposed to know that I was in New York. I'd been certain that I could get in and out of the city in a matter of days without seeing any of the crew or dealing with any of my emotional baggage. For one of the people who was the cause of all of it to stride right into my meeting, I couldn't even begin to process it.

And Lewis was definitely one of the causes. Penn's best friend and one of his crew who had been in on the little bet I was the subject of last year.

Admittedly, Lewis was a Warren. There had always been a chance he'd be here. But I'd thought it was so small as to be infinitesimal. I'd always gotten the impression from him that publishing was almost a hobby for his family of billionaires. A fun pet project but nothing with which to be concerned. They had much more important things to concern themselves with. Lewis had once likened his real family business to putting hotels on Boardwalk.

Except…now, he was here.

In my meeting.

And it couldn't fucking be a coincidence.

"Olivia, you know…Lewis Warren?" Gillian asked with a mix of shock and apprehension in her normally cheerful voice.

"Olivia," he drawled. He arched an eyebrow at my pen name.

"No," I answered at once.

"No?" he asked from those too-perfect lips and that too-handsome face.

"We're acquainted," I corrected. "Briefly."

"Now, that is a story I'd love to hear," Gillian said.

"It's not really that interesting."

"Oh, don't be shy, Olivia," Lewis said. "Tell everyone how we met."

I stared daggers at him and wondered what sort of world I lived in to have to endure this torture in front of everyone who mattered for my career. I couldn't just tell him to go fuck himself here. Not like I wanted. Not without questions getting hurled at me.

But what could I say that wouldn't give away that he was part of my book?

"He…went on a date with my friend Amy." Not exactly a lie.

"Ah, yes, Amy," Lewis said with a laugh. "Does she still prefer broke artists?"

"She does."

"And will she still love you after your book releases tomorrow and blows up all the charts?" His eyes twinkled as I squirmed.

"I'll have to ask her," I said with a fake smile on my face.

Gillian laughed at our exchange. "What are the chances that you would know Lewis Warren? Well, I cannot wait to hear the full story later. Why don't we all take our seats and get started with this meeting?"

"Yes. Let's." My eyes narrowed in his direction.

"Great idea."

Lewis promptly took the chair directly across from my seat and winked at me. My cheeks heated as my anger lit like a fuse. Forget nerves for this meeting and enter cold, hard fury that this moment was being ruined by an Upper East Side prick who had been involved in the *bet* on whether or not I'd fall in love with his best friend. It wasn't enough that the only book I'd gotten published was *about* this event. He had to be here to witness them discuss it.

I tried to block him out and focus on the meeting at hand. But I couldn't seem to get it together. I wanted to know how he had known. Because he had to have known. And, if he had known …did that mean the others did too? Did Penn know?

I recoiled from that thought. He couldn't know. I didn't want to think about him or deal with him or see him.

"Olivia?" Gillian asked, clearly repeating herself.

I'd been so zoned out, thinking about the past, that I didn't even hear her question. Or much of anything that had come before that. Had we been discussing the marketing strategies? Or preorder numbers? Had someone mentioned the *New York Times*?

"Sorry. What was that?"

"We wanted to discuss your next project," Gillian said. "It's not often we have the whole team together with the author."

"Oh, right. What I'm working on next."

I chewed on my bottom lip and glanced back to Lewis. His eyebrows were raised as he waited for my response. He actually looked…interested. Was that legitimate or fake enthusiasm about my book? Was he mocking me? Surely, he hadn't *read* my novel.

"We're all dying to know what's next," my publicist, Kathy, said.

"It's still in the beginning stages." I flicked my eyes back to Gillian. "I'm not sure it's ready for anyone to see. Might disrupt the flow."

"Oh, come on. Not even a morsel?" she encouraged.

I fidgeted in my seat. How the hell did I get out of this?

"We can't rush brilliance," Lewis interjected. "If she's not ready to share, then it's clearly not ready for the public eye. I'm sure, once the book is in working condition, she'll wow us all."

I shot a relieved look in his direction for saving me from continuing. He likely didn't know that it was because I had *no* idea what to write next and no muse. But he had kept me from having to say that, and for that, I was grateful.

"You're right, of course, Lewis," Gillian said.

"We're just enthusiastic," Kathy piped up. "If it's anything like Bet on It, then I know we're going to have a best seller on our hands."

I paled and managed to push a smile through. "Let's hope."

"All right, well, that's all we have for today," Gillian said. "Do you have any questions for us, Olivia? We know tomorrow is a magical day for a debut. We want to make everything as seamless as possible."

"I don't think so. I'm just excited to go into a store and be able to actually hold a copy of my book," I told them.

"You'll have to take a picture and send it to us. We'll put it up on our social," Kathy said hungrily.

"Sure," I told her. Though I had no intention of showing my face for the camera, I'd send them something to use.

"Okay. Well then, we're through here. See you tonight at Twig for dinner," Gillian said.

I stood and shook hands with the rest of the team. I'd been working with them off and on all year, so it was nice to have faces to go with the names. They probably felt the same way about me, if I had to guess.

But, by the end of the meeting, it was just me, Gillian, and...Lewis.

"I can show her out," Lewis said with a broad smile to Gillian.

"Oh. Of course. I need to get back to work anyway," Gillian said. She raised her eyebrows once at me as if to say, *Have a good time*, and then disappeared through the conference room door.

Once we were finally alone, I whirled on him. "What are you *doing* here?"

"Last I checked, I'm a Warren," he said with a grin.

"You don't work in the publishing arm," I accused.

"No, I don't."

"So, what are you doing here?"

"I thought that was obvious, *Olivia*."

"Don't," I snapped.

"I came to see you."

"Well, I don't *want* to see you."

He shrugged as if that fact didn't matter to him. "Yet here we are."

"How did you even know I was going to be here? My identity was tightly guarded. Only Gillian knows."

"Are you sure?" he teased.

"Clearly, I was wrong."

"Go to lunch with me, Natalie."

I scoffed in disbelief. "No."

"Come on. It'll be like old times."

I shouldered my purse and headed for the door. "Might

have escaped your notice, but I have no interest in old times."
I turned back to look at him with anger in my blue eyes.
"And no interest in seeing you."

I yanked open the conference room door and headed for
the elevator. My hands were shaking, and I clasped them
together to make them stop. My heart was hammering in my
chest. It was a reminder of what I was running away from.
That stupid smirk and confident air. The way he seemed to
own the room. I'd always found Lewis handsome. He and
Penn were two sides of the same coin. They both took up too
much space, and worse, they knew it. I would not be caught
in that web again.

Fool me once, shame on you. I'd been eighteen and in
Paris and fallen instantly for Penn. I'd given him my virgin-
ity, and he'd repaid it by ghosting on me. Granted…it was
because his father had died. Though I'd only learned it years
later.

Fool me twice, shame on me. The bet. Penn, Lewis,
Katherine, Rowe, and Lark had bet on me. And I'd fallen in
love with Penn and made an utter fool of myself anyway.

Fool me thrice—well, I didn't even know who I could
blame for that. So, I was getting as far away from the Upper
East Side and all the many charming men in it.

"Wait!" Lewis slid his hand in the elevator before it could
close, and then he walked smoothly inside.

I pressed my body against the opposite wall. "Leave me
alone, Lewis."

"Go to lunch with me."

"Go to hell," I quipped.

"I guess I deserve that."

I glared. *Deserve?* That's the least of what you deserve."

"That's probably fair."

I crossed my arms and remained silent. I didn't have to
talk to him. I didn't have to listen to him. Their antics had

ruined my life as I knew it. And sure, I had bounced back onto my feet. But it didn't excuse what they'd done or how callous they had been about it all.

The elevator chimed, and I pushed past Lewis onto the main floor of Warren Publishing. Its grandeur was still mesmerizing, but all I saw was *him* now. I should have taken another offer. Who cared that Warren had fought the hardest and won the auction? I could have taken the deal from Hartfield or Strider or any number of other publishers that had bid on my book.

I could feel Lewis's presence behind me as I exited the building and said good-bye to Warren Publishing.

"Stop following me," I hissed.

"I will. Just hear me out."

"I'm under no obligation to do that," I snapped.

"You always did have a hot temper."

I stopped suddenly in the middle of the sidewalk. He continued moving for a pace before he realized that I'd halted.

"Natalie…"

"You and your friends ruined my life. I don't want to talk to you. I don't want to see you. I have no interest in whatever lies you're going to spin," I told him with fire in my eyes. "If you thought this would go differently and that I'd fall all over myself at your feet, you are sadly mistaken. I'm not like the simpering idiots you have on the Upper East Side. I don't care how much money you have. I don't care what your last name is. So, leave me alone."

"I'm sorry," Lewis said. His eyes were wide and revealing. A window to his sincerity, and I hated it.

"Sorry doesn't cut it."

I yanked out my phone to check my messages. I was supposed to meet Amy for lunch, but then I saw I had a text from her.

> *Ran into Enzo while I was shopping. You remember him from Paris, right? His work has gone off the charts. He even has something in the MET. We're going to get lunch. Don't wait up. ;)*

I sighed heavily at the text message. Great. There went my escape plan.

"You're right," Lewis said. "Sorry doesn't cut it. But I still would like to apologize. I know I was acting arrogant and condescending in there, but I didn't know how you'd react to me being there, and it was a defense mechanism."

"Why would you need a defense mechanism? You're the one who did this to me."

"I know. It was stupid and childish and wrong on so many levels. I begged Penn to tell you. I threatened him beyond words to do it, or I would. And I should have. I see now that I should have done it. Should have stopped it all."

I rolled my eyes. "Sure, Lewis. Why don't you save your breath for someone who might believe this?"

He straightened. "You think I enjoy throwing myself at your mercy? Knowing that you can hold a grudge for six years that runs as hot as a California forest fire? I don't enjoy your enmity, Natalie. I deserve it. We all do. But it does nothing to diminish how much I wish I could change it."

I stared at him in surprise. He was…serious.

He was actually…groveling before me outside of a building he owned. A year later, and he still wanted to make things right. A small part of me got satisfaction in his suffering. It was nothing compared to what I'd gone through. But the Upper East Side never had repercussions to their actions, and his pain was at least one consequence.

"What do you want from me?" I asked cautiously.

"Nothing."

"I don't believe you."

"I thought, if I bought you lunch, it would be a good start."

"Start for what?"

"Apologizing for what you went through."

I didn't trust him. I didn't trust any of them. But one lunch might not kill me.

"Fine. But we're getting pizza. It's the only thing I miss from this godforsaken city."

He smiled at me as if he knew how much of that was a lie.

NATALIE

3

*L*ewis insisted on paying. So, I found the cheapest pizza place and strolled inside. He looked dismayed.

"Are you sure you want to eat here?" he asked.

"What do you have against pizza?"

"Nothing. But I know a better place."

"I'm sure you do, but we're not going to the Upper East Side. We're not going anywhere near where your friends could see you. And I'm not letting you buy me a ridiculously priced pizza when this place is right here."

He sighed heavily. "Fine. But don't act like you don't like expensive pizza. That place in East Hampton wasn't cheap."

I winced at the memory. All the times Penn and I had ordered in pizza from that little place in East Hampton. How we'd eaten it cold for breakfast, clustered around the refrigerator in his parents' Hamptons mansion, and taken notes on our respective writing projects. I still couldn't distinguish if that was the best pizza I'd ever had because of where it was from or who I ate it with.

"Whatever," I muttered.

Lewis ordered us a pepperoni and sausage pizza and

handed me the Styrofoam fountain drink. I giggled at his discomfort and poured myself a Coke. I sat at one of the rickety chairs. Then, my eyes slid to Lewis at the soda machine.

We both looked incredibly out of place. He was in a thousand-dollar business suit, and I was dressed to impress in an outfit Amy had insisted on. A pair of Amy's Louboutins and a sleek dress and jacket combo that I never would have purchased for myself. Sleek wasn't typically how I described myself. More like bohemian with oversize, flowy dresses and sandals. My silvery hair long and unmanageable or in a high, messy bun on top of my head. Not stick straight to my waist like Amy had insisted on this morning. Or the makeup she'd carefully applied to my face like I was a doll.

Lewis sank into a chair across from me without complaint. Though I knew he would have preferred somewhere fancier. Lewis, unlike Penn, was a hundred percent Upper East Side. He had none of Penn's qualms about living this life. He'd been born and raised into more money than God. I knew he enjoyed it.

"So," he began.

"Yep." I took a long sip of my drink.

"I'm amazed you gave in."

"I didn't *give in.* I'm merely humoring you until Amy finishes screwing her latest artist."

He chuckled. "She found someone already?"

"You'd be amazed at how easy it is for Amy to find someone to fuck." I shrugged. "Or maybe you wouldn't."

"I'm hardly Amy's type."

"No, I do remember you being shocked because she was the only woman who had ever rebuffed you for your money." I waved my hand around. "Oh, look, happened again."

He pointed his finger at me. "You're a different case. The money makes you uncomfortable. It doesn't make Amy uncomfortable. She just doesn't want to date someone like her parents."

I was surprised at how well he'd read us both in that moment. Amy had been raised in money, and she defied it all by dating artistic losers. I'd been raised poor, and no matter how much I spent time around wealthy people, it wasn't *me*. Not to mention that I had no interest in living that Upper East Side life. Not then, when Penn had begged me to come back...and not now.

"Maybe," I conceded. "And here I thought, you didn't even like to talk about money. Isn't that right? People with money don't think about it. It just...is."

"Well, aren't you one of us now?"

I tightened my grip on my cup. "I am not one of you."

"I mean that this book is paying you handsomely."

"You and I both know that doesn't make me like you. You have to be born into your part of society. And you generally need billions...or the right name."

"That's right," he acknowledged. "A name sometimes can mean more than the money."

I shrugged and leaned backward. That wasn't my world. Character should mean more than name or money. But not for them. Not for someone like Katherine Van Pelt. Katherine, who had precipitated my downfall, all to try to get to Penn. All because her name meant something, yet she was penniless. She'd entered into an arranged marriage with Camden Percy, the most despicable person I'd ever met, and thought Penn was her way out. It was all so backward. If I didn't hate her so much, I'd almost feel bad for her. Almost.

The pizza arrived then—thin crust, covered in toppings, and steaming. I took the time to eat and collect my thoughts. So far, this lunch hadn't been that horrible. It could have been worse at least.

"So, BET ON IT, huh?" Lewis asked with a raised eyebrow.

"Yep."

"Are you ready for it to come out tomorrow?"

"Honestly?" I asked. "I'm really nervous."

"You? But why? It's gold."

"Oh, don't flatter me."

I took another bite of pizza, so I didn't have to look into those big brown eyes. I'd long wondered if Lewis had had something to do with the fact that I'd gotten the deal with Warren Publishing. Even though Hartfield had offered first and the entire thing had gone to auction with thirteen publishers, Warren had still won. It made me wonder. But I knew that I couldn't ask him. I didn't want to know. Not right before release day. I'd always wanted to believe I'd won this on my own merit despite years of rejection saying otherwise. I wasn't sure my fragile heart could handle it if it was the other way around.

"I'm not flattering you, Natalie. I've read the book. It's outstanding. Your prose is so sharp, so biting. The story… well, we both know how much of it is based on a true story. But it's the way you weave it together and bring fact with fiction that really shines. It's the in-between moments that make you pause and really think. I was captivated from page one until the very end. And not just because I'm a character in this story."

My jaw fell open at his words. He'd actually read the book. I couldn't believe it. I had known that Lewis enjoyed reading, but I hadn't thought he'd pick mine up for anything more than morbid curiosity.

"Well, thank you." A blush graced my cheeks. "I didn't think you'd read it. I'm a little amazed anyone has read it."

"You've had glowing reviews in all the major journals. Of course people are going to read it. And I'm glad they are. Clearly, you knew it was a story worth telling."

"I started it when I was in the Hamptons," I confessed. Though I had no idea why.

He ran his thumb across his bottom lip and leaned back. "That makes sense."

"You're not going to tell anyone else, are you?"

"You mean, Penn?"

I winced at the abrupt use of his name and all the pain that accompanied it. Yes, of course, I meant Penn. But truly, everyone. This was the real reason I'd chosen a pen name. I needed to fly under their radar.

He must have seen it in my expression because he sighed. "What would you like to be a secret? That you wrote the book? Or that it's about the crew? Or that you're here and I saw you and we had lunch?"

I nodded. "All of it."

"Your secret is safe with me. I will not divulge that you are the great Olivia Davies." He furrowed his brow. "Not even to Penn."

"Thank you."

"But…"

"Oh god," I muttered.

He grinned devilishly at me. "I would like to see you again."

"I don't think that's a good idea."

The more time I spent with Lewis, the greater chance that someone else in his circle was going to find out. Even if he kept his promise that he wouldn't tell anyone. Which seemed doubtful to me.

"I think it's a marvelous idea. You're only here a couple of days. I'm sure your schedule is packed. I could fit into it rather seamlessly."

"You don't seem to be giving me much choice."

"There's always a choice. I want you to make the right one."

"Rather ominous," I chided.

He laughed and reached across the table, snagging my hand in his. "Why can't I want to spend time with you?"

"You can." I slipped my fingers out from his. "Maybe I don't want to spend time with you."

"No lies between us anymore. You're enjoying yourself. We've always had fun together. Why don't we continue? I could take you to dinner tonight."

I shook my head. "I'm going with the publisher."

He arched an eyebrow, as if to say, *I am the publisher.* "No one would object to me tagging along."

"I would."

"What about your release day party tomorrow? I could escort you. Amy could even come with. Bring her strapping new artist along."

"Why are you pushing this?" I asked suspiciously. "I said no."

"You haven't actually."

"I just did then."

He sighed and nodded. "All right. But I want you to know that I missed you this last year. You weren't the only one who was upset by what happened. You're a breath of fresh air, and losing your presence was a blow. You can't fault me for wanting to have you back in my life."

Despite myself, I was moved by what he'd said. I hadn't thought anyone in their circle had feelings. Or that they would miss me. I had believed that it was all a game. One they had played many times before and would continue to play for all eternity. I was a pawn, and they had moved the pieces how they saw fit. No matter who got hurt.

But Lewis hadn't made it seem like that. He'd made it seem like real lives were involved and real feelings were injured. Not just my own.

I blinked down at my cup and tried to banish these

unwanted feelings. I didn't want to feel bad for Lewis Warren. How could you feel bad for someone who had everything?

Because...he hadn't actually placed the bet. Yes, he'd been there that day. But it had been between Katherine and Penn. And the wager had been in their favor. Lewis hadn't been an unwilling participant, but he hadn't really had a stake in the matter in the same way. And we *had* become friends.

No.

We hadn't been friends. Christ. A few minutes in his presence, and already, he was twisting my thoughts. Bringing down barriers I'd put up for my own security. Lewis was an Upper East Side prick. He'd known about the bet. He'd done nothing. He deserved nothing from me.

"Is that all?" I finally asked.

He sighed and nodded.

"Good. Then, I need to get back."

I stood, and he followed suit. He cleared the table for us and then we walked out into the November chill.

"I don't want to blindside you again. I will be at your party whether I escort you or not," Lewis let me know.

"Okay."

I could probably avoid him at the party. There were going to be enough people. Hopefully.

We stood on the sidewalk, watching the madness of New York City zip by before us. Then, he turned and held out his hand. I stared down at it in surprise. A handshake. Huh.

I removed my hand from my coat pocket and shook.

"It's been a pleasure, Natalie. I'm glad that you've found success."

"Thank you."

"If you change your mind about...anything, you have my number."

It seemed doubtful, but I nodded anyway. "Thank you for lunch."

He smiled brightly. "Anytime. Now, I suppose, I should get back to work as well."

"Good idea."

He hailed a cab, which pulled up right away in front of us. He opened the back door and then held it for me. "You first."

"Oh, thank you."

I slid into the backseat of the cab, and he closed the door behind me. A sad smile graced his features, as if this whole encounter hadn't gone as planned. And for a second, it was like I could see how much he *had* planned all of this. He'd been excited to see me. He'd been expecting anger but thought that he could break through it. He'd been wrong.

The car pulled away from the sidewalk, and I leaned back in confusion. Lewis wasn't what I'd been expecting either.

4

"Natalie!" Amy yelled as she entered the hotel room that Warren had put us up in.

"In here," I called back.

My fingers were flying across my keyboard. They were hardly keeping up with my brain, which was spitting ideas at me faster than I'd seen in a year. Everything was coming together. The entire year of a dry spell had ended.

Words.

Beautiful words.

They had finally returned to me.

I almost wanted to cry with relief.

I'd thought I was broken. For so long, I'd believed that I didn't have it in me anymore to write a novel. My whole life, I'd wanted to be a writer. And, now that I was finally being published, I couldn't write a damn thing. How cruel!

And yet, here they were again.

Bright, shiny, glorious words, sentences, paragraphs, even pages.

"I had the most incredible day," Amy said. She twirled around in a circle with shopping bags dangling from her arms. She honestly looked like a cartoon character with her excitement and many expensive purchases.

"Me too."

Amy dumped all the bags on the floor. "Enzo was...as sexy as I remembered. Luckily, no whiskey dick this time. And he made up for all that lost time in Paris. And, dear Lord, I swear, he is a god." Her head popped up. "Wait...what are you doing?"

"Writing."

Amy squealed. "Writing? Really? Your day must have been amazing. Since when do you have a muse?"

"Since today."

"Oh my god, we both had sex."

I snorted. "Not quite."

"Oh please, we both know writing is like sex for you."

She wasn't wrong.

"What brought this on?" she asked, looking over my shoulder. "Wow, this is really good, Nat."

"Thanks. I'm not sure what it was. Maybe it's this city."

"Maybe...but you didn't write yesterday."

I finished the sentence I'd been working on and turned to face my best friend. "I saw Lewis today."

"What?" she gasped. "Where?"

I quickly filled her in on everything that had happened this afternoon.

"Holy shit. That's crazy. And now, you've written five thousand words in a matter of hours? Natalie, that's huge!"

"I know." I nodded and leaned back in the chair. "I don't know if it's him or my rising anger through the entire interaction. Or if it was just bringing back all those memories of last year, which helped me write BET ON IT to begin with."

"You wrote the last one in a couple of weeks after leaving all of them behind," Amy said with raised eyebrows.

I huffed. "I know."

"Hey, when you have a muse, you have a muse."

"But does it have to be him?"

"Lewis or Penn?"

"Yes?" I asked with a wince.

"Look," Amy said, sinking into a seat next to me, "the crew, as horrible as they were to you, gave you something. Inspiration and passion and drive. They took what you fantasized about and gave you the ability to put it on paper. They're larger than life, and there's a reason people want to read about them. It's not surprising that you're reacting to that same feeling again."

I hated it though. I didn't want the crew to be my muse. In any way.

"I guess this is what people mean when they say writing is easy. Just open up a vein and bleed."

Amy snorted. "Well, either way, you're writing. Who cares why?"

"Maybe," I said unconvincingly. "Of course, I'm not writing the book I should be writing. This is that literary novel I've always wanted to write. This isn't even in the same realm as my Olivia book."

"Well, beggars can't be choosers," Amy said.

"Yeah, but what do I tell them? I want to publish this one under my name."

"Then do it."

"I guess I'll ask my agent tomorrow."

"I can't see her saying no to you since this one is going to be a smash success."

"Maybe." I chewed on my bottom lip.

"Why so glum?" Amy asked, stroking my hair.

"What if the words go away again?" I asked morosely.

"If you were able to write after seeing Lewis, whether or not he was the reason, what does that tell you?"

"That I'm an idiot?"

She laughed and nudged me. "No, silly. It means you see him again."

"Ugh," I groaned. "I don't *want* to see him again. He's complicated. And he reminds me of Penn."

"He is Penn's best friend. That's true. But what is the worst thing that could happen?"

"Oh god, don't ask that again." I stood and paced away from her.

I slung open the curtain and looked down at Central Park below us. It was a beautiful day. I should be out there. We both should. But I couldn't stop the flow of the words even if I wanted to, and I definitely didn't.

"Last time was different."

"It's *always* different."

"Okay," Amy said with a huff. "The worst that can happen is, you see Penn again."

I glared at her. "Don't even joke about that. It isn't funny."

"I know. I'm sorry." She sighed. "But Lewis isn't Penn, and he promised to keep your secret. What's the harm in milking every last drop of muse out of him while you're in town? It's only a few days."

I bit my lip. "I'd be using him."

"No, you wouldn't. You're an artist, Natalie. Artists need their muses. He'd be flattered. Plus, he did ask to see you and escort you to your party. Doesn't sound like a boy who would care why you said yes."

It was a bad idea. But this was for my craft. Not for pleasure. I wasn't going to see Lewis so that I could see Penn. Because I didn't want to see his stupid, pretty face. And Lewis was going to be at the release party anyway. So, I would have to deal with him either way. It wouldn't harm anything to take him up on his offer.

"All right. Fine."

Amy whooped. "Limos and champagne and caviar, here we come!"

"We do not know that he would do any of that."

Amy laughed and twirled around in a circle. "He's a Warren, Natalie. He absolutely will!"

I COULDN'T GIVE Lewis the satisfaction of calling right away. Not that I was going to walk away from my computer when I was writing again. I stayed glued to it up until the last minute before I had to head out the door to see Gillian for dinner at Twig. And I raced back to my computer screen as soon as it was over.

Amy knew better than to complain to me about the whole thing. I told her to make plans with Enzo, and she happily disappeared to his apartment in the Village. I lost track of time from there. My fingers started to cramp, and my eyes got blurry. I knew that I had plans for tomorrow, but I also wasn't going to stop once I was on this train.

Finally, at about three in the morning, I fell into bed and slept soundly.

I awoke the next day and stared down at my phone in confusion. I had about five hundred notifications on my phone.

Today was release day.

"Oh my god," I gasped.

In my fever dream of writing yesterday, I'd actually been able to push out the fear of release day. And now, my book was out in the world. People were buying it. They were reading it. It was on shelves.

And I might vomit.

I was glad that I had lunch with Caroline at noon or else I might just stress-pace the room all afternoon. Forget the bliss of writing last night. I wasn't going to be able to do that today. Not on release day.

I scrolled through the messages. Most of it was posts on my Crew social media account for Olivia. But also texts from family and the handful of friends who knew that I'd published. The pen name was to protect myself from the crew and the Upper East Side, not the people I cared about. And, between having the crew blocked on social media and living on my Olivia page, I didn't think they'd have a way of finding out.

I spent the next half hour replying to texts and liking post after post from people sharing it. It was kind of overwhelming. Then I stopped on a text message that I'd gotten early this morning from Lewis.

Happy release day, gorgeous! Excited for everyone to finally read this book.

I stared down at it in surprise. He really was excited for me. And maybe...he did want to apologize for what had happened in some way. I'd thought he was bullshitting me yesterday. No real part of me had hoped that he was for real. This was Lewis Warren after all. I wasn't dumb enough to think that there wasn't a catch.

But damn, that conversation with Amy was too real. Maybe I hadn't had words in the last year because I'd found that muse in the crew. In the group of five Upper East Siders who had hurt me. And it didn't matter if I didn't want them to be my muse. They were. Somehow, Lewis was.

And it might be worth it to see him if I could write again.

I sighed and sent back a response.

Thanks! It's a bit surreal. I can't believe the day is finally here.

I like to see people succeed who deserve it.

Then, a minute later…

A bit surprised that you responded, but I'm glad you did.

I think I surprised myself.

What changed your mind?

I don't know. I feel like there's probably a catch here with you.

No catch. Just me. I'm happy for you. You deserve this and more.

I grinned at the words on the screen. I couldn't believe I was actually doing this. That I was actually going to invite him to the party with me. Fuck, I couldn't even believe we were even chatting. Amicably.

Except…Lewis and I had always gotten along. We certainly had never had a problem talking or hanging out. Maybe it would be okay for a night when none of the other crew would be there.

I've reconsidered. Pick me up for the party tonight?

I'd like that. See you tonight.

I tossed my phone onto the bed and stretched my arms overhead. I couldn't believe I'd actually done it. I was really going to use Lewis Warren as my writing muse. It was yet to be determined if this was the most brilliant decision of my life or if it was going to backfire spectacularly.

I headed into the shower and washed off my long night of writing. After a quick blowout, I hustled from my hotel room to the meeting with Caroline. We were meeting at Norma's. I was both giddy with excitement, as it was my favorite restaurant in the city, and sick that the only times I'd come here were with Penn. I could practically feel his blue eyes on me as I slipped in from the side entrance of the Parker Hotel, past the bar furnished with red velvet chaises, and into the marble interior of the lobby.

Caroline stood from where she'd been seated on a small wooden bench. "Natalie, so good to finally meet you!"

"Oh my god, Caroline!"

She pulled me in for a hug like we were long-lost friends even though this was our first official meeting. We'd talked on the phone, in text message, and email constantly for the last couple of years, but we hadn't met up the last time I was in the city, and now, we finally were.

"I'm sure you're starving," she said in her thick New York accent. I never got tired of hearing it. She flicked her shoulder-length bleach-blonde hair, whirled a purple scarf over a shoulder, and then looped arms with me. "Let's go inside and get you a big, hearty lunch."

The hostess seated us at Caroline's usual table, and we both shucked off our layers from the cold. After a quick perusal of the menu, I ordered a bagel and lox while Caroline got two eggs, over easy, and a grapefruit.

"Damn diet," Caroline muttered. She took a long sip of her black coffee. "My husband will *know* if I get the waffle."

"You should definitely get the waffle," I said with a smile.

She waved her hand. "Another time. Now, how does it feel? You're a published author now."

"Amazing and terrifying. Not quite real yet," I added.

"That all sounds completely normal. I'm so glad to be the one to get this book into the right hands. It's one that needs to be read."

"Thank you." I flushed and took a sip of my own coffee.

"So, tell me about the new book. What do you have in the pipeline?"

"Well," I said, meeting her steely dark gaze, "it's not what I thought it would be."

"That happens."

"It's not exactly…an Olivia book."

Caroline merely arched an eyebrow.

"It's a literary novel about a family and their relationships. How different paths shape who they become. It's not exactly commercial, like BET ON IT."

"All right. I'm listening."

I took a deep breath and told her the whole story. Everything that I had worked out for the new novel and how easily it was coming to me. Caroline nodded along the whole time, but I couldn't exactly *judge* her on it.

"And I'm so obsessed with the story. But I don't want to publish it as Olivia. I want to publish it as me. As Natalie. I feel like Olivia is great for the kind of book I wrote, when the true story aspect was behind it, but I don't want to hide behind Olivia forever."

"Look, Natalie," Caroline said, plunking her mug down on the table, "the people at Warren, they love you. You're a rock star for them. I'm sure they'd publish anything of yours. But you have to decide if it's Olivia or Natalie. For the long haul."

I swallowed and nodded. "Right."

"It's nothing personal. It's just business. They're going to want your book, but they spent a lot of money building you up. Olivia has starred reviews in journals, and hopefully, you'll hit a major best-seller list. That's something they can use. If you write as Natalie, then you start over. You're another debut. Unless, of course, you out the pen name."

"No," I said at once. That was a hard no. The last thing I

wanted was for the rest of the crew to get a whiff of who I really was or what I'd written about them.

"So, long-term, choosing one or the other is going to be the way to go."

"Okay." I didn't really like that answer, but there it was.

Natalie or Olivia?

The books I really wanted to write or the one that had brought me success?

Lord help me that I made the right choice.

NATALIE

5

*M*y stomach was in knots. I stood outside of my hotel with Amy and Enzo. He kept sliding his hand to her ass, rippling the red sequined material. She'd swat at him and giggle. And I just stood there, wringing my hands and trying to decide if I'd made a mistake.

"Stop fidgeting," Amy muttered. She knocked her hip into me, and I teetered on my strappy black heels. "He'll be here."

"Uncertain if that's the problem or not."

But I didn't have more time to overanalyze that as a black limo slid up to the front of the hotel.

"Told you," Amy said under her breath.

The back door opened, and every delectable inch of Lewis Warren stepped out of the backseat in a tailored three-piece suit. I swallowed hard and took a small step forward in response.

"Fuck," Amy said next to me.

Yeah. Fuck.

His dark eyes slid up the slinky royal-blue dress that hugged all my curves in all the right places, taking me in like a feast he was prepared to devour. A sensual smile tilted his lips as he straightened to his considerable height. He exuded confidence that had been born from years of getting everything he had ever wanted. He wore it like a second skin. And I loved as much as hated how good he looked with the considerable arrogance and charm wafting off of him.

"Natalie," he finally murmured. "You look beautiful."

I flushed expectantly. "Thank you. You look pretty good yourself."

"Pretty good?" Amy asked. She brushed past me and stepped up to the limo. "You're wearing a Savile Row suit. You look hot as fuck."

"Nice to see you again, Amy."

"Good thing you're not my type."

"Such a charmer." He tilted his head at Enzo. "Your date?"

"Enzo, Lewis. Lewis, Enzo." She shot Lewis a daring smile. "You'd better have champagne in there."

"I don't disappoint."

Amy grinned and entered the limo with Enzo, leaving us alone for a minute.

"After you, Miss Bishop," Lewis said with a grin.

"Thank you for picking us up," I said as I stepped up to him. I had always considered myself relatively tall, and still, I barely reached his shoulder. I looked up into his open expression. "I appreciate it."

"It's really my pleasure." He gestured for me to enter. "Don't let Amy drink all the champagne."

I laughed and shuffled into the limo. As expected, Amy had popped the champagne bottle, and she and Enzo were already imbibing. Lewis followed behind me, and we started off as soon as the door was closed.

"You really went all out," I told him.

"How could I not?" Lewis took the champagne bottle and poured each of us a glass. Then, he raised his champagne flute. "To Natalie and the release of her debut novel!"

Amy and Enzo raised their half-drained glasses, and I held mine up too. I downed most of mine for liquid courage. Today had been a day of nerves. I didn't know if it was worse or better that my book was doing well. I couldn't imagine feeling any worse about the release. Despite the fact that, after I'd left my meeting with Caroline, Amy and I had dragged ourselves all over Manhattan. We'd peeked into every bookstore to find my book. And to my amazement, it had been there.

In every bookstore.

On every main display.

With giant letters of recommendation to patrons and rave reviews from booksellers and displays in the front of Barnes & Noble.

I was blown away. It was more than I could have ever dreamed of.

"You really do look beautiful," Lewis whispered, leaning close to my ear.

I flushed at his praise. "Thank you. It's all Amy's doing."

"Don't be modest."

"I'm not. It just doesn't really feel like me."

His eyes swept down my body to the place where the short hem barely grazed the top of my thighs and then back to my face. "Why didn't you wear something you were more comfortable in?"

"We're celebrating. So, I got all dolled up."

"This might not be what you normally wear, but it suits you."

"Thank you," I whispered.

I bit my lip at his searing look. It had been easier when I was on guard with him. Now that he was within my realm of security, I was off-kilter. And those looks…I probably shouldn't like them as much as I did.

It was a short drive to Club 360, which was situated on

top of a Percy hotel. As in Camden Percy, Katherine's fiancé and the most despicable person I'd ever met, owned this hotel. This was Katherine's stomping grounds, and I'd been here with Penn. Unease bit into me at the memories.

Club 360 was the place where I had decided I was going to move forward with my relationship with Penn. Put my heart on the line. And that night was the first time we'd had sex since Paris. The start of a new beginning.

And a new end.

It didn't matter that Warren had rented the place out for a couple of hours before the club's official opening time or that it was a Tuesday night. I couldn't stop the nerves that jolted through me.

"Are you okay?" Lewis asked, as if he knew how terrifying this was for me. He had been there that night after all.

"Fine. Just nervous, is all."

"It's going to be great." He offered me his arm. "New memories."

I nodded reluctantly. That was what I wanted. New memories to replace the ones that were now tinged in sadness whenever I got too close to them.

Lewis and I entered the Percy hotel and took the elevator up to Club 360 with Amy and Enzo. It was exactly as I remembered it. Open-air club with a large dance floor buffeted between a horseshoe bar and VIP booths. Only, now, a retractable glass roof had been put in place over top of most of the dance floor, and heat lamps lined the room. The room was crowded with people here for the event, and I picked out my agent, editor, and some of the Warren staff in the crowd. A sign hung across one wall that read, *Congratulations, Olivia!*

"Oh my god," I gushed. "This is so amazing. Thank you all so much for coming."

Caroline peeled away from the group and pulled me into a hug. "It's all for you."

Gillian appeared beside me. "And look." She drew me over to a round table at the back. "We even have a cupcake tower where you can add your own icing. Just like in the book when Lacey eats icing straight out of the container."

I laughed in surprise and delight. "Icing saves the world again. I'm obsessed."

"We're so glad that we could convince you to come up to the city to do this," Gillian said.

"Me too," I admitted. I'd tried to get out of it so many times. And now, I was here and so glad that I was. "This is beyond anything I could have envisioned. This entire launch has been perfect. I couldn't have done it without you, Gillian."

She hugged me. "I am so glad that I was the one who was able to put this story out into the world. BET ON IT is just the beginning. Caroline has been whispering in my ear that your next book idea is even more amazing. I'll be thrilled to look at it."

"Oh, Gillian, that will be wonderful."

Of course, I didn't know what book Caroline had been telling her about. We'd put together some kind of pitch for both my literary idea for Natalie and the bare bones idea I'd had last year after BET ON IT but hadn't been able to work on. Caroline had said that Gillian would probably buy either, but I really, desperately wanted to sell my Natalie idea. I loved what was happening for Olivia, and this party was proof of that. But I wanted it to be for me, too.

"I can't wait to read what you have so far. Caroline said she'd send them over when you were ready. I'm sure it's going to be another masterpiece."

I blushed. "Thank you. Let's hope so."

"I've read your work. I know it will be," Gillian said with a wink. "Now, enough chitchatting. Let's introduce you around to some of these people that you don't know."

I met so many new people that I knew there was no way that I could remember them. Even with my prodigious memory and my writer's curse, people were starting to blur together. I'd lost track of Lewis early on, and Amy and Enzo were conspicuously absent. But I put all of it out of my head because this was a once-in-a-lifetime sort of event, and I planned to enjoy it.

"So, Olivia," a woman said, who I was pretty certain Gillian had introduced as Jessica, "are you ever going to reveal *who* exactly the book is based on?"

Gillian gasped in mock shock. "A lady never kisses and tells, Jessica."

I laughed at Gillian's response. Jessica wasn't the first— and likely wouldn't be the last person—who had asked me that.

"And it isn't about you?" Jessica pried.

I laughed and shrugged. "Do you think I'm that glamorous?" I hedged.

"Well, we did notice you walking in with Lewis Warren," another woman, Grace, said conspiratorially. "He's one of the most eligible bachelors in New York City."

"Lewis is just a friend," I assured them. Or was I assuring myself?

"She's the darling of Warren Publishing," Gillian said, wrapping a possessive arm around my shoulders. "Of course a Warren is showing interest."

Grace and Jessica went on to gush over the novel. Recounting what *they* would have done in my place after finding out about the bet. As if the situation were so easy when you were the one in it.

Of course, the book wasn't a hundred percent autobiographical. There were embellishments for the story's sake and changes to protect the guilty parties involved. But I still thought the strongest thing I'd ever done was walk out of that party.

"Oh!" Gillian said with delight. "Sorry, girls, I need to steal Olivia for a minute."

"We'll talk later!" Jessica said with a wave.

Gillian gently tugged me away from the two women. "There's this incredible woman that I want you to meet. She's so well connected. I've truly never met anyone else like her. She's bold and confident and daring. And she's slowly building an empire here in New York. I met her at a museum opening a few weeks ago and invited her to come to this event. I had no idea if she would actually show."

"She sounds amazing."

"Truly, she is. And I think she could only help with the upward trajectory of your career." Gillian sipped her champagne. "Here she is—Jane!"

My stomach dropped. Oh god.

Jane Devney.

She was shorter than I remembered with ash-blonde hair to her shoulders and wide, unassuming hazel eyes that seemed to shift in color right before my eyes.

"Natalie!" Jane cried in surprise and delight. A slight accent highlighted her word. Though I couldn't exactly place it. She leaned forward and kissed each of my cheeks.

Gillian's mouth dropped open, and she glanced between me and Jane in shock.

The last time I'd seen Jane Devney was at the Kensingtons' Hamptons mansion when I broke it off with Penn. And worse…she had been dating his brother at the time. I had no idea if she was still dating Court Kensington. It seemed unlikely, knowing the train wreck of a man he was. But I still looked uncertainly behind her to see if he was there. I didn't see him though.

"I had no *idea* you were going to be here. I'd heard that you left the city," Jane went on.

"I...I did," I said.

"Well, you look fabulous. I was speaking to Elizabeth Cunningham only last week about the state of the market and how we need more originality. I was thinking specifically of you because I remember you wore her, correct? And this hair. Well, no one forgets this hair."

Gillian gaped at me. "You wore Elizabeth Cunningham?"

"No," I said hastily. "That must have been someone else you're thinking of, Jane."

"Certainly not. I never forget a face. We met in Paris two summers ago at a Harmony Cunningham party after all." She turned to Gillian to explain, "I was working at the French Fashion Institute at the time while I was interning at *Vogue Paris*, and Natalie was staying at a flat nearby. She's a gem, this one. You are lucky to have her here."

"That is not exactly what happened—"

"She's the author I was telling you about," Gillian managed to get out.

"Oh, *you're* the mysterious Olivia Davies," Jane said to me as if all the pieces had just fit together. "Well, that makes perfect sense then, doesn't it?"

"Does it?" I muttered.

"Well, I can't stay long, but I'd love to catch up, Natalie. We never got enough time together when you were last in the city. I thought you were so charming and really going places. And look, I was right. Let's exchange numbers, darling. Then, I won't be without your company any longer." Jane thrust her phone into my hand, and I dutifully put my number into her phone. She took it back and then handed it to Gillian. "Photo op."

Gillian took the phone in surprise and obediently snapped a picture of the two of us together.

Jane showed me the image. "So glam. I'm going to text it to you now."

My phone dinged, and there was Jane Devney's number on the phone with our picture. And she was right. We practically looked like models.

"Jane, if you post this, will you please not reveal my pen name?" I looked at her with wide eyes, willing her to understand.

She tapped her finger to her lips twice. "I got you, darling."

"Thank you," I said in relief.

"But let's hang out. Seriously."

"Definitely." I'd do anything for her if she didn't let anyone on the Upper East Side know that I was Olivia Davies. I wondered then if she saw that desperation in my expression.

Jane turned from me to Gillian. "Thank you so much for inviting me to this," Jane said with a kiss to her cheek. "It's been grand. I'll make sure to mention it to Marcie at the *Times* and my friend Hanna at *USA Today*. I think we could do a write-up about it."

"Thank you, Jane," Gillian gushed.

Jane twirled her fingers at us both and then disappeared.

Gillian turned to me with wide eyes. "Why do I have a sudden feeling there's a lot that I don't know about you?"

NATALIE

6

I barely was able to steer the conversation with Gillian away from what had just happened with Jane.

I didn't know why I'd thought it would be possible to keep everything a secret. I should have never agreed to come to New York. No matter how big the city was, my world was too small. It wasn't possible for me to flit in and out and have no one recognize me. The people I knew here were the ones who could make or break a career. They were the Lewises and Janes of the world. Of course I would run into them when my publisher was trying to make *my* career.

I sighed and carried one of the containers of icing out onto the balcony. Amy's mother had always kept a pint of icing around in times of trouble, and we had frequently found her seated on the couch in the living room, eating straight out of the container. I'd put it in the book, and here I was, living it again.

I'd forgotten to snag my jacket, and I was immediately frigid as I hit the open air. But I didn't care. I needed a minute to sulk.

"Why so glum?" a voice asked from further down the balcony.

I glanced over and saw Lewis walk out of the shadows. He looked unbelievably handsome. It was amazing how much I'd forgotten from last year. Like the way his shoulders filled out his suit or the tilt of his full lips when he smiled or the hollow of his cheeks that revealed sharp cheekbones.

I turned my attention back to my container of icing. I didn't need to think about him like that. "Just had a weird interaction."

"What happened?"

"Jane Devney was here."

"Court's girlfriend?"

"They're still together?" I asked in surprise.

He shrugged and leaned against the stone railing. "Depends on who you ask. But it seems so from the outside."

"That's surprising." I hadn't thought that Penn's brother kept anything or anyone around for long.

"It is. Court doesn't normally have real relationships."

"Yeah." I stuck a huge dollop of icing in my mouth and then offered him the spoon. "Want some?"

He laughed and shook his head. "All you."

I shivered against the cold that was eating its way deeper into my skin.

"You look like you're freezing. Here." He removed the jacket from his suit and slid it over my narrow shoulders. The warmth from his body sank in, and I actually sighed in delight as it radiated through me.

"Thank you."

He smirked deliciously. "Anything to get that reaction from you again, Nat."

I flushed and turned back to my icing. Lewis was a flirt. I knew that. I'd always known that. He'd been like that with me from day one. But then…why did it suddenly feel like more?

Not that I was about to ask him. The last thing I wanted was to get mixed up in the Upper East Side again. Let alone with the crew and the dangers that came with their inner circle. Especially when I was the one who felt guilty about being here with him tonight. For using him to get more writing in.

"So, what did Jane want?" He leaned against the railing and sweetly stared at me.

"Nothing. I guess Gillian invited her for her contacts. She wanted her to get someone to write about the event and my book. But Gillian didn't know, of course, that I already knew Jane. And that Jane knows me as Natalie, not Olivia." I winced again at the thought of the encounter. "Just pure bad luck."

"Ah, how did you explain that one?"

I shrugged. "Poorly, I think."

My eyes slipped back to my container of icing. Lewis was being so nice to me. Not just in the incredibly arrogant and charming way that I knew he could be. The way he had been in the office of Warren Publishing. He wasn't putting on a front here. He was just being…nice. Standing here and listening to me vent.

It was refreshing in its own way. Even if I didn't want it to be. He hadn't been wrong when he said that we'd gotten along so well before. We had. As friends…I'd thought. Now, here as…I had no idea what.

And the heat and tension between us made me feel worse about the reason I had agreed to be here with him tonight.

"That wonderful mind of yours is thinking hard again." He leaned in closer. "Care to share with the class?"

"I shouldn't have come to this party with you tonight," I

told him truthfully, setting the icing down on the balcony railing.

"Oh no, I definitely think it was the right choice."

"No, I mean, I'm using you."

He laughed. "Natalie Bishop, using me? Come now." He brushed my silvery hair off my shoulder. "We both know that you are too sweet for such things."

"I'm serious, Lewis."

He tried to rein in his laughing grin but couldn't quite manage it. "Maybe I want to be used by you if it means more time with you."

"You don't want to be used," I murmured dryly. "Trust me. I know."

He straightened, taking me in, in a glance. "This isn't about Penn, is it?"

"What? No," I spat. I shuddered at the thought.

"Well, if you're not using me to make him jealous, then I don't see how you could possibly do something that would offend me."

"I wouldn't do that," I gasped out. "Why would you even think that?"

He shrugged. "Wouldn't be the first time."

I frowned at that. I hadn't even considered that option. That he would think I would see him just to get back at Penn in any way. I wanted nothing to do with Penn. Thinking about him was still too painful. I hadn't even wanted to come to New York, knowing I might run into him. Maybe it made me a coward that I didn't want to face him, but I couldn't help it.

"Well, it's not that. It would never be that."

"Then, tell me."

"I haven't written in a year," I confessed.

He raised his eyebrows. "So, *that's* why you didn't want to talk about it at the meeting yesterday."

"Yes. Thank you for saving me from that."

"Anytime. Though that doesn't explain how you're using me."

"Well, after I left lunch yesterday, I finally was able to write for the first time. This bright and vibrant literary novel that I desperately want to publish under my real name and not Olivia. Something that is an all-passion project and—ugh!" I sighed in pleasure. "I'm loving it."

"And you got all of that out of one lunch?"

I nodded. "So...I asked you to come with me today because I hoped that I'd be able to write more after."

Lewis met my gaze for a moment and then burst into laughter.

"What?" I gasped, swatting at him. "I'm serious. I'm using you for a positive word count."

"Use me away." He pulled me closer against him. "Use me for more writing. I'm desperate to read more. Natalie, Olivia —be whoever you want to be as long as I get more out of your beautiful brain, and if that means more time with you, I suppose I could sacrifice myself for that."

"You are outrageous," I told him. "Here I was, all worried that I was using you as a muse, and you don't even care."

"How could I care?" He leaned forward into me. Our lips mere inches apart. His voice pitched low and seductive. "I want to be your muse."

"You do?" I asked huskily.

A tingle ran through my body as he brushed the shell of my ear and dragged his finger down my neck.

"I do." His hand trailed over my shoulder and down my arm before finding my freezing fingers. His thumb drew circles into my skin.

"What are you doing?" I whispered.

"What I should have done a long time ago."

My breathing was ragged, as he cradled my neck in his

hand, tilting my head up to look at him. I knew what was about to happen. I could see the longing and desire painted on his face. That need that had been there all night but had never been more blatant than that moment, that single, solitary moment before his lips brushed against mine.

And to my surprise, desire flared red hot in me. An ache that I'd ignored for the last year. One that said I wanted this, and I wanted more of it. That I could never have enough of it. Of the easy way it was to be around him and the sweet taste of his lips on mine.

I hadn't felt desire like this in a year. Not with the aimless blind dates that Amy had insisted on setting me up on. Or the gentle pursuance from one of the guys I had known from high school. There had been nothing but emptiness.

But here was Lewis.

Lewis.

A fucking Warren. An Upper East Sider. Penn's best friend. All of these things that I didn't want.

And yet, my body responded like a lit fuse.

I should back away. Walk away and never look back. I definitely shouldn't slide my arms around his neck. Or press my body harder against his. Or open my mouth and let his tongue ravage me.

But, without even a thought, I was doing all those things. A soft moan escaped me as his fingers dug in deeper, and our lips danced against one another. His lips were soft, tender, persuasive. His body dispelled the lingering chill in the air. From my now-very-heated body.

I hadn't been kissed in a year.

A long, cold year.

Yet here I was, on a rooftop in New York, with snowflakes falling from the sky to kiss my lashes, and I was kissing one of the most eligible bachelors in the city. It felt like a fairy tale.

If it wasn't so incredibly wrong.

Why did my first kiss in a year have to be with Penn's best friend?

I pressed my lips to his one more time, and then with great effort, I pulled back to look up into those deep, dark eyes. "I shouldn't," I sputtered.

"I know." He kissed me again, slowly and luxuriously. As if we had all the time in the world. As if the reasons I shouldn't do this didn't matter.

"Lewis," I pleaded. "I can't."

"Can't? Or won't?" He dragged my bottom lip between his teeth and then pressed us together again.

My mind was saying, *No*, but, dear god, my body was saying, *Yes, yes, yes*.

I broke away again. My hand flew to my lips as if I could somehow undo that magical moment and the hot feel of his lips against my own. "Won't," I finally settled on. "I'm sorry."

"Natalie…" he muttered. "You can see this for what it is."

I shook my head. "We both know that this is wrong. That I shouldn't do this."

"Why? This was perfect. You know it was."

I didn't say anything because, otherwise, I'd agree with him.

"Because of Penn?" he demanded when I said nothing.

I winced again at his name and said softly, "He's your best friend, Lewis."

"He destroyed you," he hissed. "He used you and wrecked you and then tossed you aside. Did he even try to see you after you left New York?"

He had.

He'd tried. And obviously not told anyone else about it.

But it hadn't been enough. It would never be enough. The pain of that confrontation still hurt. And afterward, I'd told him not to contact me. He'd listened. He'd stayed far away. I hadn't had one single message from him since I kicked him out of Charleston.

That had hurt, too.

Lewis stepped into me again. "Let me be the one to put you back together."

"I don't need anyone to put me back together," I whispered.

"Surely, you know how I feel about you, Natalie. I don't hide it very well, even then."

"Lewis," I whispered.

"I fell for you," he said. "A year ago. I've never stopped thinking about you."

"This could never work…for so many reasons."

"You don't know that."

I sighed heavily. "But I do."

"Just let me try. Let me prove to you that what I feel is real." He reached out and grasped my hand. "Give me a chance."

I shook my head and pulled away. "I'm sorry. But I dated Penn. Maybe if I'd met you first." I closed my eyes. My heart shuddered.

"I hardly ever see Penn anymore. Things are different now."

"But none of that is true," I continued on. "And you still participated in the bet."

"*Participated* is a strong word."

"You lied to me about it," I reminded him.

"I thought you were happy," he explained earnestly. "Yes, I lied. I told you what you wanted to hear because I couldn't imagine being the one to break that news to you over the phone. Penn should have been the one to do it. To man up and tell you the truth. But the last thing I wanted was to shatter your heart when you seemed so happy."

"I was happy," I whispered. "And, now...I'm not, and this is too much. I don't want to be a part of this life. I'm sorry..."

And I was sorry.

I was sorry to see the pain in his eyes. To see his feelings shine through. I hated wondering if it could have been. If the circumstances had been different. But they weren't.

So, I left Lewis standing alone on that balcony.

Left it all behind. Again.

PART II
EVERY ARTIST NEEDS
A MUSE

PENN

7

"Okay, that's all for today. I'll see you all on Friday."

The students in my lecture class began to pack up their books, and my teaching assistant, Chelle, hurried forward from the back row. I turned away from the lectern to collect the remaining papers that hadn't been picked up from that class.

"Great class, Dr. Kensington," Chelle said.

"Thank you, Chelle. Though I think it was lost on most of the students."

"Yeah, well, undergrads," she said with a shrug.

I stuffed the papers in my bag. "I wish more of them showed up to class. Otherwise, I wouldn't be failing so many people."

Chelle huffed. She had been dealing with the brunt of the students this semester. Apparently, I was intimidating. Though…it hadn't kept the small number of female students from relentlessly hanging around my office hours.

My eyes lifted as another presence entered the room. It was a slight shift in the room, as if the air were suddenly charged. I sighed when I saw who was standing there.

"We're going to have to postpone our meeting, Chelle. Let's reschedule for Friday."

Chelle glanced behind her and raised her eyebrows. "Sure thing, Dr. Kensington. Let me know if you need anything else before then."

"Of course. If you'll excuse me."

I left Chelle where she was standing and strode across the room. I'd been anticipating this encounter for the last couple of weeks. I'd been purposely, conspicuously busy. Finalizing a hopefully groundbreaking book on philosophical ethics had that tendency. Though…I had used it as an excuse more than was strictly necessary.

"Katherine," I said warily.

"Hello, Penn," she said with a formality that I knew meant she was angry with me.

"To what do I owe the pleasure?"

She tilted up her cherry-red lips and tossed back her supermodel mane of dark waves. "So, seeing me is a pleasure now? That's why you've been avoiding the crew?"

"I've been busy."

She arched a perfectly manicured eyebrow. "Sure you have."

"What do you want, Ren?"

"You know what I want. You haven't responded to my RSVP."

I shot her a knowing look. Then, I pushed past her and out into the brisk New York morning. The click of her high heels followed me onto Columbia's campus in the heart of the Upper West Side.

"Why must you make this difficult?" she asked, walking as if she were on the prowl in a short black dress and fur jacket that I knew her father had left for her. She was lucky to still own it after all of their assets had been frozen and liquidated to pay his securities fraud.

"Am I making it difficult?"

"Yes. You know that you are."

I glanced over at her as we walked brick pathways around manicured lawns toward the library. "You want me to go to this sham of a wedding?"

Katherine gave me a flat look. "Well, you're not about to change your mind and sweep me off my feet, are you?"

"No," I said, mirroring her tone.

"I didn't think so."

"You're really going to marry him?"

"A bet's a bet."

I halted my steps. "Katherine…is this really what this is all about?"

"I don't want to talk about this with you, Penn. The wedding is set for the Saturday before Christmas. It's happening in St. Patrick's Cathedral, and no expense has been spared," she said sharply. "Are you coming or not?"

I searched her face. I didn't know why I'd expected to find anything in her eyes. She didn't love…or even *like* Camden Percy. Who could love that egotistical, manipulative asshole? And, with the tragic downfall of her parents' own marriage, how could she envision anything else for herself? She'd dug her own grave with Percy. Now, she had to lie in it.

"Yes," I said finally. "Of course I will be there, Katherine."

She released a breath as if she hadn't actually been sure what I would say.

"Good." A real smile graced her features then, and she looped our arms together. "I wouldn't have known what to do if you hadn't shown up. You're my oldest friend, Penn Kensington. We've had our differences, but we're practically family. I wouldn't take no for an answer."

I eyed her suspiciously. "Why do I feel like you're about to do something vicious?"

"Wouldn't you like that?" she said with a wink.

"You're being too nice. What do you know?"

"Well, I thought you already knew, and that's why you were being so mopey." She tilted her head onto my shoulder and fluttered her eyelashes. "But I see that this is just who you are. All broody and self-loathing. No wonder she didn't tell you she was back in the city."

I jerked Katherine to a halt. "Who…is in the city?"

"Natalie, of course."

My mind whirred to life. She was here. In my city. What was she doing here?

"You truly didn't know? I thought she'd have already come by to torture you some more," Katherine said dryly.

"How do you know that she's here?"

"Wouldn't you like to know?" she cooed. Her bright red lips turned up into a smile. Her dark hair blowing in the early morning breeze.

"Tell me," I said flatly. I knew that begging would only make her more stubborn. I'd give her a minute, and if she didn't tell me, I'd fucking figure it out on my own.

She stared me down, absolutely loving that she had the upper hand. I counted out a minute and then started walking away from her.

"Penn," she groaned, rushing to catch up with me. "It's all in good fun."

"Sure it is."

"Fine. It was Jane."

"One of Court's girls?"

"They've been together a year, Penn. You think you'd have an interest in your brother's girlfriend."

"I think he's had enough interest in mine for the both of us," I grumbled under my breath.

Katherine rolled her eyes. "Anyway, Jane posted a picture of herself with Natalie at Club 360 last night. I guess they're friends now."

"Why would she be hanging out with Jane?"

None of what Katherine was saying made any sense. Natalie had no interest in the Upper East Side or any of the people in it. Why would she have gone to the club with Jane?

"How should I know?" Katherine asked. "I don't keep tabs on her. I merely thought it was funny that she was here, hanging out with our people and not seeing you."

"Hmm," I murmured noncommittally.

I was too focused on the fact that Natalie was here. In New York City.

Katherine sighed in exasperation. "I don't even know why I bother with you."

My eyes swept up to hers. "Because you wanted to see my face when I found out."

She shrugged. "Fine. Now, can we move on? Let's go get lunch or something."

"I'm going to have to pass," I told her blankly.

"Whatever," she spat in frustration. "But this whole thing is a bit pathetic at this point. Natalie doesn't want to see you. You ruined her life. You wrecked whatever was between you. Honestly, if she came all the way here and didn't see you, doesn't that say something?"

I slid my hands into my pockets. "What does it matter to you, Katherine? You're getting married soon anyway."

She glowered at me. "Thanks for the reminder."

"Anytime."

"I wish things could go back to the way we were."

"We both know that you were the one who fucked that up."

Katherine laughed morosely. "The only person who ruined it came to the city and didn't see you. She's a virus, a plague. One day, you'll see that, too."

She brushed past me and across the brick-lined sidewalk. The click of her high heels the only sound as she stormed away from me. Her mission had backfired. And now, she was more pissed than before.

Still, her presence here had left me with more questions than answers.

I veered away from the spot where Katherine had left me. If I'd thought I was going to get any more work done today, that was completely ruined. Now, my mind was a restless place, itching to put the pieces together.

Why was Natalie here? What had she had doing at that party? Why had she been hanging out with Jane? Why here? Why now?

Why?

Anger blasted through my body. Anger that I had held on a leash for the last year. That I'd buried, trying to forget, trying to move on, trying fucking anything to get her out of my head.

I'd been a goddamn fool and flown to see her, and it hadn't made a difference for us. She'd wanted out. I wasn't selfish enough to pull her back in. Even if I wanted to be.

But I wasn't above finding her in my city if she'd ventured in it. None of the other shit had worked. Maybe I needed to stop running from the one good thing that had happened to me in my fucked up life and start running toward it.

I just had to figure out how the hell to get the answers to my questions. How the hell to find her.

A cab pulled up in front of me, and I hopped in as I pulled up Crew. First things first. I needed to see this picture that Katherine had mentioned. Make sure that she wasn't lying. I put nothing past Katherine at this point. She knew that I had nothing to do with Jane because of Court. I couldn't even believe they were still dating a year later. What sort of arrangement had they worked out for that?

As expected, Jane and I weren't connected on Crew. I pressed the button to follow her. It was a matter of minutes later when Jane Devney's name appeared at the top of my phone. I clicked on the notification, and her profile opened for me. It was as I'd expected. Her profile shot was of her in some kind of Chanel jumpsuit, looking away from the camera. Her ash-blonde hair framing her face in the carefully constructed way that made it appear effortless. I scrolled past the latest image of her breakfast artfully placed next to Dior sunglasses and an Hermès shopping bag.

I rolled my eyes and went to the next image. The shot knocked the breath from my lungs.

Natalie.

It had been a year since I saw her in anything other than my memories and the scarce pictures that we had together. But here she was in a bright blue dress that clung to her skin like liquid silk. Her utterly unique and wonderful silver hair flowed in waves down nearly to her waist. Her makeup was flawless, which I had to assume meant someone else had done it. Natalie hardly ever wore makeup. She didn't need it. Her blue eyes were bright and unwavering. The smile small, not quite meeting her eyes. I'd seen her give me that smile. It always came with a question.

They looked like models. Fashion models at a premiere or during Fashion Week. Natalie, who hated this life so much, fit in without even trying.

I turned my attention to the status underneath.

Missed this girl so much. Seeing her at Club 360 tonight was just a bonus. Hope I see more of her face. #besties #girltime #modelworthy #cunninghamcouture #gucci #designerlife

I frowned. What the hell did that mean? Were they friends? Had they just run into each other? And what the hell was this party? Designer life was hardly Natalie's style.

I shook my head, more confused than ever.

The cab driver pulled over in front of my building, and I hurried inside, taking the elevator to the top floor. A tiny creature came skittering around the corner, racing right for me.

I laughed and dropped to my knees. "Come here, Totle."

Aristotle, my ten-pound gray Italian greyhound puppy, was all legs and full of love. He harmlessly tackled me to the ground and licked my face with all the ferocity of a puppy who hadn't seen its owner in hours. Didn't matter though. He reacted the same way when I'd only been gone minutes.

"Yes, I do love you," I said, dropping another kiss onto the top of his head. "All right, chill out, crazy."

I scooped him up into my arms and grabbed his leash with the promise of a long walk through Central Park to clear the cobwebs. Totle had no objections as we strolled through the park, giving me time to think about Natalie.

Maybe she was here on vacation. She'd happened to be in the same place as Jane. I had no idea what her life was like now. Where she was working or who her friends were or…if she was dating someone. And it was none of my fucking business. I'd ensured that by participating in that fucking bet. It didn't matter that it was all a farce for me just to get close to her. But, of course, she had been right…I hadn't needed a reason. I could have just gotten close to her.

It was the Upper East Side billionaire, playboy stupidity, which I couldn't seem to escape, that had trapped me back into its relentless pull. Like trying to escape quicksand. The harder you tried to get out, the faster it pulled you back in.

Still…I wanted to see her.

And there was only one way to find out what she was up to. I needed to use my resources. If I couldn't go to Jane…I could always go to Rowe.

PENN

8

$\mathcal{M}$y feet carried me to his building a few blocks down from mine. I let myself in the elevator that took me up to his residence. I wasn't sure if he was home, but he hardly ever left unless he had to. He'd opened up Crew headquarters in Manhattan a decade ago and then promptly redesigned his home to include his own office space with a wall of screens to videoconference into meetings. The little introvert.

"Rowe!" I called as I let Totle off the leash, who took off running.

A muffled reply came from his office and then a laugh. I followed behind Totle and found Rowe exactly where I'd expected him, sitting at a white minimalist desk covered with computer monitors. He'd pulled Totle into his lap. No one was immune to my dog's charms.

Rowe nodded his head at me as the only invitation to enter his sacred workspace. I stepped across the hardwood floor and sank into a bare white chaise that never got used.

"What's up?" I asked.

Rowe shrugged. "Work. Shit. You know."

"I do."

"You're here for a reason," Rowe said intuitively.

Totle curled up in his lap and promptly fell asleep. Ridiculous dog.

"I can't just visit?"

"I'm not Lewis."

I snorted. "No, you're not."

Rowe went back to his keyboard, typing away at the speed of light. The best part about Rowe was that he always gave me space. He never forced me to talk when I wasn't ready. He never expected conversation when it was better held with silence. He sometimes missed social cues and was entirely obsessed with his creation and all things tech. But he was a great guy, a great friend.

"So," I said a few minutes later.

Rowe arched an eyebrow.

"Katherine paid me a visit."

"Pleasant."

"Yeah. I guess Natalie is in town, and she was photographed at Club 360 with Jane Devney. Katherine came to gloat."

"Huh." Rowe slid his chair down to face another monitor and started typing. "This?" He swiveled the monitor, so I could get a good look at it and see Natalie's face blown up on an enormous computer screen.

"Yeah," I said softly.

"And you want me to look her up?"

"No." I sighed and met his gaze. "Yes."

"Cool."

"Wait, no. She has me blocked on Crew. If she wanted me to know that she was in New York, then she would have told me, right? Clearly, she doesn't want me to know."

"I think, if you'd wanted someone to tell you no, then you would have gone to Lark. But you came here instead."

He was right. Damn it. I hated how well he knew me sometimes.

"Yeah, but is it a breach of privacy?"

Rowe's smile was strictly villainous. "If people wanted privacy, they wouldn't put everything on the internet."

We all had our own moral qualms. Mine always dealt with sensuality and sex. Katherine's was in her cunning, devious scheming. Lewis's was his obsessions and how quickly he could destroy them. Lark had long since relinquished that side of her personality, but at one point, she could manipulate people better than even Katherine. Better than even me.

But Rowe. Rowe's had everything to do with technology. And the way people used it and how he could use it to bring others down.

"And anyway, no one can block me on Crew."

Put that way, it was mildly terrifying. I was glad he was on my side.

"I don't know if it's ethical."

"Did you want moral advice or tech support?" Rowe asked. He leaned back in his chair and stroked Totle's head. "Morality isn't really my area of expertise, Professor."

I wavered on a precipice. Did I give in and find out what she was doing here? Or wait around in perpetuity, wondering?

Rowe shrugged and turned away from me, back toward the computer. "I'm too damn curious now. You can watch over my shoulder or not."

His fingers flew across the keys. And I knew that he was giving me an out. He was going to do it either way. So, I might as well find out. And I struggled with my own moral issues. They'd gotten me to this place with Natalie to begin with. But fuck, I needed to know.

"All right. Here's her account," he said.

I leaned in and watched the last year of her life scroll past on the screen. It took about a minute.

"What the hell?"

He pulled up a side screen that featured her activity. "Looks like she's gone dormant. The account is active, but she's not on it. Her last sign-in was several months ago."

"Why would she do that?"

He didn't say anything. We both knew the reason anyway. Me.

"She's added a handful of connections. Let me check those out." He skimmed through the new people she'd added to her account. "Almost all of these are from Charleston. One lives in Savannah and one in New York City. Does the name Gillian Kent sound familiar?"

I shook my head. "Never heard of her."

Click.

We entered Gillian's profile.

"She's an editor for Warren," Rowe said.

My eyes narrowed further in confusion. "Why would Natalie be friends with a Warren editor? Do you think she published a book?"

Rowe pulled up a second screen and searched to see if there was any news of Natalie publishing, but it came up empty. "Doesn't look like it." He went back to Gillian's profile and did a cursory scan. "But…"

He zoomed in on a picture she'd posted yesterday at Club 360. It was a full party with a giant sign that read, *Congratulations, Olivia*. I scanned the picture but didn't see Natalie or Jane in attendance.

"Who the hell is Olivia?" I asked.

Click.

We entered the page that Gillian had tagged for Olivia Davies.

I froze when I saw the shadowy headshot on the page.

The woman was wearing a wide-brimmed hat and wide sunglasses. She wasn't quite looking at the camera, but she was smirking while remaining in the shadow. It was clever. No one would be able to guess who was in that picture.

Except for the hair.

Even if I couldn't pick out her face in a lineup, I knew that hair anywhere.

Silvery-white locks that fell in long tresses to her waist.

Hair I'd run my fingers through and grabbed in fistfuls and worshipped.

Natalie was Olivia Davies.

"Whoa," Rowe said. "Didn't see that coming."

Click.

The book cover filled the screen. BET ON IT in stark white letters against a blue background with the words *Based on a true story* in a corner. I pored over the attached synopsis. My eyebrows rose and rose as I continued to read.

"What the fuck?" I breathed.

This sounded familiar. Beyond familiar. It sounded like I'd lived this.

Holy fuck.

"Looks like she wrote about us," Rowe mused.

"Fucking fuck, fuck," I spat.

He scrolled through the page and then clicked over to Amazon. "And it's got great reviews. Dude, I wonder what my character is like!"

I narrowed my eyes at him. "You wonder what *your* character is like?"

Rowe shrugged. "We already know what she's going to say about you."

Yeah. We sure as hell did.

I stormed across the room. If I'd been at my place, I probably would have shattered something. As it was, I was this close to letting the characteristic Kensington fury boil over, setting it loose on Rowe's monitors. I needed to rein it in, control it. Figure out why this set me on fire and compartmentalize it.

"She wrote about us," I growled.

"Yeah, dude."

I put my hands down on his desk and leaned over. "Why am I even surprised? She's a writer. That's what she does. She puts her own experiences onto paper. And who can blame her for taking a pen name when Katherine Van Pelt would skin her alive if she found out?"

Rowe nodded. "Could be worse."

"How?" I snarled.

"She could have forgotten you."

I stilled. My blue eyes lifted to meet Rowe's. "What do you mean?"

"You think a girl who spent the last year writing and releasing a book about her time with you has *forgotten* you?" He snorted. "I thought you were the one who was good with women."

I slowly straightened. Rowe was incredibly right. He'd somehow seen what I hadn't. I'd only seen the slight. How she'd clearly expunged all of her anger onto the page. Her last-ditch effort to get back at us all.

"I have to see her," I said at once.

Rowe grinned. "You're in luck. Looks like she's still in the city. Having a book signing this afternoon." He gestured to the computer.

"That's right now."

"I'll watch Aristotle," Rowe said.

"Why does this feel like a conspiracy to steal my dog?"

Rowe just grinned.

"Okay. Okay. The Strand. See Natalie." I nodded to myself and was about to walk out when another thought struck me.

I turned back to Rowe. "If this was published with Warren, does Lewis know?"

"What do you think?"

A shudder of anger shot through me. No wonder the asshole had been acting so strange around me. I'd have to deal with him later.

"Can you wipe all of this? I don't want Katherine to find out."

"Easy."

"Thanks, Rowe."

He was already back at his computer, hiding all the connections we'd made that led us to this moment. And damn, I was thankful for him. I just hoped that Katherine didn't ever discover this. I couldn't imagine the fallout.

I was out of his place and in another cab in a matter of minutes. The Strand Bookstore in the Village was packed with customers even though the space was ten times as big as it looked on the outside. I'd thought it was a cozy little independent bookstore, but this was a behemoth, storied structure with miles of books on its shelves.

I didn't see anything resembling a book signing though. Just floor-to-ceiling bookshelves, tables and tables piled high with books and recommendations, and bookish swag. A display showed BET ON IT at the front of the store, and I picked up a copy.

"Are you here for the Olivia Davies signing?" a female employee asked enthusiastically. She gestured to the book in my hand.

My head popped up. "Yes. Yes, I am."

"Wonderful. She's signing on the third floor."

I thanked the woman and then carried my book up to the top floor. I had no idea what I was going to say. A year ago, I'd rushed from New York to Charleston to sweep her off her feet. I'd thought that, if I put myself on the line, then all would be right between us. But it hadn't worked.

Now, a year later, I had no idea if she would even want to see me. All I had was this book that said she hadn't forgotten me. That she might still want this.

I took a step inside and froze.

There she was.

Natalie.

A year had passed, and she looked exactly the same to me. Radiant. Effervescent. She was dressed in boho attire I'd seen her in for weeks on end. Though the dress was different, it felt right to me. Her hair was wavy, down her back, and she kept messing with it as she spoke to the excited woman standing in front of her. Her eyes lit up as they chatted back and forth, likely about the book and how much the woman clearly enjoyed it. Natalie tilted her head back and laughed. An unbridled laugh that brought me back to nights in the Hamptons with her. All those nights I'd taken for granted.

And she looked so…happy.

So very happy.

Suddenly, everything else left my head. Her book. What we'd had. Why I was doing this. All I saw was the woman who'd had a dream to become an author and succeeded. Damn it all if it was a book about us that had gotten her here.

If she saw me, then I would undo all of *this*. This whole life she had built. The life she had always wanted. I could only ruin it. Like I'd ruined our relationship.

Natalie had made it clear a year ago that she didn't want any part in my world. That, if it were just us, then sure, this might work. Maybe. But I was a full package. I came with the expectations of the Upper East Side, which she had made perfectly clear that she did not want. She didn't want my life. Fuck, I didn't even want my life. So, there was no way I could drag her back into it.

Coming here was selfish.

Her happiness and success meant more to me than anything else I was going to say to her in that moment. If there had been something I could do or say a year ago to change it, I would have done it. But there wasn't.

And there wasn't anything now either.

So, I took a step back, walked through the door, down the stairs, and out of the bookstore.

And let her live her life without me in it.

NATALIE

9

I glanced up from the book I was signing. My eyes drifted to the entrance to the room. To the place where I was certain a dark-haired man in a suit had been standing moments earlier.

"What is it?" the woman in front of me asked at my puzzled expression.

"I thought I saw someone at the door."

She turned and looked with me. "No one's there now."

"I could have sworn…" I trailed off as my brain ran away with itself. I pushed the finished signed book back to the woman.

"Thanks for coming," I told her. I glanced back to the bookseller at my side. "Sorry. I will be back in a minute."

"Olivia," the bookseller said softly, "there's a line."

"I know. I have to use the restroom. Just…give me a minute."

Before she could say another word, I stood up and darted out of the room.

"Was there…someone standing here?" I asked the woman at the top of the stairs.

"Oh. Hmm…yes. A man just left."

My feet took off before she even finished.

I wasn't crazy.

He was here.

He was here.

He was here.

I ran down the stairs and through the bookstore, ignoring the puzzled looks of the customers and employees. Then, I was out on the sidewalk without a jacket in my sleeveless dress. But I hardly felt the cold.

I looked left and right. Desperate to catch a glimpse of the dark hair or a shock of baby-blue eyes. A man in a suit with his hands stuffed in his pockets. A look of contemplation on his face as he found me.

But there was no one.

It could have been anyone in that doorway.

I'd just hoped…

I thought I'd squashed all hope long ago.

Penn Kensington wasn't going to come and sweep me off my feet. He'd tried a year ago, and I'd rebuffed him. Now, my brain kept envisioning him running down here to make everything right. A sick, twisted fantasy that would never come true. Because he could never make it all right. I didn't even know if I really wanted him to.

But, until this moment, I hadn't even known I'd wanted to see him.

And I couldn't seem to fight away the disappointment that I did.

And he hadn't shown up.

10

"*I* still cannot believe that the publisher was able to get us tickets to *Hamilton*," Amy said giddily as we stood outside of Richard Rodgers Theatre in Midtown.

"Pretty kick-ass perk if I do say so myself."

"Tell me about it."

We had our tickets scanned and then entered the theater. I was finally in the room where it happened. My inner nerd was squealing with delight. After the weird feeling I'd gotten at the bookstore earlier this afternoon, I needed this. Just me and Amy and Alexander Hamilton.

We found our seats in the orchestra level and spent the next couple of minutes taking pictures together. Amy disappeared to get us drinks while I waited anxiously for the curtain. I fiddled with my phone, scrolling through my Olivia page on Crew.

Suddenly, my phone started buzzing, and Jane's name flashed on the screen.

"Hello?" I asked uncertainly.

I hadn't thought that Jane would actually reach out to me. I'd thought she was just being nice the other day at the party.

"Natalie, darling! It's Jane."

"Hey, Jane. How are you?"

"Lovely as always. I was about to walk into dinner with an investor for my little pet project. But I know this incredible martini bar that has the best bartenders in the city. I want to steal them all away. And I thought you should come with me. My treat for celebrating your fabulous book release."

"Oh, well, I'm in *Hamilton* right now with my friend Amy." I glanced around, hoping that Amy would show up any moment and help me make the decision about this.

"More, the merrier. I'll text you the deets."

"Thanks. I'll have to see if we can make it."

Jane's laugh was soft and raspy. "You won't want to miss this place. I have to walk in for dinner now. See you later, darling." She made a kissy noise and then hung up.

I stared down at my phone in confusion. Jane Devney was a bit of a force of nature. She was seeing an investor? For what? So bizarre. And now, she wanted me to meet her for martinis? I did not understand her one bit.

"What's that face?" Amy asked. She passed me a clear plastic cup of red wine.

"Jane Devney asked us to go out for martinis after this."

"Oh, I've been meaning to tell you that Enzo invited me to this art bar in SoHo with some friends. They're showcasing a new talent."

"That sounds like you."

"But I can cancel if you want me to come with."

"No, you're head over heels for Enzo. Plus, that sounds like it'd be good for business, too."

"I'm head over heels for his dick. Let's not get too ahead of ourselves."

I laughed as the lights flickered overhead, announcing the

start of the show. Everyone hustled to their seats, the lights dimmed, and the curtain rose. Showtime.

THREE HOURS LATER, I brushed tears from my eyes as I rose to my feet for a standing ovation. Amy and I barely had words as we stepped out of the theater and back into reality. It felt too surreal to even be here when I felt like I was still living that moment.

"I just…" Amy murmured.

"Yeah."

"Life-changing."

"Genius."

Amy shook her head. "I can't believe I'm leaving you after that experience."

I laughed. "Go have fun. Just make our flight in the morning."

Amy kissed my cheek. "You're the best."

She grabbed the first cab that stopped for her and was off to SoHo for the night. I pulled out my phone and had a message from Jane with an address for the martini bar, Tilted Glass. I stared down at the message and shrugged. This was going to be interesting.

Tilted Glass ended up being only a few blocks from the theater. Even though it was cold, I walked through the throng of people and into the bar. It was tiny with only a smattering of two- or four-person booths and an L-shaped bar. Everything was dark with black leather seats, hardwood, and dim lighting. Still, I could pick out Jane Devney with her large fur coat and mile-high heels. Her signature oversize sunglasses were next to a half-empty martini glass with two olives.

I strode to the seat next to her. "Hey, Jane."

Jane turned to face me. Her hazel eyes wide and unassuming. "Natalie, you made it. I'm so glad." She snapped her fingers at the bartender. "Kendrick, this is Natalie. Treat her like a princess. And make it extra dirty."

"Will do," he said.

"Thanks," I said.

"You do like dirty martinis, right?" She slid a hundred-dollar bill to Kendrick and winked at him.

Kendrick took the bill without comment. As if Jane Devney giving him hundred-dollar tips was totally normal. Maybe he was used to it since he was handsome, tall with dark brown skin and a shaved head. He wore a white button-up with a black vest over it. Looked to be the uniform, but he filled it out.

"I do actually," I confirmed.

"Excellent. Kendrick here is the best damn bartender in the city. Natalie, tell him to come work for me at Trinity." She fluttered her eyelashes at him.

"What's Trinity?" I asked as Kendrick slid a dirty martini in front of me.

"My club," she said nonchalantly. "I forget that you've been out of the city. I'm hoping to soft-open next month. It's a testament to my love of the arts. Trinity is for art, music, and fashion, and I want to do something revolutionary with the space. Fashion shows and art exhibits and concerts, all within a classy, unforgettable club space."

"Wow. That's amazing. Is that what the investor meeting was about?"

Jane nodded and downed the rest of her martini. "I'm working with all the best minds. You know John Forrester on Wall Street?" I didn't nod, but she continued as if I had, "Well, he has a friend, Jeff Mathers, who works with bankers, and they've been setting me up with the right investors within the arts fields and on the club scene to pull it off. Already, I have a dozen fashion designers anxious to use the space and only the best celebrity entertainment."

"Wow. Sounds like you know what you're doing."

"It's been a struggle. You'd be amazed at the number of people who don't want to work with a young woman." Jane rolled her eyes and popped an olive in her mouth.

"I don't think I would actually."

"Yeah. Well, I'm going to prove them wrong."

"I have no doubt. It's pretty amazing to me that you're not resting on your laurels," I confessed. "So much of the Upper East Side is content to be rich and stay rich. Nothing else really matters."

Jane twirled the new martini glass Kendrick had set before her. "I'm a driven woman. Much like you, I assume. I mean, your debut novel is killing it right now."

"Thanks. It is doing pretty well."

"And with Warren."

I nodded.

"I'm so happy for you. Now, tell me everything. I want to know the real Natalie Bishop. Who are you seeing? You were with Penn for a while, right?"

"I…" I sputtered over my martini. "Uh, yeah, like a year ago. I'm not seeing anyone now. Just focused on my career."

"Smart. But no one at all? All work and no play makes for a dull girl."

"Well, what about you and Court?"

"Oh, you know," Jane said dismissively.

No, I really didn't.

"Is he going to meet us out?"

"He's busy tonight, I'm afraid. Weekly poker game. You know how men are. No girls allowed." She rolled her eyes and then reached out to grasp my hand. "You're holding back. I heard you were seen with Lewis Warren. Tell me. Tell me."

I tensed. "Who…who told you that?"

Oh god, had it already gotten out? Did everyone already know?

"It was nothing, I swear. Someone mentioned at the party that you showed up with him. I assumed it was more than it was."

I deflated. My fear fleeing as quickly as it had come.

"I don't know about Lewis."

Jane laughed, squeezing my hand. "That sounds like you like him."

"Well, it's complicated. With my history with his friends, it feels like I'm crossing a line."

"Your history from…a year ago?" Jane asked with an arched eyebrow. "That was forever ago. If you like him and he likes you, you're both adults. You can do whatever you want."

"I know, but…I did date his best friend."

Jane shrugged. "So? Penn has moved on. Why shouldn't you?"

My heart twinged at the words, and I suddenly felt like I was going to be sick. "He…he's dating someone?"

"Oh, I don't know if it's serious. I've just heard all the rumors."

"What rumors?

"Apparently he's fucked half of the Upper East Side in the last year. He's back to his old ways, seducing socialites and bedding every beauty who crosses his path. A modern rake."

A piece of my heart shriveled at the news. I hadn't kissed anyone in a year. My first kiss in all that time had happened only two days ago. But Penn? Penn hadn't pined for me. He hadn't even cared. He'd given up that shred of morality he'd claimed to have and dived headfirst back into the pool.

I shouldn't have been surprised. He'd been writing a book on why casual sex was philosophically moral. That the standard view that said relationships were safer and all-around better wasn't accurate any longer. Of course he'd taken his own advice.

"Well, that's interesting," I finally managed to get out. "Here I was, feeling bad that I'd kissed Lewis. And maybe that was just stupid. Why would Penn care?"

"You kissed!" Jane gasped in delight.

"Yeah. I mean, I pushed him away because I thought it was wrong."

"But it felt oh-so right?" Jane waggled her eyebrows.

I laughed despite my pain. "Oh-so right," I agreed.

"I've got the best idea," Jane said. "You should invite Lewis out for a martini."

"Jane…"

"It'll be fun. You can decide then if you really like him without all that guilt weighing you down. Or you can have a damn good martini from Kendrick here with the most eligible bachelor in Manhattan and *moi*, of course."

"He might not even show up," I argued.

Jane's smile was electric. "Don't know until you try."

What did I have to lose really? I'd done the right thing over and over. Always the right thing. Always the smart and good thing. Where had that gotten me? Maybe I'd just forget about that and take Jane's advice. Nothing was holding me back any longer.

"All right. But, if this turns out to be a bad idea, I'm blaming you."

She clapped her hands. "I take full responsibility."

I withdrew my phone and wrote a text I never thought I would compose.

Hey, I'm at Tilted Glass with Jane. Any interest in meeting us out for a drink?

My stomach was in knots as I hit the Send button. My brain going through all the reasons I shouldn't have sent that. But then a text came in almost instantaneously, and all the nerves dissolved.

I'd love that. See you soon.

NATALIE

11

I had just finished my second martini when I noticed Lewis walking into the bar. Eyes turned to him. He attracted attention by his very presence in that dark gray suit. His black button-up opened at the neck. His eyes found me across the room. A slow smile spread across his face as he sauntered toward me, ignoring the looks that he drew from all sides.

"This was a nice surprise," he said by way of greeting.

I tipped my martini at him. "You can thank Jane."

He turned toward Jane and grinned. "I don't know what you did, but I feel as if I'm going to owe you a favor."

Jane laughed. "Favors are my favorite currency."

"I bet," he said with a grin as he slipped into the seat next to me. "What are we drinking?"

"Dirty martinis," I informed him.

"As dirty as they come," Jane said. "I'm trying to convince Kendrick to bartend at my new place, Trinity."

"I haven't heard that it's been green-lighted," Lewis observed.

Jane shrugged. "Minor kinks. It'll come through. You'll be at the opening, yeah?"

"Wouldn't miss it. Maybe we can convince Natalie here to go with me."

"When is it?" I asked, a flush tingeing my cheeks.

"December thirteenth. Friday the thirteenth felt lucky," Jane said with a chuckle.

Kendrick slipped me my third martini and passed one to Lewis, too. I was feeling the side effects pretty strong from the first two. I must have been to even consider going.

"I'll be back in Charleston."

"You could fly up for it," Jane said.

"Or," Lewis said, "you could just move here."

I laughed unexpectedly. "I can't move here."

"Oh my god, yes!" Jane said. "That would be a fabulous idea. Move to the city, Natalie."

"I can't just *move* to New York," I told them.

"Why not?" Lewis asked. "You're working as an author and making decent money, and you write better here. You told me yourself."

"I...I mean...yeah, but," I ventured.

Jane's grin widened. "You write better in the city? Well then, you have to move here. We could hang out all the time. Get coffee while I work on my business and you write. Shop at Bergdorf and Barneys and go to all the best parties. It would be fabulous."

Except...that wasn't the life I wanted or even *could* live. Just because I'd published my first book didn't mean I could suddenly shop at Bergdorf. God, I couldn't even imagine what it would cost to move to the city and get my own apartment. It was unreasonable.

"It's my first book. I don't even have the next contract."

Lewis brushed that aside. "You're a superstar at Warren. They'll buy anything you put forth now."

"Yeah, and if they don't, I think we know someone who might have a say," Jane said with a pointed look.

"Whoa, whoa, whoa, slow down," I said. "First off, no one is helping me get my book published. And even if they buy the next book, I don't know if it's a fluke that the first did well. There are so many variables. Too many variables to just move to New York."

"Oh, come on. Where's the girl who used to hop vacation homes for fun while she was writing?" Lewis asked.

"That girl got *paid* to do that and wrote on the side," I reminded him.

"What's the real issue?" Jane asked, leaning in.

I took a steadying sip of my martini. "I don't know. I... don't want to live here. I don't fit in here. The Upper East Side isn't my home. It's this other universe that I'll never belong to. I learned that the hard way."

Jane frowned. "Who told you that you didn't belong? Because they're wrong."

"I know who told you that," Lewis said grimly.

Penn. Penn had said it that first day on the beach when he saw me there. Katherine had said it later. And they weren't wrong. No matter what Jane or Lewis thought. I didn't have enough money or the name to fit in with this crowd. I was an outsider. Maybe less of a fish out of water than the first time I'd stumbled into that Hamptons cottage with the crew and their fabulous lives. But it didn't change the fact that this world had hurt me. Walking back into it would be foolish.

"Listen," Jane said, "the Upper East Side is its own world. I'll grant you that. But the only way you can survive it is by thinking you belong. The minute they see weakness, they'll eat you alive."

That, she knew for a fact.

"So, you're saying...fake it till you make it?" I asked.

"Fake it till you don't give a fuck," Jane said. She raised her martini glass.

Lewis laughed. "I'll toast to that."

We all clinked glasses together, and I sipped my martini more carefully. I was drunk enough to consider this. That was absurd. I couldn't move to New York. And I most certainly was not going to become Upper East Side by sheer force of will.

"So, what do you think?" Lewis asked.

"About moving?" I shook my head, still shocked we were even having this conversation.

"Yeah. Do it, Natalie!" Jane agreed.

"I mean, my interest is purely selfish," Lewis said, leaning forward into my personal space. "I want you here. I want you close."

"I don't know. I'm going back to Charleston in the morning. I've just been planning to write from there."

"Ugh, Charleston," Jane said. "That's somewhere in the South, right?"

I arched an eyebrow. "Yeah, it's in South Carolina. It's beautiful."

"I bet it is. But it's not New York."

"And you said you couldn't write there," Lewis reasoned again.

"I did say that, but maybe now that I have my inspiration back for the story, I could work on it there."

Maybe. Hopefully. Fuck, hopefully.

"What's the new book about anyway?" Jane asked.

"Oh, it follows this couple and their relationship over time. Starts with them young and falling in love despite the fact that they're total opposites. Then, it shows the descent of their relationship and the way family and outside influences mold and sharpen it. It's told from multiple points of view so that you see the relationship and its issues from every side. But you never quite know the truth."

"Sounds dark." Jane's fur coat slipped, revealing the bare shoulder beneath.

"Sort of. Realistic is what I go for," I said with a shrug.

"It sounds amazing to me," Lewis said. "How much do you have?"

I shrugged. "Like, fifteen thousand words. It's, like, thirty single-spaced pages."

"That's a hefty amount in a matter of days."

"It is." I leaned into the bar, wondering if this third martini was a huge, huge mistake. "Most I've written in a year."

"Rock star," Jane said. "What about you, Lewis? Any fascinating new adventure?"

Lewis's eyes crawled over me as if to say that I was the new adventure. But, when he spoke, he was all business. "I'm working with a slew of new investors that looks promising. As you are probably aware, I manage hedge funds. We're looking to rapidly increase return on investment by purchasing a new real estate opportunity." He shrugged with his perfectly casual smile. "It's all really dry and boring unless you know more about how they work."

"I've invested in a few before," Jane said with her own shrug. "Real estate seems safe."

"It can be." His tone suggested that what he was dealing with was anything but.

I, on the other hand, had no experience with hedge funds. All I knew was that they were incredibly risky, and if they paid off, you made a shit-ton of money. Also, only super-fucking-rich people could use them. Which counted me out.

"I'm going to…" I pointed toward the restroom.

As soon as I stood up, my knees wobbled, and I thought I might fall over.

"Oh shit," I said with a laugh. "I didn't think I was this drunk. How strong were those martinis?"

Jane took another sip of hers, looking utterly unfazed. "Strong. As they should be."

I blinked rapidly as I tried to get my legs to cooperate and then teetered toward the restroom. After seeing to my needs, I checked my phone, shocked to see that it was past midnight already. Time to go home. As much fun as it had been—and it had been more fun than I'd thought—if I wanted to make my seven thirty a.m. flight, then I needed to sleep off my impending hangover.

"Okay, I think I'm out," I said with a laugh. "It's late, and I have a crazy-early flight."

"So soon?" Jane complained. "Come on. One more drink!"

"One more drink, and I'm going to black out," I said with a laugh. I stumbled toward her and pulled her into a hug. "I had a great time. Thanks for inviting me out. I will see if I can make it up for the opening of your club."

"Yes! You have to be there. Or you know, just move here." Jane winked.

I laughed. "I don't know. Maybe."

Lewis had gotten to his feet and was slipping cash onto the bar. "Let me take you back to your hotel."

"Oh...I can get a cab." I took a step and nearly fell into him.

He smiled and caught me with ease. "Better safe than sorry, Miss Bishop."

"Let him take you." Jane flitted her hand. "I'll be fine here. I have more convincing to do with Kendrick."

"All right. That would be nice."

Lewis took my hand and gentlemanly placed it on his elbow, and then he whisked me out of Tilted Glass. A black Mercedes appeared in front of us. Lewis held the door open for me, and I all but fell inside.

"I think I'm drunk," I told him when he sank into the seat next to me.

He chuckled and brushed a stray strand of hair from my shoulder. "I noticed that."

"I wasn't going to invite you tonight."

"Well, I'm glad that you did."

My blue eyes met his dark depths. He was so fucking hot. It was ridiculous. How did they make the men on the Upper East Side? Was it just the outstanding wealth? Or were they somehow their own breed entirely?

"Why do you want this?" I muttered. A question I never would have had the guts to ask while sober.

His hand slid up into my hair, fingering the silver strands. "Because you are entirely you, unequivocally you. Fearless, stubborn, brazen, and strikingly independent. You say what you mean and mean what you say. There are no games with you. No questions about where your head is."

"Right now, my head is spinning."

He just grinned at me. "You want this, too."

"Maybe," I whispered.

"I can tell in the way your eyes find me and the soft pant in your breath as I hold you and the rise of your chest when I get near."

His lips were nearly upon mine. And all those things he'd said weren't wrong. I wanted to kiss him. Fuck, before, I'd never wanted to stop kissing him. Only my conscience had gotten in the way. And now...now, I'd left that with the second martini.

I pushed forward, capturing his lips. Yes, I wanted this.

My hands wrapped around his neck, dragging him closer, closer, closer. There was too much space. Not enough skin.

I dragged my leg over his and straddled him in the backseat of the car. His hands slipped down to my waist as our kisses turned even more feverish. Tongues tasting, testing, knowing. Lips urgent and aggressive. I could feel his thickness through the soft material of his suit pants. My core pulsed at the feel of him. Wantonness took over as my body awakened, yawning open and suddenly remembering in sharp clarity how good this all felt.

I reached for the buckle of his belt when his hand clamped around my wrist.

"Natalie," he exhaled, leaning his forehead against mine.

"What?" I asked breathlessly.

"Not like this."

"You don't want to?"

He coughed a laugh. "Oh, I do. I really do. But…you've had too much to drink."

"Not that much." I knew it was a lie even as I said it.

He kissed me once more, soft and tempting. A kiss that left me aching for more.

"Too much," he said. "I won't take advantage of your inebriation. Move to New York, and we'll have plenty of time."

"Lewis," I groaned.

"It's selfish. I want you here. But, beyond that, it's good for your career." He pulled back to look me in the eyes. "At least tell me that you'll consider."

I sighed, giving in to that gaze and those lips and the red-hot desire still hitting me like a freight train. "I'll consider it."

NATALIE

12

I didn't move to New York, but I couldn't stop thinking about it.

Even as my sister, Melanie, and her douche boyfriend, Michael, argued in front of me as if I weren't present. Or as Amy went about her normal routine in Montgomery Gallery as if she hadn't had the most amazing weekend with Enzo. Or as I tried to act as if everything were back to normal.

But I wasn't back to normal. I was still stuck on this damn novel. The inspiration I'd had while in New York had vanished as soon as it had come. Caroline wanted a full synopsis and to read the pages, but I seriously wasn't ready for that.

"Oh my god, would you two shut your mouths?" Amy yelled, finally blowing a gasket.

Melanie's mouth snapped shut. Michael whirled on Amy as if he was going to give her a piece of his mind.

"Don't even think about it." Amy pointed her finger at him. "You're in my gallery, and you can get the hell out if you so much as use the wrong tone with Melanie again."

Michael schooled his features into disinterest and began

to speak to Melanie less erratically. Melanie had come over straight from her last class at Grimke University, Charleston's resident Southern Ivy, to pick me up to go to dinner at our parents' tonight. Michael had shown up, unannounced, a few minutes later, and yelling had ensued. I didn't even know what they'd been arguing about. It felt like everything lately. Ever since he'd dumped her to go to homecoming with her best friend last year, things had never been the same. And only Melanie didn't see it.

"Now that I have some peace and quiet, I have to get back to work. Are you having any luck writing?" Amy asked me.

I shook my head. "Like, another chapter, but that's it."

"Another chapter is better than nothing. Maybe this book will just take longer to write."

I shrugged. "Maybe."

My phone dinged in my hand, and I grinned at the picture Lewis had sent over. It was him in a black peacoat, standing in Central Park with the Bethesda Fountain in the background. There was only one line under it.

Miss you.

A grin split my face before I could think better of it. Amy leaned over my shoulder when she saw it.

"Jesus, he is smitten." Then, she glanced up at me. "And he's not the only one."

I laughed and closed out of the picture. "I don't know if *smitten* is the word. But he's something."

"He's totally into you."

"Too bad he's a thousand miles away."

"He did ask you to move to New York," Amy conceded.

"Yeah, I'll add that to the list of horrible ideas I have."

"Why would that be a horrible idea besides the fact that you'd be leaving me behind?"

"A hundred percent because you'd be here," I said with a laugh. Amy nudged me. "I mean, first, money. Second, I don't even know if I'll get another book contract. Third, I hardly know anyone there. It would be insanely impulsive."

"First, you have money. Second, you're going to get another book contract. Third, you know *enough* people. And impulsive *works* for you."

I waved a hand at her. I couldn't stop thinking about it, but I always solidly came down on a maybe. There were a million more reasons to stay than to go. But New York called to me, and I couldn't ignore her siren call.

I was about to respond when my phone started ringing. "Hello?"

"Natalie, it's Gillian."

"Hey, Gillian. How are you?"

"Girl, I am out of this world. Do you know what today is?"

"Uh…" I glanced at my phone. "November thirteenth?"

"Wednesday," she said as if that were more obvious.

"Okay…"

"*New York Times* released their best-sellers list."

"Oh my god," I whispered.

My stomach dropped. I hadn't known that it came out on Wednesday. Or that I should even be looking for it. I'd *hoped*, of course. Who wouldn't hope? But I'd never thought it would be my reality. It was my debut. It was a dream. This just didn't happen.

"You hit at number three on the hardcover list."

A buzzing filled my head.

I'd hit. I'd hit. I'd hit.

I didn't know what to say or think or feel. All of a sudden, I burst into tears. I couldn't stop it even if I wanted to. I sobbed uncontrollably as emotions jolted through me. As all my dreams seemed to come true at once. My hands were shaking. Distantly, I saw Amy turn to me with concern. Melanie brushing past Michael to find out what was wrong. But I couldn't process it. Any of it.

"Oh, Natalie! Congratulations! I knew this book would be huge. And, now, you're a *New York Times* bestselling author! So well deserved. It's been such a pleasure bringing this book to life."

"Thank you, Gillian! I can't even believe this is real."

"It is. You're brilliant. I'm so proud of you."

I blubbered incoherently a few more minutes before hanging up the phone. I glanced up into the startled faces of my friends.

"What happened?" Melanie gasped. "Is everything all right?"

"I…I hit the *New York Times*."

"Oh my god!" Melanie shrieked at the same time as Amy. They jumped up and down and then threw their arms around me as one.

"This is amazing, Nat," Amy said, squeezing the life out of me.

"I'm so excited!" Melanie cried. "We have to celebrate."

"Drinks on Natalie," Michael said with a chuckle.

A sign of how immersed I was in my news was that I actually laughed at Michael. "Drinks on me. But, first…I need to tell Mom."

"She's going to flip out," Melanie gasped.

"I know."

"Let's go to her shop now! She'll never expect it!"

"Damn, I wish I could see her reaction," Amy said. "Stupid gallery!"

"Let's do it," I said.

Melanie hugged me again. "I have the car."

"You're just going to leave?" Michael asked.

She waffled for a minute as if she had to think about how to respond to him. "I'll call you later."

He narrowed his eyes. "Seriously?"

"Michael, it's for Nat."

He looked like he was going to breathe fire.

"We're leaving. Come on, Mel," I said, stepping between them and pulling her toward the gallery exit. "See you, Amy!"

As soon as we were out of the gallery, Melanie jammed her finger down on the open button on the clicker for her Honda Civic. She basically ripped open her door before dropping into the driver's side.

I slipped in after her. "Michael is…something."

"I don't want to talk about him right now, Nat. I know you don't like him."

"You're right. I don't."

Melanie shot me a look to tell me to shut up and then put the car in reverse. I promptly shut up. She knew how I felt about Michael. It wasn't a secret. No need to keep discussing it.

She zipped across town to our mom's New Age shop, Ascension Books & Gifts. I'd always thought that the *books and gifts* part was a little misleading. It was primarily full of crystals, incense, tarot cards, special teas, and other metaphysical tools of her trade. The books mostly consisted of instructions on how to read crystal balls, interpret cards, and clean chakras. I still hadn't discovered what she considered gifts. It just looked like a magic shop on the inside.

My mom had a slew of regular patrons who kept the shop open. And tourists who wanted their palms read and fortunes told usually made up the rest of the customers. Right now, thankfully, it was empty.

"Welcome to Ascension," my mother said as the bell jangled overhead.

"Hi, Mom," Melanie said.

"Oh, my daughters have graced me with their presence and at the same time. What must be the occasion?"

I hugged her and then pulled back to admire her beautiful, celestial blouse. "I like this. Where did you get it?"

"You always had style," my mother said with a laugh then gestured to Melanie. "You, on the other hand."

"Hey, I'm the one with style!" Melanie said. "I'm the one *studying* fashion."

"The seventies were so much more fetching," my mother said. She winked at me as Melanie huffed. "Now, tell me why you're here. Something momentous I feel. I read it last night. I see you're here now to tell me. What is it?"

"I hit the *New York Times*."

"Oh, baby," my mother said, "congratulations! I drew The World in tarot last night, and here it is. You'll begin your new journey after this."

I laughed. It was no use interpreting my mother's predictions. She always had them, and only half of them ever had any semblance of truth.

"Thank you, Mom. I wanted to tell you first."

"Have you told your father?"

I frowned and shook my head. My father didn't exactly support my decision to be an author. He'd been aloof about the whole thing since I got an English degree.

"No, of course not," she said, easily reading me.

I shrugged. "I'll tell him at dinner."

"He'll be happy for you, I think." My mom waved her hands about. "Now, sit. Sit. Both of you. I just put tea on. We'll read."

Melanie and I shared a look that said we both knew there was no point in turning her down. So, we sat with her and waited for the tea.

"Why aren't you happy about this?" my mother asked as soon as the tea was in front of us.

"What? I am happy," I said.

She gave me a shrewd look. "We've all noticed. Haven't we, Melanie?"

"True," Melanie agreed.

"What is this, an ambush?"

"She's not wrong, Nat. You've just been kind of skating by."

"You've been at college. How would you know?"

"Just think that I've been at college, and I've still noticed."

My mother nodded. "You have everything you've ever wanted and no joy. Is it because you haven't been working on your new book?"

I frowned. Maybe my mother was more intuitive than I gave her credit for. Or…maybe her readings were right. Sometimes, I wondered.

"Well, I was writing when I was in New York, but I came home, and everything got all muddled again. I'm not sure what I'm doing."

"Have you considered that maybe this isn't your home?" my mother asked.

I laughed. "Of course it is."

"No," Melanie said. "It's my home. You didn't grow up here, and you were happier when you were traveling."

"Well, I can't do that anymore, can I?"

"Can't you?" my mother asked. "What's stopping you? Money? You have that now. You could live wherever you wanted or travel the world."

"Alone?" I asked softly.

I couldn't believe that my mom and Melanie were saying the same damn thing that Jane and Lewis had said. It was like the universe was pointing me in one direction, even as I fought it at all costs.

"Would you truly be alone?" Melanie asked with a wink. "I saw that picture you were sent."

"Oh, shush you," I said with a laugh.

"Look, no matter your differences, you are your father's daughter. You shouldn't stay in one place too long. You need travel and adventure. Melanie and I are homebodies. Her world is here. As is mine. Yours isn't."

I took a long sip of my tea while I took in their words. Maybe they were right. Maybe I'd just been skating around the real issue. I wanted to move to New York. I wanted to live that life. But at the same time, I didn't want to be part of the Upper East Side. Was there a way to live the life I wanted in New York and not be a part of the Upper East Side?

"Did you already read for me before this?" I finally asked.

My mother shook her head with a smile. "It's painted on your face."

I handed over my empty teacup. "Well, what do you see?"

My mother took the cup and stared down into the leaves at the bottom. She smiled softly. "Birds."

"Birds?" I took the cup back and looked in it. And there it was...birds mid-flight. Even I could see it.

"Do I even have to tell you what that means?" my mother asked with a raised eyebrow. "Fly, my darling. Fly."

NATALIE

13

I flew.

And, two weeks later, I was standing in my own apartment on the Upper West Side. New York City might have ruined my life. But it had also brought me everything my heart had ever wanted. It was the city of dreams, and I intended to dive in headfirst.

It did nothing to dispel the nagging bit of fear that said that this was too good to be true. Or that moving here wouldn't even work. Maybe I couldn't write in New York City either.

I smothered the thought. It'd do no good, fretting on that. I had moved to New York to write, and write I would.

As soon as I finished unpacking. It was amazing, the amount of stuff I *hadn't* accumulated when living out of a suitcase for a year and a half and then hunkering down in my best friend's guest bedroom for a year. I really had nothing and was lucky that I'd been able to bring what I could to try to fill the small apartment.

But, by that afternoon, I thought I'd done a decent enough job unpacking. Writing would likely have to begin tomorrow since I'd promised Lewis that I would celebrate with him when he got off work. He'd been texting me all day, and I couldn't deny that I had something like butterflies of anticipation in my stomach.

For the first time ever, the buzzer sounded from the apartment door. I squealed in excitement and rushed to answer it.

I pressed the button and said, "Hello?"

"Natalie, it's Lewis. Buzz me up."

"Yay! Doing it now." I pressed the button and paced in front of the door until I heard a knock.

I wrenched the door open. Lewis Warren stood in the doorway, looking sexy as hell in a white button-up, rolled to his elbows, his peacoat folded over his arm, and a bottle of champagne in his hand.

A wide grin split his face. "Hey, gorgeous."

"Hey," I breathed.

I'd been anxious and excited about this meeting all day. Worried that the spark between us hadn't been real. That he'd see me differently. Or that it wouldn't really work out now that I was here because I wasn't Upper East Side...or whatever. That it would start to feel wrong again. Like we shouldn't be doing this.

But now, standing here with him, all my doubts vanished.

He scooped me up into a hug. "I'm so glad you decided to move. The last three weeks have been torture."

"I'm glad I moved, too," I said with a laugh. I stepped back and gestured for him to enter. "Come on in. It's small, but I'm in love."

He strode inside and then held up the bottle of champagne. "Housewarming gift."

"Oh, wow. Thank you." I stared down at the yellow label with wide eyes before putting it in the empty refrigerator. It was much fancier than the cheap stuff Amy and I celebrated with. "I know what I'm having for dinner now."

He chuckled as he dropped his black peacoat onto the sofa. "So, this is the place."

"Yep," I said, suddenly seeing the tiny place through his eyes. "I know it's not much, but…"

"Hey." He held up his hand. "You don't have to diminish it for me. I was the one who helped you find it, after all. And it's exactly what you wanted, right?"

I nodded. Because it was the exact apartment I'd been looking for. I'd been amazed when Lewis had stumbled across it. "Absolutely. I mean, look at this exposed brick." I gestured to the living room wall. "And…and…I live in it all alone. So, no roommates or anything."

"Pretty spectacular for your first New York City apartment. I think most people have a minimum of five roommates. I had four."

"What? No way. You're a Warren."

"So are my parents and two younger sisters."

I chuckled. "I wasn't counting Charlotte and Etta."

"That means that you clearly haven't lived with them. They're hellions."

"You weren't much better at that age, were you?"

"Oh, worse, much worse," he said with a wink.

"Why am I not surprised?"

I could only guess based on what I knew of Penn's past. I slightly shriveled inwardly at that thought. When I forgot that Penn and Lewis were best friends, it was much easier to be in his presence.

I turned away from Lewis to shrug my jacket on. I didn't want to ruin our night. We'd both been looking forward to it.

My face was carefully blank as I faced him once more. "Well, what do you say we get out of here?"

Lewis nodded, but I didn't think that he had missed my

uncomfortable moment. He pulled his jacket back on, and then we took the stairs down to the ground level. I shuddered at the frigid temperature. So much colder than it had been in Charleston this morning. I tugged gloves on, preparing for the walk.

But Lewis gestured to a black Mercedes idling in front of my building. "My driver is waiting."

"Oh, you have a driver."

He nodded as he opened the back door. "How do you think we got back to your hotel when you were here for your book?"

"You know…I was drunk enough not to have given it a thought."

"I remember that very clearly."

A blush tinged my cheeks as I slid into the backseat. I'd been rather forward the last time we were alone in the back of his Mercedes. It was embarrassing, considering how sober I was now.

And just reminded me of how divergent our lives were. Of course Lewis had a driver. He enjoyed the life that he had grown up in and had no moral objections to his upbringing. I needed to silence the voice in my head that said that was a problem. He wasn't Penn. And I didn't want Penn.

"Where are we going?" I asked Lewis once he was inside and the car had started to move.

"It's a surprise. I think you'll like it."

"I like surprises," I admitted.

"Good. I plan to have a lot of them." He angled his full attention to me. "Tell me about the drive up here. I still can't believe you drove alone."

"Oh, it was great actually. I love road trips. Amy and I went on one for three weeks one summer, all the way to LA. This was nothing compared to that. It's the basis for one of my books."

He contemplatively scrunched his brows together. "Have you submitted that one?"

I shook my head. "No, I was writing it before BET ON IT, and I just haven't picked it back up."

"How can you when you've been so busy with the new book? Do you have a title for it yet?"

"I'm leaning toward IT's A MATTER OF OPINION. Because it's all about never really knowing the truth and getting every side of the tale, except what really happened."

"I like it." He slid a little bit closer to me until our shoulders were touching. A shiver ran through my body. "So... when do I get to read it?"

I laughed. "Never!"

"Natalie! Come on. I'm your biggest fan."

"That sounds so weird," I told him, covering my face. "I don't even know what that means."

"It means, you're a brilliant writer, and I need more of your books in my life. Send it to me. Please, I'm dying to read it."

"No way. No one reads my books before they're done, except my agent and editor. I've never let anyone look at them ahead of time. I think I'd break out in hives if I knew you were reading it."

"It cannot be that bad."

"It is. I swear. Amy snuck a chapter once, and I nearly vomited on her."

He laughed and shook his head. "I think that's all in your head."

"Maybe, but what if I never write another word on it? Then, you'll have a half-baked idea of my writing in your head."

He rolled his eyes at me. "Natalie, that's not even possible."

"Oh, it's totally possible. But, hopefully, not with this

book since I already told my agent about it and she's already told Gillian about it and I moved to New York to finish and sell the damn thing."

"It'll all work out," he assured me. "No one at Warren wants your career to continue successfully more than I do. But I also want to think you moved here for more than one reason."

"Oh?" I whispered.

The tension crackled between us.

His hand slid across my lap, reaching for my fingers and lacing them together. His thumb gently stroked up and down as if he were learning the feel of me. And, while my mind was completely occupied by the feel of his hand in my own—the long fingers and broad palm and the amazing softness of that hand—my eyes were locked on his.

"I like to think that you're here because of me. That I helped you find your way back to writing while you were here. That I can help you even more now that you're in my city." He raised our locked hands to his lips and placed a soft kiss on my hand. "That okay with you?"

I nodded, momentarily speechless. Lewis *had* helped me be able to write again. And so had this city. Being in the city and close to him seemed like a perk to it all. If not the exact reason I had moved.

"Here we are, sir," the driver said from the front seat.

Lewis winked at me and then helped me out of the car. I gasped at the sight before me. I'd heard about it, seen it on television, and imagined what it would look like basically all my life. But seeing the Rockefeller Center Christmas Tree all lit up was even more amazing than I could have imagined.

Last year, I had left at the beginning of November before the tree was put up. It might make me the epitome of a tourist, but I was totally enamored by it.

"Oh my god," I gushed. "It's so huge!"

Lewis laughed and guided me forward. "I actually think it was bigger last year."

I rolled my eyes at him. "I bet you're the kind of person who says that every year."

His smirk said that I was right. "Maybe."

"We have to get a picture," I insisted.

"Obviously."

We spent a couple of minutes trying to find the best angle and finding someone who would snap the shot for us. Then, I made Lewis take a few shots for me to post on my Olivia Davies page. Back-of-the-head shots for anonymity and all that. Then, I oohed and aahed over the massive tree some more before Lewis guided me to the ice skating rink below.

It wasn't too packed since it was a Thursday night, and the crowds hadn't shown up yet. But the line still wrapped around the side of the rink. It had to be at least an hour wait. I wanted to do it, but I didn't know if I wanted to stand out in the cold that long.

"Are you sure? I mean…the line is pretty long," I told him.

He grinned mischievously as if he had something up his sleeve. I followed him past the enormous line and straight to the front.

"Ah, yes, Mr. Warren. Lovely to have you this evening," a man greeted us. "I have everything you requested right here."

I blinked and then blinked again. I knew he could pull strings. I knew he was a Warren. But, fuck…I wasn't used to it. Money opened doors. Money closed them in my face, too. And though I was wowed by the gesture, a part of me wished he had made us wait in the line.

I ignored the irritated glances from the people who had been waiting the last hour and followed behind Lewis. We put on skates, which were clearly not the dinky ones everyone else was wearing, and then hobbled to the rink.

"Where did you get these skates?" I asked. "And how did you know my size?"

He stepped onto the ice and held his hand out to me. "I guessed."

"Uh-huh. Yeah. Sure." I arched an eyebrow at him.

"Do you really want to know?"

I stared at him, waiting for the answer.

"You wore Katherine's shoes last year. I know her size. I deduced from there."

Katherine. My blood ran cold at her name. That was someone I absolutely did not want to see or think about.

"Come on, Nat," he said softly as if he could read what her name had done to me.

I took his hand because I had to. I was a terrible skater. And Lewis quickly figured that out. He chuckled as he skated circles around me.

"I prefer a swimming pool," I muttered as I slowly got the hang of it.

"Considering you swam in college, I would think so."

"For real," I muttered. "Water should be wet, not solid."

He chuckled and took my hands to help me around the rink.

We circled the ice a couple of times until I felt like I wasn't going to fall over at any second. Lewis was clearly an accomplished skater. Half the time, he skated backward and held my hands so that I was more stable. It was adorable in that can't-get-her-legs-under-her way.

"You're getting a lot better," he insisted.

I just laughed at him. "Sure."

He tugged me closer and skated us to the side of the rink, away from the majority of the other people. It was amazing how he was able to navigate it all backward when I could barely move forward.

"How did you learn to skate like that?"

"My family went to Central Park all the time," he told me. Then he smiled as if he was remembering a specific memory. "When Charlotte was young, maybe six, she took figure-skating lessons. She darted between activities so often that I thought it would be helpful if I took the classes with her to keep her motivated. I was sixteen or seventeen and easily the best in the class."

"Oh my god, adorable," I said. I covered my mouth as I imagined him in a beginner figure-skating class.

"Yeah. They still tease me about it."

I couldn't help it. I started giggling. It was impossible not to. This was the part of Lewis that made me forget everything else.

"I love to see that smile," he said, tucking a loose strand of hair behind my ear.

My stomach fluttered. Heat spread through my core as my heartbeat ratcheted up. His hand slipped under my jacket, touching bare skin. Shivers traveled down my spine, and I tilted my head up to look at him. He skated me forward against his chest until I was so near that I could feel his breath warm my cheek.

On reflex, I put an arm around his neck. Our eyes locked, asking and giving permission. The moment heating us despite the temperatures.

Then he leaned down and brought our lips together in a searing kiss that spoke of how much he had missed me the last couple of weeks. Dear god, the man could kiss. His lips were pouty and soft and warm. His tongue an adventure. His fingers dug into flesh.

A groan escaped my mouth, and he smiled against my lips. A smile that said he knew exactly what he was doing and how he was doing it.

"I like that sound," he murmured against my lips.

"Mmm," I acknowledged.

A whistle came in our direction, and we broke apart with a laugh as we realized that people had been catcalling our kiss.

"Got a little carried away," I said.

Then, he dipped down and captured my lips one more time. "Can't get enough of that."

I blushed at his comment and dipped my chin.

But Lewis tilted my chin back up to meet his chocolate gaze. "I know that you just got here, Nat, but I want to see more of you. I want more. I want you."

My throat tightened. I *did* want to see more of Lewis. I liked being around him. God, I'd loved our conversations the last couple of weeks and this...date and, god, that kiss. But something held my tongue like peanut butter sticking to the roof of my mouth.

His eyes darted across my face as if waiting for an answer. "You want that, too," he insisted.

"I do," I got out finally, hesitantly.

"But?"

I shook my head and glanced away. I really didn't want to talk about this. The reason I was cautious had already moved on. Why was I torturing myself by bringing it up?

"It's...I don't know...complicated."

His thumb stroked my jawline and turned my chin to make me look back at him. "It doesn't have to be complicated. Talk to me."

"It's Penn," I whispered.

Lewis sighed. "Ah. Competing with Penn Kensington. What else is new?"

"No," I said quickly. "That's not what I meant. Not at all. There's nothing between me and Penn anymore. But he's your best friend."

"He is. He's moved on. Why shouldn't you? After how he treated you, you should find someone who will treat you like

119

a goddess. And I have every intention of doing just that, Natalie, if you'll let me."

"I believe you, but it's more than just you. I don't know if I'm ready to fake it till I make it on the Upper East Side. I moved back to Charleston to get away from it."

"Not everything is galas and club openings. We could start small and easy. We don't have to do anything overwhelming. You had fun at Tilted Glass with me and Jane."

I nodded. "I did."

"I don't care what we do together. I just want to see you, and I want you to be happy. Everything else is secondary."

Something in his words struck a chord with me. I'd enjoyed myself with him and Jane. I didn't have to suddenly start a charity or become a socialite or pander to idiots. I could just be me. Go on dates with the guy who claimed to want to worship me and hang out with my friend who loved dirty martinis and just be me. While those other things happened to coincide with the Upper East Side. I could have one foot in each world.

"All right. Let's take the social aspect slow. I'd like that." I stared up at him, raw with emotion. "And...I want this."

He smiled brightly as if he'd won a grand prize and then pulled me into another fierce kiss.

PENN

14

I passed through security at City Hall and moved like a thunderstorm through the hallways. It had taken me nearly an hour to cut through traffic from Columbia through downtown before ending up in my mother's building. An hour to stew over that goddamn picture on Crew.

Thankfully, my mother was out for the day. Running into her, even in her own domain, would have been catastrophic for the both of us. When my temper ran hot, it was best to stay out of the way until it blew over. And my mother was like gasoline to my flames.

"Mr. Kensington," a woman chirped in recognition at my approach. "Lark is with someone right now. I'll let her know you're here."

"I'll tell her myself."

Then, I walked right past her desk and into Lark's office. I recognized the man seated there on sight. Thomas Prichard. An excellent choice when I felt like running my fist into someone's face. Especially since the person I really wanted to hit happened to be my best friend.

"What the fuck is going on here?" I demanded.

Thomas had both of his hands on Lark's desk and was leaning over her as if he could smother her existence even more than he already had. When he heard my voice, he whirled around to face me.

"Oh, look, a Kensington to the rescue."

"Thomas, stop," Lark said in that weak voice that I hated from her. She was the strongest of us all, except when it came to him.

"We were just having a nice chat," Thomas said. "No need to get your panties in a twist."

"I think it would be best if you left Lark alone," I said, low and menacing. "You might think you're untouchable, but you're not."

Thomas laughed and then winked at Lark. "Think about it. It could work."

"Yeah, sure," she said absentmindedly. "You should go."

"See you later, baby."

It took every ounce of my willpower not to ruin his face right then and there. The smirk he shot me as he walked out of Lark's office did nothing to help. I shoved the door shut behind me.

"What the hell, Lark? Why are you seeing him? You broke up weeks ago!"

"I know. I know." She leaned back in her desk and covered her eyes with her hands. Her dark red hair fanned out around her face, and she managed to look even smaller than normal. "He just...you know what? I don't even want to talk about him." She brushed her hair back and met me with her solid green gaze. "So...you saw the picture?"

"Of course I saw the fucking picture."

It was all over fucking Crew. Lewis and Natalie together in front of the Rockefeller Tree. He had his arm around her, and she was leaning into him with a wide, sincere smile on her face.

"Why didn't you send it to me?"

"I mean, sure...I'd love to ruin your week. Also, you've been offline and basically unreachable. You've been *out*. And I'm hardly *in* anymore. You've finally accomplished what you always wanted. You're separate from the Upper East Side. You sure you want to know?"

"About her...yes."

Lark sighed. She seemed to dread having to be the most levelheaded and down-to-earth member of my high school crew. The only other one with a real job, following her dreams of running a political campaign. "Looks like Natalie moved to the city this week and has a place on the Upper West."

She'd moved to the city. Natalie, who had told me she didn't want to be here or anywhere near me. Who had run back to Charleston as soon as she could. This didn't make any sense.

"Are they...together?" I clenched my hands into fists, anticipating the blow.

"Penn...it's been a year."

"I know it's been a goddamn year!" I shook my head and paced the small office space. "But she said that she didn't want this life. Maybe she's changed her mind. Or maybe she's dating Lewis out of spite because of that goddamn *bet*."

Lark looked at me evenly. It was why I'd come to her. I might have been pissed, but she usually kept me on the straight and narrow. Saw the logical conclusion in the middle of my flame.

"Does that sound like Natalie?"

"How should I know?" I spat. "I fucked everything up, and then she left. It's been a year. Anything is possible."

"Penn?"

I sighed and slouched down into the chair in front of her desk. "No, it doesn't. She holds a grudge, but dating Lewis... that sounds like a purely Warren move."

"It does," Lark conceded. "Maybe you should find out what's really going on."

"I'm not going to ask Lewis. That's what he wants. You *know* he's only doing this to get to me."

Lark arched an eyebrow. "I didn't suggest that you talk to Lewis."

"I wouldn't even know where to begin to get to Natalie."

"You just stormed into my office and nearly knocked my ex-boyfriend on his ass. Where's that fire for yourself?" she spat. She rose to her feet and threw a pen at my face. I dodged it but just barely. "She wants you to fight for her, you idiot."

I couldn't help but scoff. "I tried that once. Didn't exactly go as planned, did it?"

"Boohoo, you tried once. The only time you've had to try for anything in your whole life. Guess that's over. You've been in love with this girl for a year, even when she doesn't want to have anything to do with you. You know that you didn't manipulate her and that what you felt was real. That's what matters. Now that she's here, you're not going to do anything?"

Lark's words hit me fresh. I remembered that rush of adrenaline when I'd found out she was in the city and hurried down to see her at The Strand. I'd thought that I was doing the right thing by staying away. But I should have seen her. I couldn't stand by and watch this happen. Watch her be with someone else. Let alone Lewis.

"How do I find her?"

"Now we're talking." Lark pulled something up on her phone and handed it to me. "I assume that you got this invite."

I glanced down at her phone and saw the invitation to Harmony Cunningham's house party. Harmony and I had a long, varied history that had mostly ended up with major disappointment for her. I'd only had interest in her at one point because it drove Katherine crazy. She was the exact kind of person I tended to avoid at present.

"Yeah. Not going to that. Talk about a land mine."

"Well, I'm ninety-nine percent sure Lewis will be there."

"Great. He can deal with Harmony."

"I'd guess he's bringing Natalie, dummy."

I wrinkled my nose. "No way. This isn't her scene."

Lark shrugged. "It seems like it is. Jarre is going, and they're friends."

Yeah, I was still confused on how that had happened. Natalie, who wanted to be as far from the Upper East Side as possible was now...entering my world of her own volition?

There was only one way to find out the answers to my questions. Only one way to stop whatever Lewis's plan was. I had to go to the party. I had to fight for Natalie.

"Well," I said, scanning the invitation once more, "looks like I'll have to make an appearance."

"That's my boy. Back in the game."

"And you're coming with me to the party."

"Oh, yeah, no, I'm busy tomorrow night."

"No, you're not. You've been sulking as bad as me since you and Thomas broke up. You shouldn't be working twelve-hour days when you're not even on campaign right now. Even my mother would agree with evenings off, Lark."

"Ugh, I'm not getting out of this, am I?"

I chuckled and shook my head. "Nope."

"Guess I'll have to go shopping."

"Such a travesty," I joked.

"Hey, I'm saving your ass. Save your snark for someone else."

"Thanks, by the way," I told her.

"Anytime."

"Now, let's get some dinner. I'm dying for that Thai place around the corner."

Lark shot me an exasperated look. "Didn't you hear that I'm busy, and now, I need a dress?"

"Yeah…who cares? You can wear whatever you want. It's a Harmony party. Live a little."

Lark threw a second pen at my face, smacking me in the nose that time. "You're paying, Kensington."

I just laughed and held the door open for her. "Obviously."

PART III
BEST-LAID PLANS

NATALIE

15

*D*espite the frigid temperatures, I decided to enjoy my walk across Central Park rather than take an overpriced cab to Lewis's apartment. It was a breezy day, and I wished that I'd brought a hat with me. But we were heading out to a small house party later, and I didn't want to fuck with my hair.

I ducked my chin to my chest against the wind as I navigated the park. It was surprisingly full for the weather. Likely, everyone else was more accustomed to this than I was.

As I came upon the stairs that led to Bethesda Fountain, I snapped a shot and sent it to Melanie to taunt her. She was in the middle of finals, and basketball season was about to start for the dance team. Of course, she'd made the team as a freshman.

Her response was almost instantaneous.

Bitch.

I laughed and shot back a response.

You could always apply to fashion school and move up here with me.

That'd be a dream, but I couldn't leave Michael.

I rolled my eyes. Of course. Michael.

Besides Amy, that was the hardest part of leaving Charleston. I hated how Michael and Melanie were together. I'd hoped that I'd be able to convince her to dump him. But it had been a year, and they were still together.

I sighed and pocketed my phone once more. A problem for another day. I should be more worried about this party that I had agreed to go to. Lewis had insisted that it was going to be a chill thing and that the rest of the crew wouldn't be there. Ease me back into society.

I'd agreed between kisses after we left Rockefeller earlier this week, and I was second-guessing myself. The only positive was that I was writing again. Thankfully, the city and Lewis's presence had had a positive effect on my manuscript.

My fingers were half-frozen by the time I entered his building and took the elevator up to the top floor. Like most Manhattan penthouses, it opened up directly into the residence. A fact that I wasn't sure I'd ever get used to.

"Hello?" I called into the empty apartment.

"In the back," I heard Lewis call out. "Make yourself at home."

I stepped gingerly inside. I'd been here once before. The night that Penn had kissed his ex-girlfriend, Emily. It had all been orchestrated to cause havoc in our relationship, probably thanks to Katherine. But I hadn't known that, and I'd had Lewis take me back to his place. I was here for an entirely different reason this time.

Lewis's place was impeccable. All clean, sharp lines and carefully placed furniture. Art pieces that I knew Amy would covet hung on the walls, and a record player was playing a classical piece that I didn't recognize. An impressive collection of records was on display on a bookshelf next to the player. There were literally hundreds from all different genres. I ran my fingers across them, picking out artists that I liked. Almost all mainstream pop or rock with a whole shelf of classical.

"You like vinyl?" Lewis asked.

I whipped around, and my mouth watered at the sight of him. He was in a blue button-up, half undone as if he had been in the middle of getting dressed when I entered.

"My dad does," I told him. "He still has a few from when he was in high school."

"That's the best part about vinyl. It ages well," he said with a signature smile as he threaded each button into its hole. My eyes were struck by the strangely sexual motion.

"Like good bourbon."

"You've got me there. Want a drink?" he asked as he moved toward a fully stocked bar. "I can give you a quick tour before we go."

"Sure." He poured us each a glass out of a bottle that I couldn't help but recognize. "Jefferson's Ocean?"

"I thought it was your drink."

I broke out into a laugh. The first night I'd met Lewis, I'd plucked a bottle of bourbon out of the Kensingtons' bar at the Hamptons home. I'd used half of it to light my rejection letters on fire, and the other half, I'd shared with the crew. I'd had no idea what I was drinking, but it'd tasted damn good.

"It is now. I'll admit that I didn't know what it was before I drank it that first night. I stole it out of the bar." I shrugged with a wicked smile on my face.

"Scandal," he said as he passed me my drink. "Well, you don't have to steal this one. I got it for you."

"Thank you," I said softly. It was thoughtful in its own way.

"Come on. I'll show you around."

I took a sip of the bourbon, remembering the fiery flavor and all the memories that it dredged up. I hadn't had it since that night. And for a second, all I could see was Penn's face when I'd walked out of the ocean, naked. The way he'd looked at me, treated me, the stubborn, strong-willed grudge I'd held. The way he'd melted it.

I sighed heavily and hurried after Lewis. No need to think about things that didn't matter anymore.

We looked into the guest bedroom and then into his office. It was more of a library than an office, and I was here for it. Floor-to-ceiling bookcases in a deep, rich mahogany covered three walls. His desk took up the center space. Every shelf was jam-packed full of books. I could live in this room.

"Gah," I breathed. "It's perfect."

"I thought you might like it."

"This makes the yacht look like a joke," I said with a laugh.

"You should see the one my father has. It's easily triple this size."

My eyes turned into heart emojis with how much I wanted that. Lewis just chuckled and pulled me out of the room. He had a spare room filled with instruments that he claimed he could only half-play and a green felt poker table. A half-dozen baseball trophies sat on a bookshelf next to marathon medals. An impressive-looking digital SLR camera and lens sat next to a collection of framed pictures of family and friends. I hastily turned away from them before I could pick out the crew in the shots.

"You're good at everything," I told him.

He shrugged. "I like to pick up hobbies."

"Like ice skating," I said.

"Precisely."

We moved to the other side of the apartment to what appeared to be the *wing* for his master bedroom. It was enormous, taking up the size of the other three bedrooms and baths combined. The bathroom alone was a sprawling complex with a jetted tub at the center, a giant walk-in waterfall shower, and a stage-level vanity. His closet was nearly as big as my entire apartment. And the man had more suits and ties than God.

"Well, the tour is a bit different than my place. My apartment could fit inside here," I said, leaning against the bathtub.

He grinned, his eyes sweeping down my body. And I could see that his thoughts were far from pure. Thinking about all the things we could do in that bathtub.

"I'm second-guessing taking you out," he said as he strode toward me in the flawless bathroom.

"That so?" I tilted my head up to look at him.

"I kind of like the idea of keeping you all to myself." His hands slid to my waist. "Maybe we should stay in. I can get takeout, and we can use the bath. I'm sure I have bubbles somewhere." He firmly pressed his lips to mine. "What do you say?"

"You drive a hard bargain," I breathed against him. "I think you could convince me."

He tilted his head against my forehead. "Fuck. I want that."

"We can stay."

"I have to meet someone there," he said on a sigh. "It's a stupid business thing. If I didn't, then I'd say, let's skip it. But we can make a quick appearance, say hey to Jane, and then disappear. Plan?"

I nodded. "Plan."

· · ·

THERE WAS a sense of irony to the fact that the "small" house party Lewis took me to happened to be for Harmony Cunningham. That was the party Amy and I had snuck into in Paris when we were eighteen. The party where I'd first met Penn. I hadn't known it at the time. We'd only been there to meet up with Enzo. I thought it proved that their world was even smaller than I'd thought.

"You're sure the rest of the crew won't be here?" I asked. Because I had my doubts.

"Positive," Lewis reassured me with a hand on my lower back. "Harmony and Katherine hate each other. Always have. Lark doesn't come out. Rowe is an introvert unless he has to be in society, or someone forces him. And Penn...well, even if I'd seen him out in the last couple of months, he wouldn't be here."

"Why not?" I asked.

Lewis arched an eyebrow. "He and Harmony have a history."

Of course they did. No wonder he'd been at that party in Paris. Maybe he'd been there for Harmony all along, and I'd just stumbled into his orbit.

"Well, that's good at least."

I shook my hands out and tried to channel my inner Jane Devney.

Fake it till you make it. Fake it till you just don't give a fuck.

I could do it. I'd done it before. How different was it all really?

Harmony's apartment was exquisite. It was very obvious that her mother was a designer from the second I stepped in her place. Everything was soft, feminine, and cultured. It reminded me so much of the Cunningham flat in Paris that I'd been in.

"Lewis, you made it!" A tall blonde crushed herself to him.

He patted on her back and then released her. "Hey, Harm.

This is Natalie."

Harmony leaned forward and brushed kisses to each of my cheeks. "Welcome! I've heard so much about you from Jane, but we've never gotten a chance to meet."

I flushed. "We actually met three summers ago in Paris. I was there at the flat near yours. That's where I met Jane first too."

"Oh Lord, those parties are such a blur. Forgive me."

"Nothing to forgive," I said with a wave of my hand.

I had been vacation home watching the flat for Amy's parents. There was no reason for Harmony to have recognized me. It was a fluke that I'd ended up there.

"Well, come in. Come in. I'm thrilled to meet the woman who caught Lewis Warren's eye," she said with genuine enthusiasm. "And look at you. My mother would simply die over you. Do you model?"

"Natalie is a bestselling author," Lewis interjected easily.

"Wow. Forget it. Use your brains and not your beauty. Makes for a longer career, I'm told."

"And what do you do?" I asked.

Harmony snorted. "Model. Like an idiot."

I had been prepared to hate Harmony Cunningham. I'd thought she would be just like every other Upper East Side bitch that I'd endured. That she'd put me on edge with her history with Katherine and Penn. But truly, she was charming. Bright, funny, and lively. So far...she didn't seem like she was going to try to ruin my life.

"Lewis knows his way around. Grab a drink, dance, have a good time. Great meeting you."

"You too," I said and then followed Lewis to the kitchen where a huge selection of cocktails was being hand-prepared by a pair of bartenders. "She's kind of great."

"See? Nothing to worry about." He brushed a kiss to my forehead, and I relaxed a fraction more.

I took a glass of champagne and turned to face the crush of people. The music was loud, and most of the living room furniture had been moved to accommodate a moderate-sized dance floor. I didn't recognize anyone at all until an ash-blonde beauty materialized in front of me.

"You're here!" Jane crooned. She was glowing and seemed utterly in her element. "Lewis, can I steal your girl for a minute? I want to introduce her to everyone I know."

"Easy, Jane. Let her get her sea legs under her," Lewis said. "We both know that you know everyone."

"So should she," she said with a grin.

"Let me at least have a drink before I meet *everyone*."

"Fine. But we got the green light on my club, and it's officially opening next week."

"Jane, that's incredible!"

"So much happened while you were gone." She winked at Lewis. "Thanks for the help, by the way."

He raised his glass to her, leaving me wondering what exactly he'd done to help her. Had he done something for the club? Or invested?

"I'm thinking we need to shop this week one day when you're not writing. I'm too excited, and I need to blow some cash," she said with a laugh. "Need to see my three best friends—Gucci, Dior, and Cunningham."

"That'd be great for you," Lewis said. "Girl time."

As if I could afford a damn thing. But nothing stopped me from window-shopping. "Sure. Let's do it on a day when I finish my writing."

"Done."

Lewis's gaze moved from our conversation to follow a guy who had just shown up and was retreating onto the balcony. "Excuse me. I have some business to attend to. Jane, please try not to overwhelm her."

Jane grinned. "We'll be fine."

Lewis pressed another kiss into my hair. "I'll only be a few minutes."

"Don't worry about me," I assured him.

He leaned down to whisper into my ear, "The faster this is over, the sooner we can leave and use that bubble bath."

I shivered at his words, anticipation blooming through my core. He squeezed my hand and then disappeared into the crowd.

"Sexy," Jane said. She reached for my hand. "Let me introduce you around."

It was shocking how much nicer everyone was here. Maybe I was playing the part of Upper East Sider better than I'd thought. Or maybe a house party really was that much more low-key than the events I'd gone to with Katherine. It could also be how nonchalant and enigmatic Jane was.

"Oh look," Jane said as she peeled me away from some son of an investor she knew, "my boy toy has finally made it."

I turned around, and my stomach lurched. Christ, Court Kensington looked so much like his younger brother that it was torturous. Broad shoulders, trim waist, big unbelievably blue eyes, and a smile that could make nuns want to sin.

"Hey, baby," Court said. He wrapped an arm around Jane's waist and pressed a firm, lasting kiss to her lips.

Jane looked lovesick when he pulled back. "Hey, you."

"Come to the back with me. We're just getting started."

She nodded, captivated by that gaze. "Court, you remember Natalie."

His eyes swept to me when he realized they had an audience. "Natalie...Natalie," he mused. "You dated my brother."

"Uh, yeah. Like a year ago."

He shrugged as if the timeline meant nothing to him.

"She's a successful author now," Jane said. "You'll love her."

"I bet I will," Court said with a languid smile.

Jane grabbed my hand and pulled me to the back room with her. It was an office space, but it was clear that Harmony didn't use the space for anything more than display or her parties. A dozen people crowded into the space over a table with lines of cocaine.

My heart stopped. No, I stopped. Physically.

I'd been around drugs before. I'd seen athletes use them to get ahead. And loser artists use them to try to find inspiration. And frat boys use them to feel anything at all. But I'd never used them, and the scene was not something I wanted to see play out.

Just as I was about to make an excuse, an arm fell around my shoulders. "Hey, sexy."

I glanced over with wide eyes to find none other than Camden Percy. One of the last times I'd seen him, he'd been a raging asshole at a charity function. I didn't know if he was still with Katherine, but it hadn't stopped him from hitting on me before.

Jane giggled and casually flicked Camden's arm off of mine. "She's taken, Cam."

"So? Don't see her boy with her," he said, eye-fucking the shit out of me. He had to be fucked out of his mind.

"That *boy* is Lewis Warren," I told him, taking a quick step back.

"Warren, huh?" He shrugged. "Well, you know how to pick 'em. You friends with my *dear* fiancée, too?"

"No," I said boldly.

He laughed. "Look at that bitter frown." He nudged my lips with the back of his hand. "What did Katherine Van Pelt do this time?"

"Is she about to show up?" I asked.

He laughed again, louder. "I fucking hope not. No one here gives a fuck about Katherine Van Pelt. The frigid bitch burns bridges faster than her daddy ate her trust fund."

I shuddered at the way he talked about Katherine. I hated her. But still...she was marrying this asshole.

"Now, come do a line with me, love," Camden said with a wink. His hands went to my waist. "After you've had one, maybe you'll loosen up."

Court stepped in between us with a low laugh. "Dude, did you see that Tracey was here? Isn't that why you came out anyway?"

Camden snorted. His dilated pupils going even wider as if he noticed Court's interference but didn't remark on it. But he went to a busty redhead in the corner who was already using a credit card to make a straight line of white powder.

"Thanks," I murmured. I was surprised that it was Court who had stepped in. Everything I'd heard about him made him out to be horrible. Then again...I'd gotten it all from Penn.

"No problem. Camden can sometimes be a handful," Court said.

"That's an understatement."

"You don't have to do this if you don't want," Jane said. "I didn't realize Camden would be so handsy."

"Yeah, I think...I'm just going to get a bit of air."

"I'll find you after," Jane insisted.

I waved my hand in what was half-acceptance, half-dismissal and then hustled the hell out of that room. My heart was racing, and adrenaline propelled me further down the hallway.

Before I even saw where I was going, I ran smack dab into a large male figure in a crisp black suit.

"Oof," I groaned.

My eyes lifted as I prepared to apologize. But the words were stuck on my tongue.

"Penn?"

NATALIE

16

"*H*ello, Natalie," Penn said. My name on his tongue like a caress.

My brain went completely blank at the sight of him. He didn't utter another word. Just pressed open the door to the room we were standing in front of and maneuvered me inside.

The door clicked behind him, leaving us alone. All alone.

"What…what are you doing here?" I gasped out.

"Me? I live in New York," he purred. "Did you forget?"

"No," I whispered.

But he wasn't supposed to be here. This couldn't be happening.

He stood near enough to be disarming but far enough for him to devour me with his eyes. And for me to get my first good look at him in a year.

My memory hadn't done him justice.

Little details had disappeared from my mind. His strong jawline, the curve of his lips, the sheer blue of his eyes. That look that said he would own my body in more ways than I could ever imagine. The ease of his body, how comfortable he was in his skin, the seduction laced in every inch of him. He was so much larger than life, all charm and radiating energy that only I seemed to notice.

I hated how attracted I was to him.

I hated how my body ignited without even a touch.

I hated even more that he'd hurt me…and now, he was here…and I wasn't immediately walking away.

"This feels familiar," Penn said.

He stalked forward, a predator seeing his prey. I matched his steps as I stepped away from him.

"Does it?"

His grin was purely feline. "Meeting a stranger at a Harmony Cunningham party. Should I offer to show you New York City for a night?"

My pulse quickened at the memory—when we'd met in a party so similar to this one on the other side of the world. He'd shown me Paris until we ended up back at his flat. And then he'd abandoned me. It was for good reason. Though I hadn't known that until six years later.

"I think not." My back thudded against the door. Nowhere else to go but out.

"No?"

Penn brought his hands down on either side of my head, caging me in, so there was only him before me. Just that beautiful face and the wicked seduction on his lips.

I swallowed. "We're not strangers anymore."

"Aren't we?" he purred.

I pursed my lips at him. He was purposely acting coy. We had way too much history to be strangers. Seven years' worth of baggage to sift through.

When I didn't respond, he continued, "It feels like we are. It's been so long since I've seen you. And we're living such different lives. But I suppose you're right." A hand brushed my waist, and I shivered. "How can we be strangers when I'm so well acquainted with your body?"

I wanted that touch. I didn't want that touch.

"Penn," I murmured. I was going to tell him to stop. To back off. To just walk away. But the words didn't come out, and his name sounded like half a plea on my lips.

His body pressed flush against mine. My back hard against the closed door. Then his lips crashed down onto mine.

I gasped in shock. My hands moved to his chest. To push him away, surely. But as his lips reminded me of all the ways he'd drawn out my pleasure, my fingers twined in the front of his suit. Not away at all.

The bastard's scent encompassed me, trapped me. Lost me to a world I'd wanted for so long and missed so much and hated so thoroughly. It all mingled, mixed, enveloped me completely. Up was down, and down was up. It was like jumping off a diving board without knowing if you'd even make your landing.

He pulled back a fraction with the most self-satisfied look. "I missed you."

My mouth dropped open. He'd *missed* me? The goddamn bastard had *missed* me. After what he'd put me through—the lies and manipulations and stupid fucking bet—he thought waltzing in here and kissing me would somehow fix something? Charleston hadn't worked. This sure as hell wasn't.

I slammed my hands into his chest, sending him stumbling backward a step in surprise. I did it again. And then again.

"How fucking dare you!" I spat at him.

He laughed. He actually laughed at me. "Really, Nat?"

"Yes! What the hell were you thinking?"

"I think I dared. I think I dared very much. And I think you not only wanted me to, but also participated in that."

142

"I did nothing of the sort," I snapped.

"No? You didn't grab me and pull me closer." He cleared the distance again. "Your heart isn't racing?" His hand settled atop my chest, feeling the quick thump of my heart. "You're not heated from just my kiss?"

I was.

I totally was.

And his hand was drifting lower. Bold enough to find out for himself.

I stopped his descent. "What. Are. You. Doing. Here?"

He grinned, all possessive and territorial. "I'm here for you, Nat."

"And you thought *this* would be what I wanted?"

He arched an eyebrow, as if to say, *Isn't it?*

I just glared.

"I know what your body wants." Then his other hand moved to gently press two fingers against my temple. "It's only your mind that I'm uncertain about."

I slapped his hand from my body. Then I pushed away from him and stormed deeper into the empty bedroom. Being trapped against that door had been beyond dangerous. I needed space. Lots of space.

"Maybe that's your problem," I growled. "You only think with your body and not your mind."

"If I remember correctly," he said, slipping his hands into his pockets, "you were the one who begged me for a month of casual sex."

"I never begged you for anything," I hissed back.

Penn smirked in response. "Are you sure?"

My body flooded with memories of all the times I *had* begged him. Begged him for more, harder, faster. All the ways we'd come together last fall in the Hamptons. And the intimate way in which our bodies connected. It wasn't fair that I could think about those things and shiver with desire after what had come next. Anger flared inside of me, and I tried to hold on to that like a light in the dark.

"I'm leaving. Get out of my way."

"No."

"No?" I demanded.

"We're not through, you and me. We're far from through."

"What do you hope to accomplish by ambushing me? Whatever this act is, it isn't going to work."

"Who said it was an act?"

I narrowed my eyes at him. "You've done this in the past. I'm not going to fall all over myself just because you look good in a suit."

"Oh, do you think so?"

I silently reprimanded myself for saying that out loud. Yes, of course, he looked sexy in a suit, but that wasn't the point.

"Not the point," I grumbled.

"Fine. You want to know why I'm here?"

He straightened and seemed to let whatever mask he'd been wearing slide off. In that instant, I saw my Penn. The one who'd ordered my favorite pizza and gone stargazing with me. Who'd laughed at stupid jokes and written seriously, avidly about his passion. Who hadn't had to pretend with me...even when it was all a lie.

"Yes," I whispered, taken aback by the sudden change, "I do."

"Maybe I wanted to see you."

"And you thought using your old charms would change things?"

"Flying a thousand miles and begging you to come back didn't," he said bitterly. "Why not try what actually worked?"

"Nothing is going to work. Not after what you did to me. So, let me leave."

He stepped easily in front of me before I could bypass him and snagged my elbow. "Stay."

"I'm not going to play mind games with you."

"No mind games," he said, stepping closer into me. "Just me."

My heart lurched at the way he'd said that. At that look in his eyes that said, in a sea of people, he only had eyes for me. I wanted to revel in that. Wanted to trust that so much. But I didn't. And I couldn't.

"I haven't seen you in a year, and now, you want this?" I whispered hoarsely.

"I've always wanted this," he said sincerely.

I shook off that pain and shoved it back down where it belonged. I tugged my arm out of his grasp. "You put a *bet* on me, Penn. That you could get me to fall for you, and I did. How could I ever trust you again?"

"You seem to be trusting Lewis just fine."

"Don't bring him into this."

"Don't bring him into this?" he asked, fire burning in his eyes. "Are you fucking kidding me? You show up with my best friend, who I'll remind you was there for that fucking bet and didn't tell you about it either. Then you expect me to not talk about that?"

I glared at him. "I know he was involved. I'm aware."

"Good. Then you'll have to excuse me when I say that you must be out of your goddamn mind to be here with him right now."

"Him instead of you?" I quipped. "Because you two are the exact same person, and there's no difference whatsoever between the man who used and manipulated and *bet* on me and the man who *didn't*?"

Penn laughed sardonically. "You don't see through him? We're friends for a reason. Lewis is not some innocent.

You're just another one of his many obsessions. And when he gets tired of them, what do you think happens?"

"Stop. You know what? If you want to discuss Lewis, then I'm out of here." I shouldered past him and reached for the door. The knob twisted in my hand.

"Sure, just run away," he snapped, his hand coming down on the door, so I couldn't open it. "Don't address the real issue here. Let's not talk about the fact that you moved to my city after saying that you didn't want this life. Yet here you are, Natalie."

I whirled on him. "I am not in this city for you or Lewis or this *life*."

"Doesn't really look like that from the outside. Were you lying to me in Charleston when you said you didn't want to be a part of this world? Were you lying when you said it could have worked out between us? I let you go because I understood where you were coming from. I hate my life. I can't really escape. There's no hope for me, and I refuse to put that burden on someone else. But now, you're back, and you're living this life of your own free will."

My hands were trembling. I was so pissed off at what he was saying. The truth in his words and the lies in his words. The way he twisted what I'd said when he hurt me to fit the world I was living in now.

"I don't have to justify myself to you."

"No, of course not. You can walk all over my heart, but a justification is too much to ask for."

"Walk all over *your* heart?" I gasped. "After what you did, you want me to believe that this is hurting you?"

"Isn't that why you're doing it?"

I shook my head in frustration. "God, you are so narcissistic. You're just mad that you're not getting your way."

"Yes, I'm mad. I'm fucking mad that I let you go because

you didn't want this life. But now, you're willing to have that life with someone else."

The words were a slap in the face. They weren't a lie either. This life didn't feel the same with Lewis as it had with Penn. There wasn't Katherine. I didn't have ex-girlfriends trying to jump in and take what belonged to me. Or his mother firing me and calling me trash. Or a fucking bet. And I didn't have to deal with this bullshit.

I calmly met his steely blue gaze. "Maybe I realized only *your* world is too small for me to be in it."

"That's bullshit, Natalie, and you know it. Lewis and I live in the same world. That's why I'm here. That's why he's here. You might think you can escape it, but you can't. There is no in-between. No half-in, half-out. You'll get sucked in, and you won't be able to get out."

"You're wrong. This isn't my world. I'm just here to write. Everything else is secondary."

"Then why are you with him?" Penn demanded.

"I don't want to…"

"I know you don't want to talk about it. But I don't give a damn. I want to talk about it."

Something snapped inside of me. "Why do you even care?" I demanded. "You've clearly moved on. Fucked half of the Upper East Side, right? Back to your old ways?" I jerked the door against his arm, and he finally gave. The door sliding open to the hallway beyond. "I don't want to hear any more of your hypocrisy."

Penn opened his mouth to respond, but I never heard it. I just saw his face close off and his eyes narrow, and then suddenly, a throat cleared behind me.

I turned to the open door in surprise, completely caught off guard.

"There you are, Natalie. I was looking for you," Lewis drawled, his eyes fixed on Penn.

17

*F*uck.

Well, just…fuck.

I didn't know what to say. I was standing alone in a bedroom with Penn Kensington. Yes, we had kissed. Well… mostly, he'd kissed me, and then we'd yelled at each other a lot. But still. It definitely looked bad from Lewis's point of view.

"Lewis," Penn said stiffly.

"What's up, man?" Lewis said. He nudged the door open a bit wider and even held his hand out. "Long time no see. You coming back out in the real world now?"

Penn looked down at Lewis's hand, and for a second, I thought he wouldn't shake it. That he'd throw the punch right then and there. But he did take it. They shook a quick, hard shake and then released.

"Semester is over. Easier to get out. Figure society missed me. Going to be out all the time now," he said pointedly.

"Ah, just like this spring then?" Lewis asked with a grin.

Penn narrowed his eyes. "Not exactly my plan."

"Well, it'll be good to have you back. Can't stay in that ivory tower forever."

"Oh, I have no intention of staying away." Penn slid his hands into his pockets and raised his eyebrows.

"I was surprised to see Lark here. She asked me to do shots."

"That right? Both of us out in one night," Penn mused with a glint in his eyes.

"Yes, how…convenient."

They were saying more with their eyes than with words. I gathered that Penn must have sent Lark to distract Lewis, so we could be alone. It was…sneaky. Even for him.

"We should go," I told Lewis.

Lewis finally looked down at me. His depthless, dark eyes filled with warmth. "If you're ready to go, we can. But I think Jane was looking for you."

I could see Penn's jaw set at that. I didn't know if it was because of Lewis's obvious affection or because I was acquainted with his brother's girlfriend. Maybe both.

"I'll see Jane later this week. I'm ready to go." I hugged my arms to my chest.

"What's the rush?" Penn smoothly stepped in. "It's been a while since I've been out. We should open a bottle and make it like old times."

"Penn," I hissed warningly.

"I would, but I just follow where the lady goes," Lewis said with a wide, knowing smile.

I gaped up at him. Jesus Christ, what was he doing? What were they both doing? Their Upper East Side was showing and I had to admit, it didn't look good on either of them.

"Are we done here?" I finally snapped. "Are you two done measuring dicks?"

"Natalie," Lewis said placatingly.

"No, you're no better than him right now. This is stupid."

Penn snorted, and I turned my gaze on him. "Don't even start."

He held his hands up in surrender, a cheeky grin on his face. "I would never."

I rolled my eyes. How the hell had I gotten to this moment? I'd agreed to a chill evening out with Lewis at a party. I hadn't bargained for cocaine, Camden, and then Penn.

"Let's just go." I pushed past Lewis and out into the hallway.

I heard Penn curse under his breath from the room I'd vacated, but I didn't care. I couldn't even look back to see if Lewis was following as I stormed down the hallway and back into the living room. The music had gotten louder, the dancing more scandalous, the alcohol flowing freely. It was no different than any party I'd gone to in college or with Amy after. But it pissed me off way more right now.

"Natalie," Lewis said as I angled for the exit. He reached out and stopped me. "Hold on. Don't run out of here."

I sighed heavily and then looked up at him. "That interaction between you two was horrible."

"I know. I'm sorry. But I don't know how you expected me to react."

"More of the *punch him in the face* and less of the *ha-ha, I got your girl*," I spit out.

He chuckled softly. "I will keep that in mind if I see him again."

I covered my face with my hands. "Tonight has been a disaster."

"This wasn't what I wanted it to be like."

"I forgot how much I hated this part of this world."

"Look, it's not always like this. I had no idea Penn would be here. Or that I'd find you two alone in an empty bedroom together."

"Ugh! It was so stupid. Being in there made everything worse."

"What happened?"

I shook my head and looked away. I didn't want to tell him, but I had to. "He kissed me."

"Of course he did." Lewis's lips fell into a line.

"I pushed him away though," I said quickly. "And then we yelled at each other. I swear, all we do is try to hurt each other. It's exhausting."

"Well, I'd hate that the last kiss you got was one that you didn't want," he said as he slipped an arm around my waist and brought his lips down on mine.

I didn't correct him. I hadn't wanted that kiss. It had just happened. But...it was Penn. So, it was infinitely more complicated than that.

Not that Lewis seemed to care. As he kissed my lips in front of the entire party. Laying claim on me for all to see. It was a short, hot, and possessive kiss that spoke volumes.

And when he pulled back, I could see Penn stop mid-stride from the hallway. His jaw was set as he stared at the pair of us. A moment passed between us. As he came to understand that I wasn't going to change my mind. That, if anything, this had only made it worse.

I didn't trust him.

Not after last year.

And not with how he was trying to manipulate me all over again.

I understood his frustration. I had said that I wasn't interested in living this life, but that hadn't changed. Only my feelings for Lewis had. And while I probably should have chosen someone other than his best friend, I couldn't change that.

Lark came to Penn's side with concern on her face, as if

understanding precisely how wrong everything had gone. He ignored her, his eyes still locked on mine. But I'd already made my choice.

I broke Penn's gaze and took Lewis's hand, and together, we left the party.

PENN

18

I stood there, frozen, watching Natalie's retreating back as she disappeared from view with Lewis.

"Penn," Lark said. She shook my arm, trying to bring me back to reality.

But I was already in reality, and it was a cesspool, a nightmare.

"What the fuck happened?" Lark asked.

"I kissed her."

"Wait, what?" she demanded. "That wasn't part of the plan. I thought you were going to be sincere and tell her how much you missed her."

I shook my head. "That was the plan, but then we just started arguing. We run so hot together. Every horrible thing that we'd both thought in the last year spilled from our lips. Then, fucking Lewis walked in and carted her out with a sick smile on his lips."

"Oh, Penn."

How had it gone so far afield? Kissing her, yelling at her… that hadn't been my intention at all. But then her lush body had collided with mine. Her fiery eyes had looked up into my own. Those perfect lips had stared up at me. And suddenly, it was a year ago. She was in my arms. I wanted her back. She was *mine*.

My brain had ceased functioning. All there was, was the moment between getting her alone and pressing her into the door and, god, her lips. She'd said my name like a prayer, and there wasn't a goddamn thing in this world that could have stopped me from kissing her.

Then, those words. Fuck, where had they even come from? No wonder she'd pushed me away.

And now, she was walking out of the party with Lewis.

He'd kissed her. Put his hands on her. Staked his claim in front of the whole fucking party.

There was no fucking way I was going to let that stand.

"Penn, talk to me."

"I'm going after them."

I strode toward the exit with Lark on my heels.

"Is that a good idea?"

I was halfway out the door when Lark's hand landed on my arm.

"Penn…"

"What?" I snapped. "I have to go stop them. If she goes home with him tonight, we both know what's going to happen."

"Penn, you can't," she whispered. Lark sounded heartbroken. Her words were raw. Her eyes sad and sympathetic.

"Lark, I have to."

"You think she'll accept you like this? After what just happened between you two?" Lark asked. "She chose. You might not like the answer, but tonight, she chose Lewis."

I cursed violently at the thought. There was no goddamn way I was going to let this happen. "We can fix this," I pleaded with Lark. "I know we can."

"Not tonight," Lark said. "Give her some space. You hurt

her, and whether or not you want to see it, Lewis is giving her what she thinks she wants. She'll figure it out."

"Lewis is a fucking liar."

Lark shrugged. We both knew that he was. No point in arguing that.

"I'm sorry it didn't work out."

I clenched and unclenched my hands. "Yeah well, she spat in my face that I'd fucking slept with half of the Upper East Side. No wonder she had fire in her eyes. Who do you think told her?"

Lark pursed her lips. "Was it supposed to be a secret?"

I narrowed my eyes at her.

She held up her hands in surrender. "Everyone knows you did, Penn. All spring, it was a different model, socialite, long-legged beauty. I'm not sure why you're surprised that Natalie found out."

"We weren't even together!" I snapped. "And she's holding it against me when *she* was the one who said that we were never going to see each other again. That flying a thousand fucking miles couldn't change anything."

"I know," she whispered. "But look at it through her eyes. She cared for you, and then as soon as you broke up, you slept with every woman who walked past you."

"Not all of them," I said carefully, my voice on a razor's edge. "Not Katherine."

"Oh boy," Lark said. She glanced my way and waited. "I assume there's a story there?"

"Katherine ruined the one thing that was real for me," Penn said. "So, I fucked a few brainless socialites to piss her off. It was more of a chore than anything. But I was going after Katherine in the best way I could. I picked up each of the dumb friends she associated with and was seen with on *Page Six*."

"Jesus Christ, you're ruthless," Lark said.

I shook my head. "It was stupid. While it pissed Katherine off, eventually, I just got fucking bored out of my mind and gave up. It did nothing to make me forget Natalie."

"That's why you suddenly disappeared off the map this summer? You went from high society to a recluse in a matter of months."

"Yeah."

I'd thrown myself into work afterward. Put all of that behind me and tried to focus on research. On writing about how meaningless sex was moral despite the standard view that a relationship made it safer and better. All the while, I was pining for the one person I'd really wanted to have a relationship with. The person who had made me see meaningless sex was never as good as her.

Lark gripped my elbow and veered me into the elevator. We took it downstairs without a word and then out into the late New York night.

I still wanted to race after Natalie. Figure out how to make it right. Break a few of Lewis's bones. But I'd probably only do more damage than I had. It was hard to think about that when my body was saying, *Go, run, fix it.*

"Well, if you still love her, then this isn't the end," Lark said as we fell into step together, heading back toward my place.

"Yeah. This definitely isn't the fucking end," I swore into the night. "I might have lost the battle, but I'm not going to lose the war."

NATALIE

19

*W*e were silent on the ride back to Lewis's apartment.

I didn't have words for what had just happened. The night was a blur of bad decisions, and once again, I felt out of my depth with this world. Exhausted from trying to keep up with the nightmare unfolding before my eyes.

Thankfully, it was a short ride, and we were back in the comfort of his home once more. I was seriously regretting having ever left this house. I should have told him to deal with work tomorrow and stayed in. That bubble bath was sounding awfully appealing.

Lewis went to the record player and switched out the vinyl to something soft and romantic. A balm to the hectic night we'd had.

"Wine?" he asked with a smile that said he wasn't the least bit affected by the evening's events.

"Sure," I agreed easily. I slid out of my heels and sank into a seat on the sofa. It was more comfortable than it looked. I could fall asleep right then and there as the adrenaline fled my body.

Lewis returned with two glasses of red wine and took the seat next to me. I was shocked that he wasn't angrier. I'd been alone in a room with Penn Kensington. I'd admitted that he'd kissed me. And he didn't seem upset. I'd thought that he'd be murderous after that.

"Can I ask you something?" I took a careful sip of my wine and then turned to face him.

"Anything."

"Why aren't you mad at me?"

He arched an eyebrow. "Do I have something to be mad at you for?"

"Penn and I kissed. You found us alone. I mean…most guys would be mad."

"I am mad," he conceded. My stomach flipped as I waited for his wrath to finally be unveiled. "But not with you."

"Oh," I said. Just a breath escaping my lips.

"What happened tonight wasn't your fault. Not any of it. Not even dealing with Camden."

My face flushed. "How did you hear about that?"

"Jane mentioned it when I went looking for you. Camden Percy is a right bastard who was high as fuck. I'm sorry that I left you alone to deal with him. With all of it."

"Camden was…I don't know," I said, shuddering to think of what might have happened if Court hadn't stepped in. "Why is he marrying Katherine if he hates her?"

Lewis snorted. "You've got me there."

"I mean, she deserves it. But it seems like not a wise choice. He knows that she's marrying him for the money. He said tonight that her dad ate her trust fund. Whatever that means. And he still doesn't care?"

"Ah. That is a little known secret," Lewis confided. "Most people don't know how broke Katherine is. Her trust fund should have been safe from the IRS. But, before her father transferred it to her, he made a huge withdrawal—in the hundreds of millions—to try to cover his ass. Then, everything went under before he could replace the money."

My mouth hung open. "Shit. How does she still live the life she's living?"

"She already had the apartment, and there's been enough money in there to manage, but it's almost gone."

"Hence, Camden," I muttered.

It all made sense now. I had known that Katherine was in a tight spot with money, but I hadn't known the specifics other than her father's securities fraud. No wonder she was desperate to tie the knot. Though it still didn't explain Camden. I had no idea what he was getting out of it.

"Yep." Lewis drained the last of his wine and then set it down on the glass coffee table. Then, he moved closer to me, reaching for my hand and lacing our fingers together. "But all that really matters to me is that you're okay."

"I'm fine," I told him. "Just...tired. Drained."

And while I was utterly exhausted, Lewis seemed different. Almost keyed up from the ordeal. I didn't know if it was the adrenaline still racing through him or what.

"You don't seem tired," I said on a laugh.

He grinned wider and brought my hand to his lips. He set lazy kisses across my hand and around my wrist before drawing the tip of my thumb into his mouth and nipping it. "I'm not."

"I'm surprised that you're so happy after everything that happened." It was one thing not to blame me. Another thing entirely to be practically giddy after all that.

He ran his tongue along the pad of my thumb. All the while, his eyes were locked on mine. Offering everything without words and making me squirm in my seat.

"You came home with me," he said.

I tilted my head. "Why wouldn't I have?"

He arched one eyebrow. His other hand slipping to my bare thigh. Teasing the flesh on the inside of my knee. "I know what Penn meant to you. I wasn't looking forward to that first interaction between you two. He's a smooth bastard."

"You thought I'd fall all over myself for him?" I asked in disbelief.

"You wouldn't be the first."

"I'm not a simpering idiot." I pulled back, offended that he'd thought I'd be so thoughtless. "I haven't forgotten what he did to me."

"I don't think you're a simpering idiot. But I know Penn, and I know how women react to him. That the first time you saw him would be difficult. But see, you're still here with me." He released our joined hands and tipped my chin to look into his eyes. "After all that."

Seeing it from that point of view, I understood why he was happy. Some part of him must have been preparing himself to lose me. Yes, I was attracted to Penn, and we had history. But I hadn't fallen for his words. And the look Lewis was giving me then said everything else. I'd passed some sort of test. And now, he wanted more. He wanted me. Just me. All of me.

He tugged my leg over his own, sliding us closer and closer together. His hand fell into my silver locks, and then his lips were on mine. Tasting, testing, caressing. He was delving into me, taking all I would give him. And it was easy to give in. To let tonight slip away and be in the moment with this sexy man.

"Natalie," he groaned against my lips. His hand ran from my knee up my leg, sliding under the material of my black dress and caressing my inner thigh. Up, up, up.

"Yes," I breathed.

I trembled at the lightest brush of his knuckle against the thin material of my thong. The feel of a finger running along the outline where my skin met the underwear. He skipped over my hot core to trace the other side. I bucked against him, kissing him that much harder, deeper, needier as my body thrummed to life.

When I thought I would combust from anticipation, he hooked his finger under the material and tugged my panties over my hips before tossing them to the ground.

"Oh god," I moaned at the first touch of his finger against my clit.

Desire flared through me, molten hot and unyielding. I released his lips and tipped my head back. My eyes closed in surrender as he slicked a finger through my already-wet center and then caressed me in slow, agonizing circles.

He slipped me down, so I was lying flat on the sofa, spreading me wide for better access. All conscious thought fled the second he inserted a finger into me. And then another. He stroked me from the inside, warming up my primed body. Then, he curled his long fingers into me, reaching depths that made me shake. It had been a long time since I felt anything besides the feel of my own fingers. And, oh dear god, this was infinitely better.

"Fuck," I breathed desperately.

I was seeing stars when I felt the first kiss on the inside of my knee. My eyes flew open. He was just grinning at me as he placed a second kiss higher on my leg and higher. My pulse quickened. Thumped loudly in my ears as I watched his ascent.

Then those tempting lips were on my core. Kissing my most sensitive area. Licking the bud of my sex until I couldn't keep my eyes open anymore, and I lost all thought to anything but exactly where his lips were placed. The way he teased me with fingers and lips and tongue, drawing out my climax.

"Lewis," I groaned.

I was so close. I was seeing stars. Stroking, moving, taking, needing, aching. I was on fire.

Lewis knew exactly what he was doing. It didn't come as a surprise, but damn, he could work my body to a fever.

"Come for me, gorgeous," he breathed. "I want you to take all of this pleasure. I want to see you come undone. To feel like you've never felt before."

And, at his last word, my body hit the apex. I gasped as energy cascaded through my body. It radiated from my core all the way through my legs and down to my toes. My back arched off the sofa as I came apart at the seams. Then I collapsed backward, breathing heavily.

"God, you are so beautiful," he whispered. He straightened my skirt and lifted his head to see the aftereffects of my dizzying climax.

I laughed as I came back from outer space. "That was…"

"Amazing?"

I smiled lazily up into his beautiful face. "Yes."

"I could watch you come over and over and over again." He leaned forward and pressed a kiss to my lips. "I will tonight if you let me."

I believed him. And I wanted to. But, as the haze of my orgasm wore off, I knew that it couldn't be tonight. Not with the events that had unfolded, clouding our relationship. I wanted it to be right. Not because Penn had pushed me into Lewis's arms.

"It's been a long night. Maybe we could just sleep instead?"

"Of course. Stay here with me. It's late, and I already sent my driver home."

"You think we'll do much sleeping if I stay here?"

"I can control myself," he said with a laugh. Then he kissed me again, slow and delectable. His hands splayed across my hips. "But I'd be lying if I said that I didn't want to try to seduce you in my bed."

"Don't tempt me," I murmured.

He seemed to take that as a challenge. His knee coming between mine, his body sliding atop me. One arm sinking underneath my lithe body and firmly pressing us together. I could feel the length of him through his suit pants. And for a second, I could think of nothing but grinding against him to relieve that pressure once more.

His cock moved against the space between my legs, and a desperate moan escaped me. His hips circled, increasing the friction. Tempting me with every movement as his lips claimed mine. We breathlessly tangled together on the couch. Nothing but heat and tension crackling between us. Classical music reaching a crescendo.

I knew that if I didn't stop him now, I would never stop him. We'd go all the way tonight. And I might regret how we got here.

"Lewis, please," I purred.

"Yes?"

His hand slipped to my ass, drawing me harder against him. A strangled gasp released from my mouth.

"We should...stop," I got out.

And he stopped instantly. His eyes fluttered open, and they met mine. "Whenever you're ready."

I swallowed and stopped myself from saying, *Now*. Because logically, I didn't want it to happen tonight. But my body simply didn't give a fuck.

He straightened and helped me to my feet. I wobbled, my legs still weak from my orgasm. He brushed my wild hair out of my face, cupped my cheeks in his hands, and kissed me.

"We have all the time in the world," he told me. "We're in no rush."

I nodded. "I like that."

"But you're mine," he whispered against my lips. He circled my waist, and I wrapped my arms around him. "All mine."

NATALIE

20

The good thing about staying in all weekend after the disaster at Harmony's party was that I got so much writing done. In fact, it was starting to shape up into a real story. And while Lewis worked during the day, I had taken to wandering Central Park or finding a café to get more done.

Jane had messaged me this morning to meet her for coffee, and I'd promptly slung my messenger bag over my shoulder and headed her way.

The patisserie was everything I hadn't known I was missing. I'd spent hours writing in little cafés in Paris my first summer after college while house-sitting Amy's parents' flat in the city. Jane had picked the perfect place with rows upon rows of French pastries. I ordered a café au lait and a *pain de chocolat* and then found Jane seated at a corner table by a window.

She rose to her feet when she saw me approaching and kissed me on each cheek. "Natalie! Here, take a seat. Don't mind my mess. It's all for the opening next weekend."

"Thanks." I took my seat and then booted up my computer.

"So many last-minute things to get done though. I have a whole team working on the venue and making sure everything is up to code. It's taking way more time than I thought." She laughed this light, tinkling laugh. She sounded frazzled, but she looked relaxed. She was even dressed down in designer athleisure attire with black leggings and a hooded pink jacket that probably cost a small fortune. Her enormous Cartier sunglasses were perched on her head.

"You'll get it all done," I assured her.

"No doubt." Jane grinned. "Just like you and your book."

The next couple of hours were spent hunched over my computer, typing and deleting at equal paces. I finally had a passable intro. Now, I needed to work on a synopsis so that Caroline could sell this thing. But I didn't want to interrupt the flow to work on that instead.

"Oh my god," Jane groaned. She'd hung up the phone on her fifth call since I'd gotten here hours earlier. "I am wrecked. This is going to make me break out, I swear. I need retail therapy. Bergdorf?"

I found myself nodding. I wasn't going to buy anything, but it'd be fun. Plus, I needed a break.

"Excellent." Jane stuffed everything back into her Hermes handbag and then hurried us around the corner to the enormous designer department store.

Half the saleswomen seemed to know Jane on sight. We had a personal shopper, Sandra, in a matter of minutes and mimosas a second after that.

I tried on everything that Jane and Sandra handed to me. It was like playing dress-up with things I could never afford. Jane talked the entire time about everything she had to do for the opening, who she'd invited and hadn't heard from, and all her friends who were flying in for the event. It sounded like it was going to be huge.

"But the best part is the fashion show," Jane told me.

"Fashion show?" I asked.

"It's part of my grand plan. I'm going to have Elizabeth Cunningham showcase her designs at the opening. It's going to be so chic." Jane ran her finger over a silver sequined dress. "Just imagine a dozen models wearing original designs on a runway in my club. I'm dying."

"I've never even heard of something like that."

"Exactly!"

But something was nagging at me. A little flutter that wouldn't leave me alone. I'd already agreed to go to this party. I'd agreed long before we even knew it was a definite thing that was going to happen. So, I couldn't back out now. Still … the first time that I'd seen an Elizabeth Cunningham dress was with Katherine. I knew that she didn't model. She was a socialite, so being seen in designer clothing was a perk for the designer. But Elizabeth's designs were Katherine's signature.

"Can I ask you something?" I said carefully.

I liked Jane. We were becoming fast friends now that I was in the city. But I didn't really know her relationship with Katherine.

"Of course."

"Is Katherine Van Pelt going to be at your opening by chance? I know that she wears Elizabeth's designs quite frequently."

"Haven't you heard the gossip?" Jane said with wide eyes.

Jane always knew everything about everyone.

"No."

"Elizabeth Cunningham eloped with Carlyle Percy last month. Which means that the owner of Cunningham Couture is now married to Katherine's future in-laws. It's not being reported yet. I guess they're denying it," Jane said with a wave of her hand.

Wow. Two empires coming together. Cunningham and Percy under one roof. And if Katherine ever finally married Camden, then...the Van Pelt name would be there too. A lot of concentrated income in one place. Though I didn't know exactly what their elopement had to do with Katherine coming to the party.

That must have shown on my face.

"Katherine was wearing Cunningham designs before the elopement, but I'd guess it had been in the works for a while."

I stared at her blankly. Not quite putting the pieces together.

"Well, she didn't start putting Katherine in her designs until she was engaged to Camden."

Lightbulb. There it was. So, Elizabeth and Katherine must have worked out a deal. They were both marrying into the Percy line. Maybe Elizabeth had already been having an affair with Carlyle before he divorced his last wife. So, future Percy women needed to stick together.

"Anyway, it's all speculation. No one is coming out and saying it," Jane said. She laughed. "Except me to you. But Elizabeth always designs for Katherine, so I'm sure she'll be at the party."

I frowned. "Great."

Jane noticed my expression and sighed. "Hey, don't worry about her. You'll be there with me. I know you have history, but show up with me and on the arm of Lewis Warren, and you'll be untouchable."

I didn't think it worked that way, but I liked the sentiment. "And Penn?"

Jane frowned. "He was invited. There are certain names on every guest list."

"It's amazing how much the Upper East Side is like a small town."

"Girl, do not let anyone around hear you say that." Jane giggled and then waved her hand at Sandra.]

She handed me three different outfits, including a stunning dress that I had coveted but couldn't even bring myself to look at the price tag.

"We'll take these, Sandra. Put them on my account."

"Of course," Sandra said, taking all of the clothes.

"Oh, Jane, I can't accept that."

"Don't be silly. That's what friends are for. And anyway, you must wear that dress to my opening."

Sandra came back a moment later and spoke privately with Jane. Jane sighed exaggeratedly as if she was being put out. Then she opened up her enormous purse and passed Sandra a giant wad of cash. My eyes widened in shock. Who carried that kind of cash on them? Jane must be even wealthier than I'd thought. Jesus!

"Yes, that should cover it. Sorry for the inconvenience," Sandra said apologetically.

Jane rolled her eyes. "Some error with my account. I'll have to call the bank."

"That's annoying."

Jane huffed. "Tell me about it."

When Sandra came back with the packages, Jane passed them to me and refused to take no for an answer. "Take the packages, Natalie. Wear the dress to my event and don't think twice about it."

"It's too much, Jane."

"Stop thinking so much. Just live."

That was how I walked out of Bergdorf Goodman with clothes that cost more than most people's monthly salary. And I felt a bit sick about it.

· · ·

I CARRIED the packages up the elevator and into Lewis's apartment. I was pretty certain that I was going to return them before the day was officially up. Even bringing them up the elevator made me feel guilty. It had been different when I was borrowing shoes from Amy or a dress from a rack at Katherine's apartment. These were now mine. I was probably going to have to go to Target and find some kind of knockoff to replace it with.

Lewis turned to face me when he heard the elevator ding, walking out of the kitchen. His eyebrows rose in surprise when he took in the various bags I was carrying.

"Well, well," he said, "I feel a different person has just walked into my place. Bergdorf, huh?"

"Jane," I said in response.

He laughed. "If I'd known you were so amenable to shopping sprees, I would have suggested I take you."

"Trust me," I said, tossing the bags down onto the couch. "I wasn't amenable. Jane is just more convincing than you."

"That so?" He moved to stand in front of me, sliding his hands down my hips. His lips met mine with deliberate slowness. "I think I can be pretty convincing."

I couldn't help myself. I laughed. "You're ridiculous."

"Is that what you think? You issued a challenge, Miss Bishop. What did you expect from me?"

I shrugged. "I hadn't really thought it through. And anyway, I'm probably going to have to return all of this stuff."

A voice cleared from the kitchen, and I turned in surprise to see two people standing at the island bar. I immediately recognized them—Charlotte and Etta. Lewis's sisters.

"Brother, do you care to introduce us?" Charlotte said.

"Or are you just going to stand there, looking sheepish all day?" Etta asked.

Lewis huffed. "You two are insufferable." He turned back to face me. "Natalie, these are my sisters. Charlotte." He gestured to the taller of the two. Then the shorter. "And Etta."

Charlotte was stunning with dark brown skin and unbelievably long eyelashes. Her black hair was parted in the middle and curled alluringly to her shoulders. Her style was model perfect—dark wash jeans and a plain white T-shirt. She needed nothing else to accentuate her beauty.

Etta was all black leather leggings and moto jacket, gold studded bracelets, and dark red lipstick. She had replaced the bob I'd seen her in last year with a high ponytail of box braids that nearly went to her ass. She was curvy where Charlotte was trim, edgy where Charlotte was delicate.

They were a dynamic duo. And I couldn't believe that they were only twenty-one and eighteen years old respectively. Upper East Side girls were from a different planet.

"They showed up, unannounced, in an attempt to ambush you, I'm afraid," Lewis said, shooting me a look of frustration. "They have been bugging me nonstop since we started dating."

"Bugging you?" Etta asked. "Is it too much to want to meet the woman you're dating?"

I was taken aback. They'd wanted to meet me. I hadn't heard a word of that from Lewis. Maybe he was worried that it would freak me out. Which maybe, if I'd had time to think about it, it might have, but here, when they were together, it just made me happy. A sharp contrast to a mother hating me so much that she'd fired me and blacklisted me from ever getting work again.

"It's fine. I'm glad I get to meet you again," I told them.

"Well, excellent," Etta said. She darted over and looped our arms together, dragging me to the bar. "We've been dying to meet you."

"Etta, give her room to breathe," Charlotte chided.

"She can *breathe*," Etta grumbled.

Lewis buried his head in his hands. "I should have made you leave the moment you walked in."

"As if you could make us leave," Charlotte said with a sly grin.

"Brother, make us a drink," Etta said. "We'll be a while."

Lewis shook his head in disbelief. "What am I your bartender now?"

"Yes," Charlotte and Etta said at the same time.

I started laughing right along with them.

"Oh dear lord, they've already converted you," he said with his eyes lifted to the heavens. "I will play bartender just this once, but do go easy on her. I know you two."

"Us?" Etta said, touching her chest, as if offended he would suggest that they'd be anything but nice.

Lewis gave them *the look*. A brotherly thing that clearly said he didn't buy the innocent act. Still, he went to the wet bar to make us drinks.

"Now, tell me all the dirt. Lewis is so tight-lipped about you two." Etta's eyes were an intense hazel color, and they looked excited and maybe a bit devious. "Are you *dating*, dating? Has he *defined* the relationship? You know how guys are these days. They're all about that *let's just see where it goes*, which we all know is code for sex."

I opened my mouth to respond, but Charlotte cut in, "Ignore Ettie here. Tell us more about you. All we know is that you're a famous author. Where did you grow up? Where did you go to college? What do your parents do?"

I heard Lewis curse from where he was mixing drinks and mutter something that sounded a bit like, "You two are the worst."

"Well, I think we're dating." My eyes caught his, and he grinned. "If anything, I'm the one taking it slow."

"Oh, flipping the gender norms. I approve," Etta said encouragingly. "Keep my brother on his toes. He needs that."

"Jesus Christ," came from the bar.

"And there's not much to tell about me. I grew up in the military. My dad retired in Charleston. I went to Grimke University and have a bachelor's in English. Now, I'm writing here in the city."

"Wow," Charlotte breathed. "You must have lived all over."

"I did. We moved every other year until I was a freshman in high school."

"And here, I'd never moved until I graduated," Etta said and then pursed her lips. "Unless you consider vacationing in Paris or the Hamptons or Ibiza for that winter or the Swiss Alps."

Lewis plunked down glasses in front of us. "It's not the same. And you sound ridiculous when you spout it off like that."

Charlotte nodded. "Rein it in, so you don't sound like an entitled brat."

"As if you're any better, Charlie."

Charlotte fluttered her fingers at them and took a long sip of the cocktail in front of her. "Oh, heavy on the gin, brother. I do approve."

"At least I'm good for something," Lewis said.

"That's a change," Etta joked.

"Anyway," Charlotte drawled, "we're glad we got to meet you. And didn't have to keep following your escapades on Crew."

"Well, it is new." I took a drink of my cocktail for liquid courage to get through this apparent interview with his sisters. I'd never liked interviews, and I hoped I was passing.

"Oh, girl, my brother does not give his affection lightly. If he likes you, then you're it," Etta said.

"Yeah. I mean, he's only ever had three real girlfriends, right?" Charlotte asked.

"Guys," Lewis grumbled.

"Yep," Etta confirmed. "Addie in high school."

"Monica in college."

"And that bitch, Alicia."

"Ugh, Alicia," Charlotte groaned.

"Would you two knock it off? We're not here for you to tell Natalie about my previous girlfriends."

"Hey," Etta said, poking him in the chest, "we're helping you out, brother."

"Yeah. We're showing her that you stick with a woman when you find one that you like. The others are just…" Charlotte flitted her fingers up.

Lewis shook his head. "Why did I think introducing you all would be a good idea? Oh wait, I didn't."

Etta rolled her eyes. "Yeah, but if you'd introduced us to Alicia earlier," Etta said, "then we could have told you she was a bitch. Would have saved you a lot of time!"

"And Natalie isn't a bitch," Charlotte confirmed.

"Well, thank god," I muttered. My eyes were wide as I kept up with their swift exchange, learning so much in the process.

Charlotte laughed. "As if there was any doubt. You're so sweet that you're going to rot his teeth."

Etta tilted her head onto my shoulder. "This is Charlotte's way of saying that she likes you."

"You three are so fun all together."

Lewis looked mildly offended. "They're trouble."

"So are you," Etta accused.

"A hundred percent." Charlotte nodded her head. "Mom is going to love her."

Etta eyed Lewis. "So, when are you bringing her home?"

I coughed in surprise. Meeting his sisters was one thing. I'd technically already met them at the Chloe Avana concert. Plus, drinks at Lewis's wasn't scary, only a bit intimidating. But meeting the parents…that was…wow.

Lewis shook his head at them. "Whenever I damn well please. You menaces should butt out."

"Just saying, Mom is curious," Etta said.

"All right. That's it. Go bother someone else."

Etta and Charlotte cackled as they drained the last of their drinks and stood. They pulled me in for hugs, promising to see me again soon and that I was welcome with them anytime. They dramatically bustled out of the apartment.

"They are…"

"I know," he grumbled.

"Amazing, Lewis. Truly so amazing. You're lucky to have that relationship with them."

His eyebrows rose. "Most people find them over-whelming."

"Well, sure. But what part of the Upper East Side isn't?"

"You're incredible. You know that, right?" He stepped into me and planted another kiss on my lips.

"Obviously," I joked.

"No really. There's no one else quite like you, Natalie."

"You make all of this seem so easy."

"It *is* easy with you." He pulled back to look at me sincerely. "Can I tell you something?"

I nodded.

"I would really like you to meet my mother. She's a wonderful, powerful, incredible woman. And the girls weren't wrong when they said that she'd love you," he said against my lips. "Is that too much?"

I found myself shaking my head. Not if she was anything like his sisters. Anything like him. "It's not too much."

"Good. I want everyone I care about to know and love you."

And I surprised myself by not only believing him…but also agreeing.

NATALIE

21

"*T*here's no reason to be nervous."

I warily glanced over at Lewis as we took the elevator up to the top floor. "That's easy for you to say. How would you feel if you were meeting my parents?"

"If you invited me to Charleston to visit your family, I think I'd probably be over the moon."

"My dad was in the military. Now, he's a cop. He's very good with a firearm."

Lewis laughed. "Well, I don't think my family even owns one. Does that ease your fear?"

"Not in the slightest."

He lightly wrapped his arm around my waist and kissed my temple. "It's going to be fine. My parents are great. Shockingly little drama for the Upper East Side."

The elevator opened into the Warrens' impressive apartment. Though it felt as if that was such an insubstantial word for their home. My dinky third-story one-bedroom on the Upper West was an apartment. Even Lewis's huge penthouse still had the feel of an apartment. This was something else entirely. The ceilings in the living room were two or three

176

stories high with floor-to-ceiling windows overlooking Central Park. Stairs led up to a second floor where I assumed the bedrooms were tucked away. Everything was monochromatic with a touch of greenery. Classy and conservative and all-around stunning.

"Mom, we made it," Lewis called into the house.

"In the kitchen," his mother called back.

We walked through the foyer, past the living room, and into the kitchen, which was as insane as the rest of the house. The island at the center of the kitchen could possibly be the size of my entire living room. My eyes doubled in size when I saw the industrial-sized stainless steel fridge and—I counted one, two, three, four—*four* ovens.

"We brought you a pinot," Lewis said, holding the wine up as we stepped fully into the professional-grade kitchen.

But it was the beautiful black woman standing in front of a host of pots on the stove that drew my attention. Nina Warren. She looked like a mix of Etta and Charlotte. Her hair in a shoulder-length inverted bob. Her designer dress fit like it had been made for her. But it was her stance as she turned in her stilettos to face us that made me see the real woman. The current ambassador to the United Nations, a woman with grace and poise in every feature.

"Oh, thank god," his mother said in response. "Pop that open. I'm going to need a glass before I finish with this sauce. It is not cooperating."

Lewis reached into a drawer to remove a wine opener. "Mom, this is Natalie."

She set down the spoon she'd been stirring with and came forward to draw me into a hug. "It is so nice to meet you. Lewis speaks so highly of you, and now, my daughters do as well."

"It's nice to meet you, too, ma'am."

She laughed. "Nina will do just fine."

"Three glasses?" Lewis asked, extracting them from a cabinet.

"Definitely," his mother said. "We all need it to deal with my cooking."

"Oh please," Lewis said as he poured the wine. "Your cooking is the best."

Nina gave me a skeptical look. "Normally, we'd have the chef over, but I wanted to do it myself. If it's burned, blame it on someone else."

Chef. Right. I hadn't thought it was strange to see her cooking.

"Mom always used to cook," Lewis said, handing me a glass. "She's too important now."

"Never trade your ambition for a home-cooked meal," Nina said.

"We just ate a lot of pizza at my house." I shrugged. "My mom burns eggs unless they're in a cake. And my dad worked late hours in the military. I learned how to make the essentials pretty young after that."

"Oh, what do you like to cook?"

"Pasta was a specialty. A lot of lasagna. I'm pretty good on a grill, too. Don't ask why I was allowed near that much fire before I was out of elementary school."

"I'm going to need to try this lasagna," Lewis said.

I laughed. "Oh god, what did I get myself into? I'm going to use your kitchen."

"Done," he conceded easily.

"Okay, you," Nina said, pointing a wooden spoon at her son. "Roll those sleeves up and start chopping vegetables. Don't think you can come in here and not work for your food. Your sisters should be here any minute. I think Charlie's bringing a boy."

"Which one?" Lewis asked. He'd already set his glass

down, and to my surprise, he was rolling his sleeves up to do exactly as his mother had demanded.

"There's more than one?" Nina asked worriedly.

Lewis shot me an amused look. Apparently, the answer was yes.

"Do you need my help with anything?" I offered.

"Absolutely not," Nina said. "You're a guest. Lewis needs to be put to work but not his lovely girlfriend. You enjoy your wine and the sarcasm that will ensue as soon as Charlie and Etta show up."

The elevator dinged then, announcing his sisters, as if summoned from her proclamation.

"Here's trouble," Lewis muttered.

Charlotte and Etta appeared around the corner, chatting about something that had happened earlier. Charlotte had her hand laced with her date, a man who made even her almost look short. He was tall and trim with black skin and close-cropped hair. He was dressed down in jeans and a T-shirt that revealed the tattoos spiraling up his left arm.

"Natalie!" Etta said excitedly. She was in black jeans that were torn at the knee, a skintight black tank top, and a cherry-red leather jacket.

She pulled me into a hug, and then Charlotte hugged me, too.

"This is my boyfriend, Brodie," Charlotte said.

Etta snorted.

"Shut it, Ettie."

"No offense, but I really can't keep them all apart. Is this the one at Harvard or the *I'm back for break* boyfriend?"

Charlotte narrowed her eyes. "I hate you."

Brodie was either oblivious or didn't care, and Charlotte carted him off to the bar. Etta came to stand beside me, taking Lewis's discarded wine glass and draining the rest of it.

"I wasn't finished with that," Lewis said.

"Guess you are now."

"Brat."

"Jerk."

"Children," Nina said with an exaggerated sigh. "All my babies in one place, and a headache is already blooming."

"I already hear your mother is frustrated. Everyone must be home," a male voice said from the direction of the stairs.

I'd been so wrapped up in meeting Lewis's mother that I hadn't thought that much about his father. I didn't know much about Edward Warren, except that he had come from a long, long line of wealthy Warrens. I didn't even know that he was white until he walked into the kitchen with all the presence of a hurricane and wrapped his arms around his wife. He planted a kiss on the space between her neck and shoulder.

"Don't let them stress you out, dove," he murmured against her skin.

Nina smiled like a lovesick puppy and turned into her husband. "Edward." She breathed his name like they were teenagers again. The love quite evident in both of their eyes.

"Ew, Mom. Can we not?" Etta grumbled.

"God, are they making out again?" Charlotte asked, striding back into the kitchen with Brodie following.

Nina laughed and took a half-step from her husband. "Edward, you remember Brodie, right?"

"Ah, yes." Edward held his hand out, and Brodie shook it.

"Sir," he said with a head nod.

"And Lewis's girlfriend, Natalie."

He turned his stern face toward me. He looked so much like Lewis but twenty years older. Handsome, regal even, and rather serious.

He held his hand out to me then. "Nice to meet you, Natalie."

"You, too." I swallowed and shook his hand.

There was nothing off-putting about him. Yet I could feel his judgment on me like a weight. Maybe it was just his intimidating presence, but I felt like he had already made up his mind about me.

"Well, are we all ready here, Nina?"

"Pretty much. Etta, help with drinks. Lewis, start carrying everything to the table. Charlotte, show Natalie and Brodie where to sit."

Everyone jumped into action. I took my seat in the middle of the table between Nina and Charlotte. Lewis took the chair opposite of me with Brodie and Etta on either side. And Edward took his place at the head of the table. Nina said grace, and then we all partook of her incredible food.

"So, Natalie, how did you and Lewis meet?" Nina asked.

My gaze swept up to his. Oh, jeez, I hadn't thought about these sorts of questions.

"Um, we met last year when I was in the city."

"I thought I'd already told you that. We met in the Hamptons. I took her on the yacht."

Nina nodded. "Right. Right. I remember now."

"You took her on the yacht, and it took you a year to catch her," Edward said with a raised eyebrow. "Maybe I need to upgrade."

The girls laughed, and I tried to force out a laugh, too, but it sounded hollow. No reason to explain why the yacht hadn't worked and the year had passed. Lewis gave me a sympathetic nod.

"How did you two meet?" I asked Nina to change the subject.

"Oh, that old story," she said.

"Tell it, Mom," Etta said. "It's our favorite."

"If you insist."

"We do," Charlotte agreed.

"Well, I was eighteen and a freshman at Harvard. I came from a banking family in Boston. So, it was home territory for me. I was pre-law, and your father was business, but we had a class together."

"Where you kicked his ass," Etta butted in.

"She always did," Edward said with a loving smile.

"And well, one thing led to another, and I became pregnant with Lewis. Everyone told us we were crazy for keeping him, but it was love at first sight. We eloped. I took a year off of school. But everyone still said that I'd never make it because I'd had a baby in college. That Edward and I weren't paired." She rolled her eyes. "A lot of people didn't want to see two successful people together, period. When you add in the fact that it was an interracial couple, it was even worse. But we proved them wrong. I still finished college and got a law degree. Then once I was a partner at my firm, we decided to have Charlotte and Etta. Proving everyone wrong again."

My smile widened at the story. "What a great story."

"True love," Nina said, reaching for Edward's hand and squeezing.

I was still thinking about that heartwarming story as the conversation shifted to the girls. Etta taking a gap year before going to Harvard next fall. Charlotte's business classes at Harvard. She'd finished exams earlier this week, and she was pretty certain she'd aced them.

"All that, and we have such a busy Christmas. Between your modeling debut at the Trinity club opening, the wedding, gingerbread houses, a handful of charity functions, and Christmas, I don't even know when I'll find time to work," Nina said. "Natalie, I hope that you're coming with Lewis to the wedding?"

"Um…wedding?" My eyes shot to his.

"I was going to talk to you about that," Lewis said across the table.

Nina raised her eyebrows. "I assumed you were bringing her as a plus-one."

"I do intend to bring her. But I haven't asked her yet."

"Sorry, whose wedding?" I asked.

"Katherine Van Pelt and Camden Percy," Nina said with a wide grin as if those two names didn't send acid through my stomach.

"Oh."

Of course.

No wonder Lewis hadn't brought it up. Not with how I felt about the pair. That was the furthest thing from taking it slow in society. The furthest thing from what I wanted to be doing with my life. The epitome of the Upper East Side. An arranged marriage between a deceptive, penniless, scheming bitch and her cheating, addicted, asshole groom. Count me out.

I didn't know what anyone said after that. I was still stuck on that one point. And how I knew for certain that there was *no* way I was going to Katherine's wedding. No way in hell.

NATALIE

22

$\mathcal{A}$fter dinner ended, I thanked Nina and Edward for their hospitality and promised to come back again soon. Lewis kissed his mom good night and then whisked me out of their mansion. He breathed out in relief as soon as the elevator doors closed.

"Well, that went as well as could be expected."

I arched an eyebrow at him.

"I was going to tell you about the wedding."

"When? When it happened?"

"You've been so anti–Upper East Side. You don't even want to go to Jane's club opening after what happened at Harmony's. And Jane is probably your closest friend here."

"I have good reason for feeling that way," I reminded him.

"I know. So, why would I burden you with the knowledge that Katherine is getting married?"

"Because apparently, everyone already assumed I was going with you. And then I looked like an idiot because I didn't even know it was happening."

"You didn't look like an idiot," he assured me as we exited the elevator and strode out to his waiting Mercedes.

I had to admit, it was nice, having a driver waiting for you wherever you went. Especially with the frigid temperatures bathing New York City this weekend.

"You could always go with me," he said with a cocky grin.

I laughed in his face. "Not going to happen."

"Wouldn't it be a victory for you?" he offered. "Seeing Katherine be miserable for the rest of her life."

"There is no victory in that. Victory implies that there was a competition, which I was never a part of," I coolly told him. "And I don't care if Katherine is happy or miserable. I just don't want to have to deal with her."

He sighed. "Fair."

We were out of the car and in his apartment again when fresh anger hit me at the situation. "Didn't I just see Camden with someone else? Tracey?"

Lewis shrugged. "It *is* arranged."

I huffed dramatically and tossed my coat on the couch. "They disgust me."

He chuckled softly and then stepped into me, tilting my chin up to look at him. "I like when you get all fiery."

"You like when I'm angry?" I asked with a disconcerted look.

"Not angry. But passionate. It's like when you discuss your book. Or when you talk about swimming. Or how you talk about any topic that you have strong opinions about."

"So...everything?"

"It's my favorite thing about you. Your passion. Most people around here lose it, learn to contain it, leash it. You set yours free. And it lights you up."

A smile came to my lips. My irritation over Katherine's impending wedding melting away. What did it matter if she got married? I wasn't going. I didn't need to ruin a perfectly good night because of it.

"Well, I had a good time with your family otherwise. Your mom is the best."

"Isn't she?"

"Your dad is kind of intimidating though."

"He has that perfected." He threaded both of our hands together and kissed me once. "He was kind of terrifying when I was growing up. But I get it now. He was preparing me to take over."

"And you wanted that?" I asked, slipping my hands out of his, up his chest, and around his neck.

He breathed out a laugh. "Not always. I wanted to play baseball after high school. We fought about it a lot. But in hindsight, he was right. I wasn't good enough for the majors, and I would have wallowed in the minors when I should have been at Harvard. So, Harvard was where I ended up."

"Why didn't you play baseball at Harvard?"

He shrugged. "I'm an all-or-nothing sort of guy."

"Oh, yeah? Is that what you are with me right now?"

"You're like nothing else that has ever come into my life."

When his lips touched mine, all semblance of restraint evaporated. No longer did he touch me with soft, achingly slow kisses. He'd deserted that with our talk of passion. And his passion for me.

Our lips moved against each other with abandon. He demanded a response and took everything that I gave back to him with equal fervor. A hand moved to my breast, squeezing me through the material of my dress. His thumb slipped under the front of my dress and flicked against my erect nipple, sending a jolt of desire through my body.

I reached blindly for the buttons of his shirt. Wanting— no, *needing* to feel his heated skin and taste that perfect physique. He pulled back long enough to reach behind him, grasp the back of his shirt, and tug it over his head. My mouth watered at the sight of him. All chiseled abdominals and bulky arms and shoulders. Hours in the gym. He must spend hours to have this kind of incredible body.

My fingers splayed over the pecs and went down every square inch of abs to the V that drove me utterly crazy. And he let me. Let me eat him up.

Then, he pressed forward into me. His hands found the zipper of my dress, and he dragged it down inch by inch until it hit the apex of my ass. His fingers tipped the sleeves off of my shoulders, revealing the curve of my breasts and then the black-and-nude bra I'd chosen for the evening. His eyes went wide when he caught a glimpse of it. His head dipped down and sucked the pebbled nipple into his mouth, heedless of the sheer material as a barrier.

I gasped, arching into him at the sensation. At the fact that he couldn't wait to even take the thing off because he needed me so badly.

The rest of my dress fell over my hips and then into a puddle at my feet. He pulled back long enough to take his fill of me. He'd seen me in nearly as little clothing. I'd worn a bra and panties into the pool the first night we met. But that had been a year ago. We hadn't been anything at the time. This was all different.

"You are perfect," he told me as he slipped his hands down my body.

Then he took my hand and guided me into his bedroom. I went willingly. My body taut with anticipation.

He flicked the clasp on my bra, and my breasts spilled forward out of the constraint. His hands went to them. Feeling the soft mounds and fingering my sensitive nipples. He explored me in no rush for this to come to a close. Just enjoying every second of it.

My hand moved for his belt, which I deftly undid. Then I snagged the button and released the zipper. His cock jutted upward in his pants, unobstructed by any kind of underwear. A soft noise escaped me at the unexpected sight.

"Like that?" he groaned.

"Commando," I observed.

"Going to be thinking about that every time we're together now?"

"Do you always?"

My fingers dipped into his pants, running gingerly across the head of his cock. He stretched into my hand as I got the feel of him in my palm and stroked.

"Fuck," he grunted. "I've wanted your touch...so long."

I did it again and then again. Up and down. Up and down.

"Natalie," he murmured.

I pushed the waist of his suit pants off of his narrow hips and then gently came to my knees before him. Pre-cum glistened on the tip of his cock, waiting for me to taste him. I leaned forward, bracing myself against his powerful thighs, and then licked the seam. The taste of salt hit my tongue at the same time Lewis's hands dug into my hair.

"More?" I teased.

"Open your mouth," was his only answer.

I did as I had been told, and he slid his cock into my mouth. Inch by solid inch. Enough to nearly make me gag on him. But he waited, patient not to hurt me before pulling out and then thrusting in again. When he withdrew once more, I licked my lips and wrestled control back from him, bobbing forward before he could fuck my mouth.

His groan was enough to make my lower half pulse with desire. I could feel wetness pooling in my panties. Taking control, making him feel everything that I was offering him, turned me on as much as it did him.

I could feel him continue to lengthen in my mouth. Growing longer, fuller.

Then, suddenly, he was out of my mouth. He hoisted me to my feet and all but easily threw me onto the bed.

My eyes were wide with concern. "You don't want to finish?"

He grinned. "I do. But you first."

Then he slipped the panties over my hips and buried his face in my pussy. The scruff of his five o'clock shadow brushing against my thighs. His tongue lapping at my clit. I was already wet and needy after the blow job. And mewling noises were coming from my mouth as he brought me to the brink.

"God, you taste like heaven."

"Oh fuck," was my response.

He chuckled as if he knew how good he was and then ate me out like it was his fucking job. I came in ripples. Shattering into tiny pieces and somehow coming back together into one.

My eyes fluttered open, and I dropped my trembling legs. "Hey, you."

He'd just hopped off the bed. His hand was in the side table drawer. "Hmm?"

"Come here."

He held up the condom that he had been retrieving. Good thing one of us remembered. I was on birth control, but it was smarter.

He slipped the sheath onto his cock and then settled between my legs. I wrapped my arms around his neck. He stared down at me as if I was the most incredible thing in the entire universe. Our lips came together, eager but tender. The tip of him slipped past my opening, and I groaned into his mouth.

"Fuck," he muttered and then slid all the way inside me in one quick thrust.

I quivered at the full feel of him inside me. The coupling that felt so complete.

"I love that," he murmured against my ear. "That first feel of you wrapped all around my cock."

My body throbbed at the words. Then, he started moving, sliding out and thrusting back in. Picking up his pace with each movement until we were both pushing our hips harder and harder against each other. Working up to that moment where we both came undone.

He braced himself over me, taking one of my legs to his shoulder to get deeper. And it was that moment, that one perfect spot, where everything fell away.

I cried out then, yelling, "Oh god, oh god, oh god," into the night. Until he gasped, hit bottom once more, and came with a powerful bellow.

Lewis dropped his head down to my shoulder. His powerful muscles heaving. His body sated and spent.

I ran my fingers across his hair and kissed his shoulder. No words needed to be spoken. Not after that. Not while we were naked and happy. All I needed was our heavy breathing and racing hearts. The evidence of how we had come together in that moment.

For I knew that nothing would ever be the same.

PART IV
DARKEST HOUR IS JUST
BEFORE DAWN

NATALIE

23

$\mathcal{T}$he limo stopped in front of Trinity for Jane's club opening. I tensed in the backseat with Lewis at the red carpet and paparazzi waiting outside. I had known they would be there. Jane had pulled out all the stops. But I was still uncomfortable with the spotlight. Not to mention that this was the first time I would be out with Lewis since Harmony's unfortunate party. Even worse, I knew the crew would be here. I knew that I might run into them. And I had come anyway.

For Jane. For Lewis. For Charlotte and Etta. For the person I was in this moment who wanted to be there for my friends...my boyfriend.

Even if the paparazzi display brought back a slew of negative feelings. I remembered strutting along behind Katherine as if I belonged here, as if Katherine liked me or cared. And it was hard to shake those feelings loose.

"I'm not nervous," I lied to him.

Lewis bent forward and placed a kiss on my cherry-red lips. "Liar," he murmured.

"I'm not nervous. I'm just remembering the last time I did this. The girl I was then."

"Natalie, look at me."

I swung my gaze away from the commotion at the entrance.

"You belong here. You belong here with me. Don't let anyone convince you otherwise."

My shoulders loosened, and I breathed out once as the words rolled over me.

His hand threaded up into my long silver hair, tugging me closer. I leaned into him, feeling his lips against my own. Glad for the lipstick that wouldn't budge and his hot presence that grounded me in that moment.

The driver tapped on our window, and Lewis pulled away with a satisfied smirk, leaving me hanging in the space between us. He ran his knuckles across my cheekbone and then winked, bringing me back to the present.

Showtime.

The driver opened the door, and Lewis stepped out first before holding his hand out for me. I took it and gingerly took a step into the spotlight. I'd had every intention of wearing the dress that Jane had purchased for me at Bergdorf, but this morning, when I'd been getting ready to leave to go write, a package had been delivered to my apartment.

I'd taken the long royal-purple garment bag in confusion. My heart had fluttered at the gold lettering that read *Cunningham Couture* across one side. I'd unzipped the bag to find the most stunning forest-green lace dress in existence. I'd shimmied into the thing and found that it fit like a dress, wrapping up and around my neck with a full open back. It hugged my waist and down to mid-thigh before fanning out to my feet. The color looked stunning against my long pale hair and my fair skin.

It had come with a small handwritten note.

Wear me.
—Jane

A pair of high heels with red lacquered bottoms that cost a fortune were also attached. And I wanted to turn it all down. I had returned everything from Bergdorf that day, except the dress since I'd been planning to wear it to the event. I could *not* keep an Elizabeth Cunningham original. But Jane had refused to even take my calls all day.

And here I was. Stepping up to the cameras in strappy black Louboutin fuck-me heels and a one-of-a-kind designer dress. It almost felt like putting on armor. Heading into an Upper East Side event felt like going into battle.

Cameras flashed. Journalists called out for questions. We walked across a red carpet. And it was over. It took only a matter of minutes, and my anxiety had been for nothing. Go figure.

I held my head high as I walked into Trinity nightclub. I was on Lewis Warren's arm. He was dressed to kill in a Tom Ford tuxedo. We were here at the bequest of the owner. I even knew one of the models in Elizabeth Cunningham's collection for the event. Maybe I did belong after all.

Then, the toe of my shoe caught on the front of my dress, and I stumbled. Thankfully, Lewis's arm was still around my waist. He steadied me before I fell on my face. Or worse… ripped the one-of-a-kind dress.

"Easy there," he said with a laugh.

My face turned the color of a tomato. "So embarrassing."

On second thought, *fake it till you make it* seemed more realistic.

I hurried with Lewis out of the spotlight and took in the club. It was enormous, even bigger than I would have guessed. A stage and runway took up the center of the room. Cunningham Couture's logo was tastefully displayed around in gold across purple banners. One entire wall was floor-to-ceiling glass with discreet exits onto a heated balcony. A long bar lined either side of the room, and waiters in tuxedos were carrying champagne flutes amid the crowd. Jane had said that DJ Damon Stone was playing for the crowd tonight, and I could hear his telltale style coming in from the speakers.

All in all, it was outstanding. Jane had really outdone herself.

"Ah!" a voice shrieked from behind us as Lewis claimed two glasses of champagne for us. "You made it!"

I turned around in time for Etta to throw herself into my arms.

"We made it," I said, pulling back to smile at her.

She was a smidgen shorter than me, even in her sky-high heels. She had on a skintight dress with studded details that showed off her curvy frame. The gold high-lighter on her light-brown cheeks was flawless. Her box braids were artfully swept into a bun. She looked like a vixen.

"Oh, look, my little sister is here," Lewis drawled.

"Brother, I was going to say that you look dapper tonight, but I take it back," Etta quipped.

"Where is my well-behaved sibling?"

Etta rolled her eyes, which were heavily lined in black coal and fake lashes. "Fuck well behaved."

I just laughed. I enjoyed their antics.

"Come on, Natalie. We can't expect my brother to be a gentleman. I'll take you back to see Charlie."

Etta looped her arm with mine and veered me toward the stage door. Etta winked at the guy guarding the door, and he opened it for her.

"Sorry, no men backstage at this point," the guy said to Lewis.

Lewis arched an eyebrow. "Do you know who I am?"

"Oh, give it a rest," Etta said with a laugh. "We'll be in and out in a minute. Go get us drinks. Something strong." She winked at him and then dragged me through the door.

I glanced back at Lewis and shrugged. "See you in a minute."

He shook his head and started speaking to the guard, who didn't seem to care in the slightest that he was Lewis Warren.

As I turned back around, the world transformed. We'd gone from bumping tunes, clientele dressed to the nines, and floating champagne to half-naked models, a strong smell of hairspray, and glitter flying everywhere. And yet, I felt more comfortable here than out there. I was going to have to thank Melanie for that one. One too many dance recitals back in the day.

"Charlie!" Etta called. She grasped my hand and then moved through the chaos toward her sister, who stood out in all of her beautiful glory. "Look who I brought with me."

Charlotte stood in six-inch heels and looked like an Amazon goddess. Her hair had been cornrowed back on both sides, leaving a soft mane of finger coils down the middle. She was being pinned or maybe sewn into the dress she was wearing, which was exotic and looked like stained glass or a painting of the inside of a kaleidoscope. Not practical for everyday wear, but clearly a piece of art.

She turned to face me with bright purple lipstick and rhinestoned eyelashes. "Natalie! Oh, I'm so glad that you were able to make it. Is my brother being an ass yet?"

I chuckled and shook my head. "Not yet."

"Well, don't let him fool you."

"I don't know how she can be fooled with us two around," Etta said, slinking her arm across my shoulders.

"Fair point," Charlotte conceded.

"You two are hilarious. You love your brother."

Both girls sniffed as if I'd insulted them even if it was the truth. I understood that. Melanie and I hadn't always been close, definitely not close like they were, but she was my sister.

"Okay, before we forget," Charlotte said, "what are your plans on Tuesday?"

I shrugged. "No plans. Just writing."

"You should come to make our annual gingerbread houses," Etta added.

"You make gingerbread houses every year?" I asked.

"It's tradition," Charlotte said with a smile.

"Our mom is a gingerbread connoisseur," Etta explained.

"Like, the best in the city. You had her cooking. It's fine. But the gingerbread houses? Those are spectacular."

"And now, Lewis can't back out of inviting you," Etta said with a pointed eye roll.

I laughed. "You two are devious."

"He'd say the same thing," Charlotte said.

I shook my head at their careful maneuvering. "You look amazing, by the way."

"It's all Elizabeth. She is a genius. Seriously, pure genius."

"Why, thank you, Charlotte," a voice said as a stunning woman appeared next to Charlotte, inspecting her dress. She pointed out a few things, and the other man working on her dress went to work.

"Oh, Natalie, this is Elizabeth Cunningham," Charlotte said.

Elizabeth turned her keen, dark eyes on me. She was a woman who was reported to be in her early fifties but didn't look a day over thirty-five. I didn't know if it was plastic surgery or amazing genetics. Her dark brown hair was artfully twisted on her head, and she wore a crisp black and white dress that was beyond stunning on her.

"So, you're the woman Jane had me send another dress over for." Elizabeth stepped forward and checked the fit on my dress. "Ah yes, the woman at Bergdorf sent over your exact measurements. It looks perfect with your hair. So unique."

"Why...thank you," I whispered, in awe of the designer before me in her natural element.

"Who normally dresses you?" Elizabeth asked. She tapped her lips, as if sizing me up.

"What do you mean?"

"For appearances. What designer do you prefer?" Elizabeth asked me with a predatory smile. "Oh, I don't care who I'm going to piss off. Let me dress you for your next appearance. I know exactly what line to pair with that silver hair. Where will you be seen next?"

My eyes shot to Etta's and Charlotte's, frozen in shock. I didn't make appearances. I wasn't a socialite. Surely, Elizabeth was mistaken. She couldn't possibly want to feature me with her clothes.

"She's going to the Percy wedding with us," Charlotte answered for me when it was clear that I wasn't going to respond.

"Oh, excellent. I'm designing Katherine's wedding dress." Elizabeth snapped her fingers at her assistant. I hadn't noticed the short man standing behind her. He placed a card in her hand, and she passed the embossed cardstock to me. "Here's my card. Get in touch with my assistant, and we'll put something together for the wedding."

"Thank you," I stammered.

Then, Elizabeth breezed out as easily as she'd walked in.

The man at Charlotte's feet interrupted my shock by saying, "You're good to go."

"Thanks," Charlotte said, stepping off her pedestal.

"I…" I blinked rapidly. "What just happened?"

"Elizabeth has excellent taste," Charlotte said.

"You're in great hands," Etta agreed.

"But…I'm not anybody. I'm not a socialite or a celebrity."

Charlotte and Etta exchanged a glance.

"You're dating our brother. That makes you somebody," Charlotte said.

Etta nodded. "This is our life. You'll get used to it."

That might have been a bit of what I was afraid of. I couldn't even believe I was wearing one original designer piece, but to have the designer specifically ask to dress me? I had no idea what that even meant for my life. Fancy house parties, shopping at Bergdorf, club openings…maybe I was falling into the Upper East Side a little easier than I'd thought. Blurring a line that I'd believed to be so solid.

Penn's words echoed through my skull, reminding me that no one could straddle the line.

But I still felt like me. I wasn't any different. Right?

NATALIE

24

$\mathcal{O}$ne of the stage managers started calling out for everyone to get to their places, and suddenly, the backstage went from disaster to utter chaos. Everyone started frantically running around as they got set for the show.

"Okay, we have to go," Etta said. She kissed her sister's cheek. "Good luck, Charlie."

"Break a leg," I said, still half in a daze. "If that's good luck in modeling."

Charlotte laughed and then waved as she somehow walked in her amazing heels. "See you after!"

I followed Etta back out of the backstage door. I thought Lewis might be waiting for us there. I needed to talk to him about what had just happened, but he was nowhere to be seen. The minute we were out of the backstage though, a brunette girl threw herself at Etta and started kissing her.

"Ava, Ava, Ava," Etta said with a laugh. "I thought you weren't coming home from Princeton for another week."

"I couldn't leave you waiting," she said in a slight British accent.

Etta introduced us as quickly as possible and then all but dragged Ava away. To where, I could only imagine. Hopefully, she made the show to see Charlotte at least.

I shook my head and then headed toward the stage in search of Lewis. But the crowd was thick. The show was about to begin, and I needed to get to my place. Without Etta as a guide, I was in a sea of strangers.

"Hey, I know you," a voice said behind me.

I turned around and came face-to-face with Addison Rowe. She was not only the twin sister to Archibald Rowe, but also Lewis's high school girlfriend. Last time we'd been in vicinity, she'd cornered me in the restroom of a charity function to warn me about the crew. Turned out that she was right.

I smiled uneasily at the woman standing there. "Natalie. You're Addie, right?"

"Yeah, that's me. We met last year."

I nodded. Instantly on guard. Getting ambushed in a restroom had that tendency.

"I didn't know that you were back in New York." Addie stepped up to my side as we meandered the crowd together.

"Yeah, I moved here recently."

"You're looking for Penn?" she asked, shifting her eyes forward. "I think I saw him over there earlier." She pointed to the other side of the room.

My stomach flip-flopped at the information. So, Penn *was* here. Somewhere. I didn't need another ambush from him either.

"No," I got out. "I'm not here with Penn."

"Oh. I didn't know. Well, forget I said anything then. You looked lost, like you were missing someone. I just assumed." She smiled sincerely.

I wondered if we could be friends if I kept my mouth

shut. But I didn't trust her. So probably not. "I was looking for someone. I'm here with Lewis actually."

Addie's smile vanished. "Really?"

I nodded.

"Well, good luck with that," she said, dripping sarcasm.

"Thanks," I said with equal derision.

"There he is." She pointed him out in the crowd. "Go running back to him."

"What is your problem?" I asked. "First, you find me in the restroom to warn me about the crew, and now, you have to make snide remarks about Lewis? Can't you keep it to yourself?"

Addie promptly stopped and jerked me to a stop, too. "Did you ever even do what I told you? Did you look them up? Ask questions?"

"I asked questions. And I got burned, just like you'd thought I would. But this is different."

Addie rolled her eyes. "It's *always* different."

"Whatever," I said, trying to brush past her.

"I mean, you're clearly just the latest."

I stilled. "The latest?" I couldn't help asking.

"Oh, you know, Lewis. He jumps between obsessions. One time, it was me, then it was baseball, then it was classic novels, then poker, and photography and on and on."

I narrowed my eyes at her accusation. These obsessions... they sounded like all the things he had on display at his apartment. He'd claimed they were hobbies. I didn't know what the difference was.

"So?"

"Well, when it's you, you're bathed in sunlight, and when you lose his attention, you might as well be on the dark side of the moon. And you're the latest," Addie said with a smile.

"You have no idea what you're talking about."

"Maybe. But, if you're not his latest, then you know about Hanna Stratton, right?"

"Who?" I had never heard that name in my life.

And Addie saw it at once. She laughed. "That's what I thought. Enjoy the sunlight while you can."

I scrunched up my brows as she swept past me. I was pretty certain that I didn't like that girl. She always had some strange, ominous thing to impart on me. If my mother were here, she probably would say that she had a dark aura. That I needed to dispel the taint of it to move on. But I wasn't my mother, and right now, I was shaken by her words. Because Addie's comments were oddly similar to something Penn had said at the last party.

My head was in the clouds when I finally reached Lewis's side at the front of the stage. Trinity had darkened considerably, and a spotlight was now on the runway.

"There you are," Lewis said with relief. "I tried your cell, but you never responded."

I touched the tiny purse I had slung over my shoulder. I'd forgotten about it. That would have been easier. "I guess I was distracted."

His eyes filled with worry. "What happened?"

I shook my head. I didn't know what to think about Addie. I had no idea if I could trust or believe a word out of her mouth. The only reason I even considered it was because she had been honest last time. But I didn't want to ruin our night, Jane's night. I'd have to ask him about it later.

"Elizabeth asked to dress me for Katherine's wedding."

Lewis raised his eyebrows. "Look at you."

"The wedding I'm not planning on going to."

"You could," he muttered. "Go as my girlfriend."

My stomach flipped at the way he'd said that word. But it did nothing to dissuade me. "I can't go. I never want to see Katherine again."

"I know. I know that you hate her for what she did."

"Hate her?" I said. "She tried to destroy my life. She got me fired from my job and blacklisted from ever working in that field again. *Hate* is not a strong enough word."

"But it wouldn't be about her. It'd be about us."

"I don't think so."

He sighed. "All right. We can talk about this later. Look, Jane is waving at you."

Jane motioned for us to stand by her at the front of the runway. Court Kensington stood at her side. He looked so much like his brother. It was unnerving. But at least, I didn't see Camden with them. Court I could handle. Camden made my skin crawl.

Jane kissed each of my cheeks when we arrived before her. "Natalie, I'm so glad you made it. And look at this dress. Amazing!"

"Thanks to you."

Jane grinned. "I wanted you in something spectacular. Plus, I knew that I had to surprise you, or you'd figure out a way to say no."

I laughed. She knew me too well.

"Court," Lewis said, holding his hand out.

They shook. Court's eyes moved from me to Lewis for a moment with a wry smile on his face.

"Haven't seen my little brother around here, have you?" Court asked, craning his neck, as if Penn would just materialize out of thin air.

"No," I breathed.

"I don't think he's coming," Lewis said.

"He is," I said before I could stop myself.

Lewis's eyebrows rose in question.

"Uh…someone told me he was already here."

"Why?"

I shrugged. Awkwardness permeated the space between us all. "Just remembered that I knew him."

"That you dated," Court needled. "Right?"

I narrowed my eyes at him. Lewis's arm wrapped around my waist and pulled me back a step into him.

"How interesting," Court said.

What he was thinking was painted all over him. Court had slept with Penn's girlfriend, Emily. And I was now with Penn's best friend. He smirked when he saw me grasp it.

"Court, darling," Jane interrupted before I could say anything else, "why don't you stand over here so that the photographer will have a better shot of me when the show begins?"

Court grinned at me and Lewis standing together as I tried not to think about what he'd insinuated. Then, he stepped around Jane and turned his focus to the runway.

"Jesus, he has a way of being such a fucking bastard," Lewis snapped.

"While saying so little."

"All that time spent with Camden, I think."

I nodded. Remembering the way Court had saved me from Camden. So, he wasn't all bad. But, right now, he wasn't exactly my favorite person either.

Lewis dropped a kiss onto the top of my head as the announcements began for the show.

And Jane nudged me when the first model walked the runway. "I'm so excited! I can't believe this day is really here!"

I let her ramble on through the entire fashion show about everything from who'd helped fund the club to all of the other celebrities who were in attendance. The number was staggering. Jane knew everyone. And everyone wanted to be here for it. It almost made me wonder why she wanted me next to her when all these other people were here. We were friends, but it wasn't like I was famous. Even if being Lewis Warren's girlfriend apparently made me somebody.

When Charlotte walked out on the stage, I ignored propriety and cheered for her. Etta and Ava on the other side of the stage did the same. Lewis laughed and joined in, too. Suddenly, everyone was cheering for Charlotte. And on her debut at that! She looked unbelievable up there. The *pièce de résistance* of the entire thing. I knew she was the spotlight. She was the one everyone was going to talk about. Cameras flashed, and she swaggered back down the stage, soaking up the energy.

"She's amazing!" I told Lewis.

"She loves what she does."

The fashion show wasn't as vibrant without Charlotte. But it ended with a final walk for all the models and Elizabeth herself. The crowd went wild. Then they were gone, the lights came back on, and the show was over.

That was when a figure caught my eye almost directly across from me.

There, standing in a suit fit for James Bond, was Penn Kensington.

And he was smirking at me.

Hands in his pockets. Cunning, wicked, delectable. He tilted his head in a come-hither motion. I knew that was a terribly bad idea.

It might as well have just been me and Penn alone in a crowded room in that moment. But I couldn't make the mistake I'd made at Harmony's party. I wasn't subject to his whims. I didn't want to have another screaming fit.

Still, seeing him like that, I wanted to go.

But I swallowed hard and shook my head. I mouthed, *No*, to him.

He raised an eyebrow. A challenge.

I held my breath for a second before letting it out again and turning away from him. There...over and done with.

"Let's go dance," I said to Lewis.

He smiled down at me, oblivious to what had just transpired between Penn and me across the room. Then he took my hand and led me out onto the dance floor.

Our bodies moved together in the crush of people. Jane flitted in and out of the picture, meeting with friends and celebrities and investors while also trying to make sure that I was having a good time. I kind of loved her. Charlotte and Etta appeared sometime later. Charlotte had changed out of her kaleidoscope dress and into a short, sleek black number. Brodie was at her side with his tongue down her throat half the time. Rowe even appeared at one point on the arm of one of the models. He awkwardly nodded at me and then went back to his date dancing on him while he stood still.

The night was everything Jane wanted it to be. And after my second glass of champagne, I was finally feeling a buzz. Enough of one to stop feeling like there were eyes burning into the back of my head. Like Penn was following us around the room...even though I hadn't seen him since I told him no.

It was probably just my imagination. But it was as if I had a sense of his presence. Despite the fact that I couldn't see him.

"Let's go get another drink," Lewis said.

He took my hand and pulled me off the dance floor. I mopped at my glistening forehead as he scooted into the bar to get us another drink. I fanned my face and looked around the large space to all the drunken revelers.

And I found him again. Penn. He was standing with Rowe, talking and laughing. Rowe was about as animated as I'd ever seen him. Which basically meant, not at all. Then Penn's eyes flicked over to the dance floor. His eyes narrowed, brows scrunched together. He craned his neck, as if trying to spot someone in the crowd.

Me.

He was looking for me. I wasn't crazy. He *had* been keeping tabs on me. My heart hammered at the realization. That he was here just to...what? Watch me? Spy on me? Wait for the moment I was alone, so he could yell at me again?

My anger flared and then dimmed. He needed to stop. I needed to stop this.

Lewis appeared then with my drink. "Here you go."

I turned back to look up at him. "I need to go talk to Penn."

Lewis coughed on the sip he'd just taken. "What?"

"I need to tell him to stop. I don't want to keep doing this at every event."

"I would be happy to go tell him that. I believe you said I should use my fist next time."

My hand touched his, and I shook my head. "No, I need to do this. He'll listen to me."

"Doubtful," he grumbled.

"It'll be fine. This is important."

"All right," he said with a sigh. "But if it looks like it's getting heated, I'm going to come intervene. I don't need him pissing you off again."

I nodded in understanding. "I'll be right back."

Then, I took a deep breath and strode toward Penn Kensington and a conversation I desperately did not want to have.

PENN

25

*W*here the hell had she gone?

One minute, I'd been talking to Rowe, and the next, Natalie was nowhere to be found.

She'd told me no when I showed up to talk to her and tell her the truth. I respected that. Even if I didn't want to. I could have shown up with some stupid model and flaunted her in front of Nat, like she was doing to me. Hurt her like she was hurting me. But that was petty and would only prove her right.

And after all, I was the one who had hurt her in the first place. I wanted her to be happy. Just not with him. She didn't get to choose Lewis and move on in my face.

Rowe nudged me and cleared his throat.

"What?"

He pointed in the other direction, and then I saw her. And she was walking toward me. What the fuck? Hadn't seen that coming. Not after she'd turned me down earlier.

"Is this when I'm supposed to vacate?" Rowe asked.

"Uh…I don't even know."

"When Penn Kensington doesn't know something about women, it is a new day."

"Ass."

Rowe smirked and then disappeared, likely to find the model he'd come with. He was only able to stand her presence in increments, as he found her relatively brain dead.

But my eyes were fixed on Natalie. That green dress that popped against her pale skin. The long, flowy silvery-white hair that stood out in the crowd. Those bright red lips that I missed and her blue eyes that said she was about to rip me to pieces.

I straightened at the fire in that look as she appeared before me. "To what do I owe the pleasure?" I asked calmly.

For all that fire, the closer she got to me, the more uncertain she looked about whatever mission she was on. But, since I didn't know what she was going to say, I couldn't prepare myself. Decide if I should wear my Upper East Side mask that she hated and deal with her or just be me…the guy she'd fallen in love with. Both came with their own problems.

"I can feel your eyes on me all over this club. I want you to stop."

I arched an eyebrow. "You're that attuned to my presence that you know when I'm looking at you?"

"Please, stop," she repeated.

I glanced over her shoulder to see Lewis standing in our line of sight, watching her, watching us. A light flipped in my head, and I stepped forward toward her.

"Ah, that's what you told him so that you could come see me?" I asked. My voice was low and seductive.

Her eyes flicked to my lips and back up.

"Don't do this," she pleaded.

"What will he do if I touch you right now?"

"Probably punch you. So, please listen to my words."

Her eyes searched my face, pupils slightly dilated. Her chest rising and falling at an irregular beat. She clasped her hands together in front of her. Probably to keep them from shaking.

"I can hear what you're saying. Your body is the one not listening," I said, taking another step forward.

"All right. Do what you want. I'm going to go. I wanted to tell you that I don't want this to happen between us at every event. That we could maybe just be normal. But you don't want to hear it."

The words broke like shattered glass in my skull. "At...*every* event?"

She flitted her hand and shrugged. "Yeah, if we're in the same company again."

I arched my eyebrows. Anger hit me fresh. She was actually going to continue this fucking charade.

"You know I wanted to talk to you to tell you the truth. But you said no, so I left you alone. You're the one who walked over here to throw your relationship with my best friend in my face. Now you want to talk about *other* Upper East Side events you're going to be at?" I shook my head, trying to keep from boiling over. It didn't work. "What the hell is wrong with you?"

"Excuse me?" she demanded.

"Where did the Natalie go who told me that she didn't want this life, to deal with my friends or a family who hated her? What the fuck, Nat?"

"I'm still the same person," she said indignantly.

"In a designer dress and heels, on the arm of a Warren. You're exactly the same. Nothing is different at all," I said sarcastically.

She winced. As if I'd hit home. She must know that it wasn't the same. That she was teetering on a precipice. Halfway into the Upper East Side might as well be a hundred percent. There was no in-between. I knew. I'd tried to get away. The only person I knew who had succeeded had to change his name and move across the country without anyone knowing. If Natalie wasn't careful, that was where she'd be too.

"Fine. It's different. I was wrong," she spat. "Is that what you want to hear? I don't see your crew. Lewis's family doesn't hate me. I've made friends here. And a designer likes me enough to want me to wear her clothes to appearances. Whatever the fuck that means."

"If I wanted to hear you say that you were wrong, I would want it to be about us," I told her earnestly.

I took her hand in mine, and she wrenched back.

"I'm with Lewis now," she whispered as if it pained her to speak it to me.

"Noticed that."

"Don't use that judgmental tone, as if you're so above it." Her blue eyes flared with fire. "I've heard all about the last year for you."

"Yeah. Want to hear more about it?" She turned as if she was going to leave, but I reached out to stop her. "Yes, I slept with other people. Because *you* said that we were never going to be together. You slammed the door shut. And the only way to get back at Katherine for fucking ruining my life was to sleep with her friends until I got bored and realized none of them could ever fill the void that was missing. None of them could make me forget you. So, I packed it up and left society and tried to get *out*. I'd half-succeeded when you walked back into New York City with your fancy book deal and my best friend on your arm."

Natalie gasped. "My...fancy book deal?"

"Fuck," I grumbled, releasing her. "I hadn't meant to play that card. I'd just gotten so pissed off that it tumbled out."

"How...do you know about my book deal?"

I sighed and ran a hand back through my hair. "Look, it was an accident. Katherine came to see me and flaunt that you were in New York after seeing the picture of you and Jane. I couldn't figure out why you'd be here and asked Rowe to look for me."

Her eyes rounded. "You did what?"

"I know. I'm sorry. I didn't realize that you were hiding your identity for a reason, but we looked through your page and found your editor, who kind of led us to Olivia."

She blanched. "Who...who else knows? Rowe? Oh god, does Katherine know?"

"No," I assured her. "No, she doesn't. I asked Rowe to bury it, so she wouldn't figure it out. I shouldn't have done it, but then I found out you were here at that book signing. I drove to the Village to see you."

"You were there," she whispered.

I nodded. "I just...you said you didn't want to be in this life with me. And you looked so happy. I wanted to respect your wishes. Look where that fucking got me."

She slammed her hand into my chest. "You showed up and didn't *say* anything?"

"Didn't you hear me?"

"I *knew* you were there. I thought I was crazy, running out of the bookstore, thinking you were there. And you were there all along."

She looked frazzled. As if I had confirmed something that had been haunting her.

"I should have talked to you. Then maybe you'd be with me instead of getting new material for your next Olivia book."

Her mouth dropped open. The spark in her heated to full fury. I liked it better than her contained neutrality.

"Is *that* what you think of me? That I'm here to get more material to write about?"

"What else should I think?" I demanded, pushing her, wanting her to fight me. "I'd rather think that you're using us than that you want him over me."

"I'm not using you for material," she snarled. "Not that it's any of *your* fucking business, but I'm not even *writing* an Olivia book anymore."

"One was enough for you?" I goaded. "Wanted to write the shit about the bet and then go on and live happily ever after on the Upper East Side?"

"I own *everything* that happened to me." She stepped into me then. Our bodies so close. Her anger so hot. Now we were standing in that in-between space where we were as likely to fuck as fight.

"Fine. Own it. Just like you do right now."

"If you didn't like what I wrote about you, then you shouldn't have been so shitty."

"I liked your portrayal of me," I said, catching her off guard.

"What?" she asked in shock. Her eyes going wide.

"Yeah. That Natalie was in love with me on every page. Every damn page."

I'd read it. Cover to cover. My character was...obliterated. She'd unleashed all her rage on the end of the book and practically destroyed me. I'd read it and only seen how much I'd hurt her. And how much she loved me. Two sides of the same coin.

"What?" she murmured softer. Her heart splintering in front of me.

"Yes, you loved me, even when you hated me. Especially when you hated me. But I'm still here, Natalie. I'm still fighting for you. Even if I can't reconcile that Natalie with the one who is yelling at me right now."

"It's because you broke that girl," she said. Her voice was

low and mournful. "You broke her, and you can't fix it. And you need to stop trying."

I slipped the necklace I'd been carrying around all night out from my pocket. Then I transferred it to her palm, closing her fingers tight around the crown charm.

A reminder of my love.

A reminder of that night we'd looked up at the stars.

A reminder that this was real to me, even then.

Then, I uttered one word, "Never."

NATALIE

26

I stared into Penn's eyes. Blue meeting blue. And I read the sincerity there. Heard it in his voice. The knowledge that he wouldn't give up on me. Not now. Not ever. Not when he still thought he had a chance.

Slowly, I peeled my fingers back and stared down at the small charm in my palm. A crown. Our crown. My throat tightened. I had the sensation like I couldn't breathe. It was too much.

Why had I come over here anyway? I hadn't thought it would be easy. But I'd thought it was necessary. Get this over with and out of the way. Then maybe we could all start to move on. But now, it felt impossible.

He knew I was Olivia. He'd read the book. And he hadn't concluded that I hated him at all. He'd concluded that...I loved him. Fuck...he was right. I'd loved him so much that I wasn't able to do anything else for weeks. Just write cathartically into the void until the book was finished. Then I'd been dead. For weeks...months. Amy hadn't even been able to get me out of the house. I'd sent him away, but he hadn't left my heart.

Now that I was finally moving on, it all came flooding back. I might think I was okay now, but fuck, I wasn't fine.

"Choose me, Natalie" he demanded.

"Penn," I said with a shake of my head.

"I know I hurt you, but what we had was real. And I have no idea how you can throw it away if you felt what I did."

I fought for words. For something to say to that. I hadn't thrown it away. He had. Fixing trust issues was infinitely more difficult than he was letting on. But as he drew closer, gripping my hand in his like a lifeline, it was hard to see anything but him. And easy to forget everything else.

"Well, well, well"—a voice laced with accusation rolled over us—"what do we have here?"

My stomach dropped to my toes as my gaze drifted up.

"Katherine," Penn said. He dropped my hand and effortlessly shifted himself in front of me.

Katherine Van Pelt. I should have known that I would eventually see her. I wasn't lucky enough to be on the Upper East Side and completely avoid her. And now, she was here... at the most inopportune time.

"Hello, darling," she crooned.

Her dark eyes feasted on the pair of us. She looked spectacular in a blood-red dress fit for a runway. Glossy, dark hair cascaded over one shoulder, and her lips were the deepest, darkest red. She was striking and treacherous and the devil incarnate. She might as well have her tail and horns from Halloween.

"Look what the cat dragged in," she said. Her eyes flicked over my shoulder.

And suddenly, Lewis was there too. He stepped up next to Penn so that they were both in between us. A solid masculine barrier that said more than words ever could. Who would have guessed the only way they could stand together would be because of Katherine?

No one said anything. Just waited for Katherine to make her move.

"Why are you all standing there like I'm about to attack someone?" Katherine fluttered her fingers at them. "We're all adults here. Aren't we, boys?"

Lewis and Penn exchanged a weighted glance and then moved back a fraction of a step. Apparently, they could work in unison when it was necessary.

"That's better," Katherine said. She settled her cool, hard gaze on me.

"Katherine, this isn't a good idea," Lewis said.

"On that at least, we are in agreement," Penn said. "What do you hope to gain from this?"

"Gain? Why would I have to gain anything? Can't someone else lose for once?" She tittered.

I huffed. "I don't have to deal with this. I'm leaving."

"Well, that solves my problem," Katherine said. She twirled a glass of champagne in her hand and cocked an eyebrow at me. "Though I don't understand why you're here in the first place."

"She's here with me," Lewis interjected.

"And even if I wasn't," I cut in, "I would have come because Jane invited me."

"Oh, be sure, I noticed you cuddling up with the owner. It seems there is a long line of people who you've tricked into feeling pity for you."

I shook my head in disgust. Only Katherine could turn around the horrible bet she had made and place the blame on me. "Okay. Sure, Katherine. Whatever you have to tell yourself. But I'm not going to just stand here and let you insult me."

"Good. *Leave*," Katherine said viciously. "Get out of my world and don't come back."

I was half-turned to go when the words hit me. *Her* world.

No. If I walked away like this right now, then she would feel like she could continue to do this forever. That I couldn't be in the same space as her. That I couldn't be near Lewis or at Jane's parties or even something as simple as walking through Central Park. There would be no end to this.

Katherine had been my friend for a brief period. Or I was a project, was more like it. But I'd seen enough of her to know how she would react to me scampering off to get away from her.

"It's not *your* world." I faced off with her. Ready to go another round in the ring. "And I can do whatever I want, including being here right now or anywhere else you happen to be later."

"Not if you know what's good for you."

I straightened and took a step forward. My eyes were narrowed in anger. "Is that a threat?"

Katherine just smirked. "If you want it to be."

"Katherine, stop it," Penn hissed. He moved forward, as if to put himself between me and Katherine in the likely event that I launched myself at her and ripped her shiny brown hair out.

I shoved him away and took another step toward Katherine. "I can go wherever I please. You don't own New York City."

Katherine laughed in my face. "Actually, I do."

"Just let it go," Lewis whispered, trying to pull me backward.

But Katherine wasn't finished. "That's what you don't get, Natalie. What you never understood. You think you can waltz in here and be one of us. That, with my clothes on your body and a Warren or a Kensington on your arm, you'll *be* someone. But you're nothing. And you'll always be nothing."

She was goading me. She wanted me to do something

stupid so that she could play the victim. But I saw through her. I shook Lewis off and straightened. My blue eyes weren't menacing but sad. Because Katherine was a product of this world. She was empty inside. And she didn't know anything else.

"I might be nothing. I might be no one. That's fine by me. But you...you can't even come to terms with who you really are. So trapped in the past that you can't see the future." I shook my head once. "You're a desperate, scared little girl who gets her kicks from hurting other people. You have no real friends, and you're so insecure that you're entering an arranged marriage for money. I'd rather have nothing than what you have."

Katherine drew in a sharp breath. And for a solid minute, it felt as if all the air had been sucked out of the room. The music seemed to go quiet. The lights focused on us. We all waited on a precipice for her response. But I was done. No matter what she said, it wouldn't matter to me. I was through with Katherine Van Pelt and her weak threats.

"Now, if you'll excuse me," I said.

I turned and walked away. Left Katherine waiting on a clever response. I might have had second thoughts about whether or not I fit into this world earlier today. But Katherine's torment proved that I did. She thought that, by belittling me, it was proof that I should run and cower. But it was the opposite. I was a threat. A threat that she had to try to squash under her Manolo Blahnik heel.

I wouldn't be squashed. I wouldn't go away just because she wanted me to. I would rise from the ashes over and over again and not look back.

I was halfway across the room before I felt an arm grasp my hand.

"Hey," Lewis said, stopping me from leaving.

"I'm fine. No, I'm not. I'm royally pissed off actually. And I want to go home."

He tucked a loose strand of my silver hair behind my ear. "I'll take you home. You were brilliant back there. No one ever stands up to Katherine like that."

"I don't want to have to stand up to her."

"You're right. You shouldn't have to. Next time we're out, we'll avoid her."

"Next time?" I felt defeated, just thinking of having that encounter over and over again.

"If you don't come back out and do the things you want to do even if she's there, then you let her win. Katherine and I have been friends a long, long time. If you give her an inch, she'll take a mile."

"I don't want to play these games," I told him.

He kissed my forehead and pulled me against him. "I know. It'll get easier."

I sighed against his chest. It mirrored what Charlotte and Etta had said. But...would it get easier? Or would it fester and rot, only getting worse and worse until we all broke?

I WANTED to be back at my place after the night I'd had. I had so much to think about and sift through. Conversations that didn't make sense, that my writer's brain needed to piece together. But Lewis took me back to his apartment, and I didn't fight it. I'd been staying at his place more often. I just wasn't looking forward to the conversation I knew we'd have to have now that we were here.

He undid his bow tie and left the first couple of buttons undone at the top before flipping on the record player and heading to the wet bar. "Wine?"

"Something stronger." I kicked off the Louboutins Jane had given me and was glad that I'd left a spare change of clothes at his place. This dress was incredible but not exactly for relaxing or to be comfortable in.

Lewis returned to my side with two glasses. He plunked a bottle of scotch onto the table and poured us each a knuckle's worth.

"I'm going to change. I need out of this dress."

He pulled me hard against him, kissing me deeply. "I can help."

"I'll just be a minute."

I was still too pissed to even think about being sexy. He must have read it in my eyes because he released me. I headed back to his bedroom and undid the buttons that held up the top of the dress and then the hidden side zipper. I hung the designer dress on a hanger in his closet before shimmying into leggings and a flowy T-shirt. I tipped my head upside down and gathered all my hair into a messy bun on the top of my head. I looked at myself in the vanity mirror, giving myself a second of breathing room before going back out there.

Lewis was waiting, pouring himself another glass of scotch, the overhead light illuminating his dark skin. I couldn't judge him in that moment. I didn't know where to even start. But I had more questions for him, and I wasn't one who held them in.

"I saw Addie tonight," I said.

Lewis turned toward me with a questioning look on his face. "I didn't see her."

"We ran into each other when I left backstage."

"From your expression, she must have said something characteristically Addie-like." He patted the seat next to him. "Come sit down. Addie has been a frequent menace in my life since high school. This wouldn't be the first time."

I walked across the room and took the seat across from him on the couch. I tucked my legs up underneath me.

"So, what'd she say?"

"She said that you're...obsessed with me. That you have these obsessions. That it's like being in the sun, but when you leave them, it's like being on the dark side of the moon. She said that I'm the latest."

He rolled his eyes. "How original of her."

"I wouldn't have thought anything of it, but Penn...might have said something like that a couple of weeks ago."

"All right. First, I do have these obsessions. I've told you about them. The things that I fall for and then dismiss when I start falling for something else. But that isn't *people*. Those are hobbies." He reached forward, gently stroking my cheek. "Second, that isn't you. Never you. I might have been like that with other things, but I could never be like that with you. You're it for me, Natalie."

My skin heated at the words. At the easy delivery and obvious affection. But something stuck out. Addie had been right before. She'd told me to look into the crew, and I had. There were skeletons and secrets, and I'd been burned.

"I just...they made it seem like more."

"Point-blank, Addie is jealous."

I wanted to give him the benefit of the doubt. What he was saying made sense. But I couldn't seem to forget everything else Addie had said. "Yeah, but...she said, if it wasn't true, then I should know about Hanna Stratton."

Lewis's back went rigid. "She said that?"

I nodded.

"Huh."

"Who is she?"

Lewis shook his head. "She was a girl that we were friends with in high school. She left middle of junior year. Her parents pulled her out of school for drug use, and she ended up overdosing before they could get her into rehab. It was pretty horrific at our high school."

"But...why would Addie think that I needed to know that?" I asked in confusion.

"Honestly, Natalie, that was what made us the crew. We'd always been close. But then leading up to and eventually losing Hanna changed everything. Addie didn't take it well, and she left the group. While the rest of us got a lot closer. It's still the defining point of our friendship." He sighed. "I understand why she would think someone who was close with me would need to know that, but I don't think it has to continue to define me. Addie wanted me to get out with her, but I didn't want to leave, and it splintered our relationship. Now, she still tries to sabotage my relationships with this kind of information. Using things that she knows about me to try to hurt me."

I still felt like I was missing a piece, but I didn't know what it was. I didn't know Addie well enough to judge if she was just jealous or trying to warn me of something. Or what even there *was* to warn me about.

"I think you're acquainted with someone else like that," he said, jarring me back to reality.

Penn.

"Yeah," I muttered.

That was definitely not a conversation I wanted to have. Not with his echoed words still ringing through me.

"Never."

"How did it go with him anyway?" he asked.

I shook off the thoughts. "Exactly as I'd expected."

It wasn't a lie. I hadn't thought it would be easy, and it hadn't been. I hadn't been sure he'd give up so easily...and he'd refused to. The only thing unexpected was how I'd reacted. The pulse that had shot through me at his words. Things I didn't want to consider and definitely couldn't tell Lewis anyway. Not with the crown sitting in the bottom of my purse as a constant reminder of us.

"Good. I don't want him to try to get between us anymore. Like I said, I'm no longer defined by my high school relationships." He gripped my hand. "I want you, Natalie. Just you."

"Yeah. Hopefully, we're both done with people throwing this stuff back in our faces," I muttered. "Dealing with Addie, Penn, and Katherine in one night makes me never want to leave this apartment again."

"I'm all for that. But you absolutely have to come to Katherine's wedding with me now."

"After what just happened?" I asked in disbelief.

"Especially after what happened. If you avoid her, then she wins."

Ugh, I hated that he was right. That this was exactly what Katherine wanted to happen with her threat. She wanted me to second-guess ever being in her vicinity again. She wanted the Upper East Side to herself. And though I didn't want the Upper East Side at all...I didn't want her to lay claim on it either. To push me out.

"I'll think about it," I finally said.

Though his answering smile made it seem as if I'd already committed.

"There is one place I'm definitely going with you though."

"Oh, yeah?"

"Making gingerbread houses with your sisters."

He groaned. "They told you?"

I grinned and nodded. "Yep. So, don't make any plans for Tuesday."

"They are seriously insufferable."

"You love them."

He nodded, but his eyes were on mine. Saying that maybe, just maybe, he was falling in love with me, too.

27

*T*he intercom in my apartment buzzed.

"Fuck," I grumbled under my breath. My finger hesitated over the Return key, and before I could think about it, I pressed Send. My stomach flipped, and then I dashed to the door. I pressed the button. "I'll be right down."

I snagged my jacket and gloves, slid into moccasins, and headed downstairs. I jogged down the three floors and found Lewis standing on the doorstep, waiting for me. He was sort of dressed down in khakis and a striped button-up. His smile lit up when he saw me coming through the door.

"I think I need a key so that I can just come up," he said with a laugh. "You have that advantage at my place."

"Oh yes, the advantage that you have your *own* elevator," I joked as I slipped a beanie onto my head.

"It is an advantage." He put his arm around my waist, bustled us through the cold afternoon air, and into the back of his car. "An advantage that you can come and go as you please."

"Well, we're never at my place anyway."

"We could be."

I placed a kiss on his lips. "But your place is so much better. My place is only great for writing."

"Which I'm going to get to read eventually?"

I laughed and shook my head. "Nope. *But* progress! I sent in the synopsis and chapters of IT'S A MATTER OF OPINION to Caroline. So, we're that much closer to you reading it."

"Or...you could just send me the proposal, and I could read it now," he said with a cocky grin.

"Or not."

It was probably the only thing that I hadn't given in to with him. The only thing that I wouldn't budge on. I knew it drove him crazy, but I didn't care. I didn't ask about his job stuff when he had to work late or take phone calls at random times or pick paperwork up at parties. It was all weird to me, but what the hell did I know about hedge funds? This was one of those quirks he'd just have to deal with.

He sighed. "I will wear you down."

"I wouldn't count on it."

"At least you turned it in even if you refuse to let me be involved in the process," he pushed.

"We'll see if she even likes it. It's not like Gillian is going to pick up the phone tomorrow and offer me more money. This could go nowhere."

Lewis looked me dead in the eyes. "That is never going to happen."

I shrugged. "Imposter syndrome?"

"You're an incredible writer. I fell in love with your writing from the first page I ever read. It's a gift."

"Thank you," I said, flushing at his praise.

It was something I wasn't used to. Even if BET ON IT was still sitting pretty on the *New York Times* and it was doing better than I ever could have imagined, it didn't make it any easier to see it as a success. But, when he spoke like that... sometimes, I remembered.

The car came to a stop in front of his parents' building, thankfully ending our conversation about my books. We took the elevator up to their mansion and found Charlotte, Etta, and Nina already in the kitchen. And, similar to the last time when my eyes had expanded at the mere sight of the kitchen, now, they did it for the sheer *quantity* of gingerbread on every single surface in sight.

"Oh, Natalie, dear," Nina said with a smile. Her apron was coated in flour, face smudged with it. "I'm so glad that the girls could convince you to join us." Her eyes turned to Lewis. "No thanks to my son."

Lewis held his hands up. "I would have invited her eventually."

"Liar," Etta said.

"We both know you wouldn't have," Charlotte agreed.

I laughed. "Well, I love gingerbread, and this sounds like a perfect Christmas tradition. So, tell me where to start."

Nina pointed out all the various pieces and the stages of cooling. The gingerbread had to be a hundred percent cool before they could use royal icing to put them together. The girls were in the process of whipping up the icing right now. Lewis and I stacked pieces together based on the number of houses we were making, which turned out to be a dozen. Plus, there were nearly a hundred cookies still coming out of the oven for some charity event.

It took us ages to get it all sorted, but by the time the gingerbread cooled, we'd all had a drink, and we were ready to get started.

"Mom, did we tell you what happened to Natalie at Trinity?" Etta asked. She was using a piping bag to expertly put her house together.

I looked like an idiot, using a knife to try to smear the icing onto my house. It would just be heavily frosted. Hopefully, it stood.

"Oh god, what happened to me?" I muttered as I thought about all the things that could come out of her mouth.

"Elizabeth asked to dress her for the Percy wedding," Charlotte said in delight.

"Really?" Nina asked with a smile. "Elizabeth is a lovely woman. You'd be lucky to have her expertise."

I glanced down at my flare-bottomed jeans and flowy purple shirt that looked like it had walked out of Free People, but I'd found it at my favorite thrift store back home. I'd gone hippie to the max. After wanting to impress them, I'd put the Upper East Side behind and gone full-out Natalie. Now, I didn't know if that was a mistake.

"I don't know if I'm going to take her up on it," I told them.

Charlotte gasped. "What?"

Etta looked skeptical.

"I already have a dress."

Lewis just raised his eyebrow, as if he knew what was coming.

"A dress," Charlotte said. "But not a Cunningham Couture masterpiece designed for you for the occasion. There is a difference."

"You cannot miss the opportunity," Etta said.

Nina sighed at her daughters. "I'm sure you will look lovely in whatever you choose. Don't let my spoiled daughters dissuade you from your choice."

"I think you'll look beautiful either way." Lewis's eyes said that he was just glad that I was going.

I hadn't agreed to go…exactly. I kept holding out on actually saying I was going, but I didn't say I wasn't either. Calling Elizabeth's assistant and asking for a dress sounded like a confirmation. Having the dress Jane had gotten me at Bergdorf on standby sounded like I could make a snap decision on the day of.

The conversation shifted to mundane topics as we finished up our houses. Mine looked like it was a bit of icing short of collapsing at any point. Charlotte's and Lewis's were passable. Much better than mine, but not professional grade. While Etta's and Nina's were beyond amazing. Etta's house was more of a mansion with candied windows and a vaulted ceiling. Nina's was definitely more castle-like. It even resembled Hogwarts.

"Well, wow," I muttered. "I feel inadequate."

"All gingerbread houses are equal," Nina declared.

"They all taste the same. That's for sure," Lewis said, plucking a gingerbread cookie from the tray and bringing it to his mouth.

Nina narrowed her eyes at him. "Lewis Edward, did you just eat one of my charity cookies?"

He crunched down on the gingerbread man's head. "Yes, ma'am."

She shook her head at him. "Boy never learns."

Charlotte and Etta had pulled out their phones and were scrolling now that their houses were complete.

"Hey, Mom, I'm going to go see Brodie," Charlotte said.

"Yeah, Ava is back already. So, we're going to hang out," Etta said.

"Try to stay out of trouble," she said. "And say good-bye to your father."

"Good-bye?" Edward asked, appearing in the living room and stalking toward the kitchen. "I'm right here. Who am I saying good-bye to?"

"We're leaving, Daddy," Etta said. She wrapped her arms around him and kissed his cheek.

Charlotte followed suit. "We'll be by later," she said.

He kissed both girls on the tops of their heads and then shooed them out of the house. "How did the annual gingerbread celebration fare?"

Nina raised an eyebrow. "I see you came down at the end."

"My architecture skills were never cultivated," he said with a grin. "But I'm an excellent taste-tester."

"You and your son both."

Edward turned his attention on us. "Well, do you two have plans? We could have a drink on the balcony."

"I have that phone call to take for work," Lewis said.

"Are you closing the Anselin-Maguire deal?" Edward asked.

Lewis nodded. "Yes, we're hoping to finalize negotiations tonight."

"Excellent. That one has been on the table too long." Edward clapped his hand on Lewis's back. "Why don't you take the call in my office? Then you and Natalie can still stay for a drink. Nina and I would love to get to know her better."

Lewis's eyes cut to mine, as if in a question. I just shrugged. I didn't have anything else to do, and it was a nice offer. Charming actually.

"If Natalie doesn't have plans, then I think we could do that," Lewis said.

"That's so nice, Edward," Nina said. "Go turn the heaters on, so we don't all freeze, and I'll make cocktails."

Edward dutifully left, and I followed Lewis back into the living room. He wrapped an arm around my shoulders and pressed a kiss to my lips. Once the heater was working, we took our cocktails out onto the balcony. I hadn't been out here on my first visit, and I couldn't believe that they had this kind of space in New York. The balcony had a giant heated pool that was unfortunately closed with a jetted Jacuzzi and a full garden. The view overlooking the park was outstanding, and I knew that they paid a premium to have it.

"You look like you're ready to dive in," Lewis noted as we took our seats across from his parents.

"If it was open, I might actually do it. I'm dying to have a pool again."

"Natalie was a college swimmer," Lewis explained.

"Well, you can use this one anytime you like once we open it again," Nina said. "Lord knows it doesn't get enough use anymore."

"Thank you. That's very generous," I said.

I leaned back into my seat and enjoyed my drink. Lewis's parents laughed and joked with each other as if they were still those teens who had fallen in love at Harvard. It was adorable.

"Okay. I have to clean up before the maid gets here in the morning. Otherwise, she is going to cuss at me in every language that she knows," Nina said.

"Nina," Edward complained.

She kissed him once. "I will be back as soon as I'm done. You know I hate a messy house."

He sighed. "Fine. But do be quick."

She laughed and took her empty glass with her.

"She's going to be at it all night," Lewis told me. "Mom is a bit of a neat freak and a perfectionist."

"Those are some of her best qualities," Edward said, raising his glass.

Lewis checked his watch and sighed. "Okay. I'm going to head inside. Shouldn't be long."

He squeezed my arm and then disappeared into the house, already dialing the number and conferencing in. Which left me all alone with his father, the indomitable Edward Warren.

"So, Natalie," Edward said. He swirled his drink. "I hear that you're a writer."

"Yes."

"And you have a book published."

"I…yes. But it's not under my name."

He nodded. "I heard that. Olivia something. We published it."

My mouth went dry. I hated when people knew about my pen name. But why should I be surprised the owner of the company knew? The owner whose son was dating one of their authors at least.

"That's right."

"Pardon me for saying, but I did a bit of research on you after you came over for dinner."

"Uh…research?"

His eyes were still stuck on the drink in his hand, and I had the sudden feeling like he was toying with me.

"It seems like you came from nothing. Lewis said you met a year ago. But you were dating Penn Kensington at the time. When that fell through, you jumped to my son." His eyes finally met mine. Hard as rocks and just as cold as stone. "So, what exactly are your intentions with Lewis?"

"My intentions?" I asked, still not grasping what he was getting at.

"Well, he already spent a cool million to get you," he said casually. "What are you expecting for him to keep you?"

My eyes doubled in size, and my jaw dropped open. "What are you talking about? Lewis didn't give me a million dollars, and I don't want anything from him."

"Your contract with Warren Publishing was for seven figures. You're not naive enough to not know who pushed for that figure at auction."

My stomach roiled. "He didn't," I whispered.

Edward arched his eyebrows. "Obviously, he did. He can be so trusting sometimes. But I've met other women like you before. And I don't want my son tangled up with someone like that."

My heart raced in my chest as I vaulted out of my seat. "Are you calling me a gold digger?"

"I didn't use that word."

"You didn't have to!"

"Then, we're at an understanding." Edward slid out of his seat, graceful as a cat, and towered over me. "This is a business negotiation. How much will it take for you to get out of my son's life?"

I balled my hands into fists. Fire coursing through me. Anger at the insinuation, at what I'd just learned, at the sheer horror of it all.

"You seriously misjudged me, Mr. Warren," I spat at him.

He laughed. "I really don't think that I did."

"Fuck you," I growled. "You can keep your goddamn money. I don't need any of it. I was fine without it before, and I'll be fine afterward, too."

NATALIE

28

I moved like a thunderstorm off of the balcony. Anger pulsed off of me like sheets of rain falling from the sky. I couldn't even *believe* what had just happened. At the sheer audacity of Edward Warren. He had clearly orchestrated this thing so that he would have a moment alone with me. A moment to accuse me of trying to take his son's money and then offering me more to get rid of me. I had never been more offended in my life.

And worse...was what Lewis had done. I wanted to scream. I'd worried that ending up with Warren was coincidental, but I'd told myself that they hadn't been the first publisher to try to buy my book. I'd thought it had been won on its merit. Not Lewis's interference. Turned out, I was wrong. I'd been stupid enough not to even ask him.

Lewis was pacing the living room when I stormed past him. "Natalie?"

I ignored him. I had no words for him. Not a single one.

"Natalie? Are you okay?" he called.

But I was reaching for my purse, slinging it over my

shoulder. Then I threw my jacket on and marched toward the door.

Lewis rushed after me, and I heard him say, "I'm going to have to call you back."

I got in the elevator and watched the doors close in his face. He jerked his hand in between the doors, stopping them from completely closing. Then he jumped into the elevator.

"Are you okay? Why are you leaving?" Lewis asked. His eyes were wide and wild with concern.

"Why don't you ask your father?" I snapped and pressed the button for the bottom floor.

"My dad? Why? Did he do something?"

I glared at him. I felt like I was going to explode at any second, and I didn't want it to be here in an elevator. I needed to get outside into the open air. Away from that cautious face. As if he hadn't done anything wrong at all.

I faced forward again and crossed my arms without an answer.

"Shit. Natalie, talk to me. I don't know what happened. So, I can't fix it."

"No, you can't fix it," I snarled.

The elevator opened at last, and I shouldered past him, through the lobby, and finally outside.

Lewis rushed after me. "Natalie, please talk to me. I don't want you to just run out of here because you're angry."

"Too late."

"Please," he pleaded.

I ignored him and headed across Fifth Avenue, toward the entrance to Central Park.

"My driver is around the corner. I can take you home. Let me take you home."

"I don't want to go anywhere with you."

Lewis huffed but followed me across the street. "You're

just going to rush out into the night without telling me what happened? This isn't fair, Natalie."

"Fair?" I screeched, heedless of who was around. "You want to talk about fair, Lewis? How about you convincing the publisher to pay me seven figures? How about how you were the one who told Warren to buy *my* book?"

He took a step back, as if I'd slapped him. "I was...helping."

"Don't try to spin this," I told him. "You can't convince me that this was somehow *good* for me. I wanted to do this book on my own. I wanted my debut to have success because of my writing. I didn't need or want a leg up. Someone else would have bought it for less money, and I would have been ecstatic. But no, you had to interfere. You had to make it about you. So, talk to me about fair."

I whipped around and started into the park. Central Park was drained of color. The winter trees empty of leaves and loomed ominously above us as I stomped through the grounds.

"I did that. I admit it. I found out that it was you, and I wanted to help. Why is helping you a bad thing?" he asked.

"If it was such a good thing, then why did you never tell me?" I snapped.

He shrugged. "It never came up."

"Yeah, because *you* never brought it up. Because you knew that I wouldn't be happy about it."

He reached out and grabbed the sleeve of my jacket, yanking me to a stop. "Everything that I do is for you, Natalie. Everything. Maybe this was the wrong way to go about it, but I didn't know that you'd be upset with me for doing this. I didn't know."

"You knew," I accused. "Or else I wouldn't have heard about it from your dad when he called me a gold digger. He said that you'd already handed over a cool mil and asked how much more it'd take for me to leave you alone."

Lewis sucked in a breath. "He didn't?"

I laughed maniacally. "Oh, he did."

"Fuck, Natalie, I am so sorry. I know that he's done this in the past, but I didn't think he'd stoop to that level with you."

"Well, excellent. Good to know I'm the one worth stooping for," I growled.

"My last girlfriend took the money. Alicia. The one my sisters hate. I thought that he wouldn't do that to you because I'm clearly in love with you."

I took a step back in horror at the words. At the way he'd used them to try to get out of this argument. When I was seething and not blissfully happy. When I wasn't ready to hear those words. Right now, it was the last thing I wanted to hear. The last thing I could even deal with.

"Well, he did. I told him to go fuck himself and that I didn't need or want your stupid money. Because I don't. But I did want the truth," I told him. My features turned to stone. "And you couldn't seem to give me that."

"Natalie…"

"Just don't. I've heard enough for one night. I wanted this on my own," I said. I hated that my throat was tight with unshed tears. "I was so proud of my accomplishments. But you tarnished it all. So, I'm going to walk home right now. And you are going to let me."

"Please," he said, stepping toward me. "Please, Natalie. Don't go like this. Don't leave angry."

"That is entirely your fault and not mine," I said before I tucked my hands into my pockets and headed toward my apartment.

I thought he'd follow, even when I'd told him not to. But he didn't.

And when I glanced back, he was gone.

I sank into a park bench, tucked my legs underneath me, covered my face, and cried. I hadn't cried in a long time. A very long time. I hated it and how weak and vulnerable it made me feel.

But this wasn't just about a boy. Or even his father's accusation.

This was about the death of my one perfect moment for my book. A matter of minutes had stripped it back to its bare bones. Merit hadn't won me that contract. It might have won me everything that came next, but now, there was a hole in it all. A black hole sucking the life out of everything that came after. I burrowed down deep, sinking into my own inadequacies. It showed me that this book was like all the others before it. Only I'd had a Warren push it through.

And I didn't like the rancid taste of it when I saw it from that angle.

My feet dropped back onto the sidewalk. I should go home. Deal with all of this in the morning. Being alone in Central Park wasn't my smartest move, but at the same time, I wasn't ready to return to my sad one-bedroom. I'd go home, crack open a container of icing, and cry.

I turned my feet in the opposite direction. Back toward the Upper East Side. It was closer than continuing to the Upper West. I turned left and headed north toward the MET. Streetlights and taxicabs illuminated my way. For a Tuesday night, the traffic was insane. The traffic was always insane.

It was easier to think about the traffic than to deal with the real issues. With Lewis and his dad and my career. Just thinking of those made me want to scream.

I pulled my phone out for another distraction and almost immediately regretted it. I had two missed calls from Lewis and a text message. I clicked off of them. I didn't want to read his apologies and excuses right now. Because I knew that was what it would be.

Maybe I'd be able to hear it when I calmed down. This moment? Not so much.

Finally, I stopped and looked around. I'd been walking for a while. I didn't exactly know where I was. Then I looked up at the light on in the apartment at the top of the building I was in front of.

I froze, realizing *exactly* where I was.

My fingers pulled up the number that I'd thought about blocking more times than I could count. But never had. I hovered over it. Indecision written through me. Then, I pressed Call.

I waited three rings before a male voice answered, "Natalie?"

"Are you home?"

"Yeah," he said tentatively. "Is everything all right?"

"Can I come up?"

"What? Right now?" he asked, flummoxed.

"Yeah. I'm…I'm downstairs."

"Uh…yeah. Come on up."

"Thanks," I muttered. "See you in a minute."

"Natalie, are you sure you're all right?"

"No, no, I'm not."

Then, I hung up the phone and walked into the building to take the elevator up to Penn's apartment.

NATALIE

29

I should have been nervous, but somehow, I wasn't. Not with Penn. He'd put me through the wringer, but being around him had always been so easy. Even back when we'd first met in Paris.

The elevator opened to his apartment, and I waited for the memories to assault me. But, before I could even process them, a small Italian greyhound bounded off the couch and vaulted straight at me.

Totle.

He knocked me so far off-balance that I actually tumbled backward. He just figured it was easier to smother me with kisses that way. His thin body pressed against me, and he wagged not just his tail, but also his entire body. His unbelievably long legs for a ten-pound dog tried to find purchase in my arms, and his wet nose brushed my cheek. He barked at me once, and then he was licking my face as if not a day had passed since I lived with him.

Tears welled in my eyes. Fuck, I was emotional. But I really hadn't realized how much I had missed him. Maybe all I needed was puppy therapy. I snuggled him tight against me.

"Hey, buddy. Oh, look how big you've gotten." He kissed me more. "Yes, I do love you. I know. I missed you *so* much. It's okay. I'm back."

Then a hand came and pressed into the elevator to keep the doors from closing on us. Penn leaned into the chamber, looking perfectly disheveled. His dark hair looked as if he'd been running his fingers through it. Stubble grew in along his jawline. And he was out of his typical suit and instead barefoot in black running pants and a T-shirt. Somehow, he still looked hot as sin.

"Did you come here to abduct my dog?" he drawled.

"I'm considering it. He clearly loves me more than you."

"He's kind of a whore actually. He gives his affection a bit too freely."

"Don't listen to him," I told Totle. "Your love is the best kind. Unconditional. You'd never break my heart, would you?"

Totle wagged his tail and licked me from chin to forehead.

I laughed and wiped my face. "That's what I thought."

"You going to come in or just hang out in the elevator?"

"I guess…I'll come in."

I stood from my seat, scooping up Totle in my arms as I entered Penn's apartment. It looked exactly as I remembered. A slight mess from all his work cluttering the space. His worn leather notebook open on the table. A glass of bourbon next to it. Indie music filtering through the speakers. His signature obscure artist. It looked and smelled and felt just like a year ago.

Penn moved to the table and cleared all of his papers into some semblance of a pile. He closed the notebook with a snap. All those philosophical musings buried away. "Sorry about the mess."

"It's not messy," I told him.

He shrugged and stepped around the couch toward the kitchen. I kissed Totle's head and then set him down on top of a blanket. He curled into a ball and plopped down.

"What's this song? I like it."

Glasses clinked together.

"'Not Over' by Cole Massey."

"It's good."

"Yeah. Mournful. The whole playlist is."

He stepped back around the island and had two glasses in his hands. "Here." He offered me the liquid. "You look like you could use that."

I took it in my hands but just stared down at it without taking a sip. I needed to say something. To explain why I was here or what had happened. But I didn't know where to begin or really what I'd expected to get out of coming up here.

"You think this is a good idea?" he asked after the silence had stretched as thin as paper.

"Me being here?" I asked. "Probably not."

He nodded thoughtfully. "Why exactly are you here?"

"Do you want me to go?" I tipped my head up to judge his words.

He didn't look like that was what he was saying, but he'd stepped back into the relative safety of the kitchen. "No."

The word hung between us. No explanation needed.

"But I thought you'd made yourself clear at the club. So, I'm surprised to find you in my apartment."

I dropped my head backward on the couch and stared up at the ceiling. "I really don't know what I'm doing here. I just started walking. I couldn't go home. Then I saw your light on. And...I don't know."

He waited for me to elaborate. I didn't.

"You feel safe with me," he said. A statement, not a question.

Despite all the shit he'd done to me. And how much I was mad at him for making that stupid bet. And the year of silence. And, and, and…the list went on. No matter what we'd gone through, I *did* feel like this was a safe place. That he wouldn't turn me away or push me. I didn't know what that said about how I felt about him that I could be so angry with him that I was seeing red but still feel safe with him. That I didn't trust him, and yet…I trusted him. It was irrational and hurt my head too much in the moment to put it all together.

"Yes," I whispered.

Penn stepped back into the living room and took a seat in an armchair across from me. He looked more relaxed. The crystal glass dangling in one hand over the side of the armrest. His foot nestled across his knee. His gaze locked on me. Weighing.

"What?" I asked.

"You look…like you."

I gave him a quizzical look. "And I normally don't?"

"No, I've only seen you in designer dresses and heels. This"—he gestured to my flares, billowy top, and moccasins —"is the Natalie that I knew."

"Yeah, well, I didn't have a big party to go to tonight. The seventies apparel came back out to play."

"It suits you."

I waved my hand at him. "You're in running clothes."

"Yes."

"And not a suit," I pointed out.

"I'm at home, working."

"On what?" I asked. Anything to delay the inevitable.

"Edits for my book. We're in the final stages of production. I can't help but tinker with the arguments while I have it."

"I know that feeling," I muttered. "When are you releasing?"

"Sometime next year. Academic books work on a different timeline than mainstream publishing."

I nodded and took a sip of the drink he'd handed to me. It was some kind of bourbon—biting and delicious. It was strange, being here. And how easy it was to talk to Penn. We had so many of the same interests. And we'd spent so many long hours together in the house in the Hamptons that *this* here felt totally normal.

"Why is it so easy to talk to you?" I mused.

"What kind of answer would you like to that?" he asked carefully.

I shrugged. "I know why it is. But you'd think there'd be some awkwardness."

"There never has been. Not even in Paris. We bared our souls that night, and not once was it awkward with you."

"Yeah, what a strange night."

"Not the word I'd use."

My eyes flicked to his, and I felt the heat across the room. "No...I suppose not."

The tension brimmed between us again. And I went back to petting Totle. This conversation was just a distraction from what had brought me here. But I couldn't work up the energy to tell him what had happened.

"You said at the club that you weren't writing an Olivia book," he said, changing the subject. "What does that mean?"

"Oh, I'm working on my literary novel again. It's called IT'S A MATTER OF OPINION. Kind of inspired by my parents' deep love despite the fact that they're opposites. The idea is that love isn't easy when you come from two different worlds, and the reader sees it all unfold from the point of view of everyone close to the situation. But never the truth."

"Hmm," he said softly. "Love wins out despite outside influences and their differences."

"Yeah," I muttered. "Sounds a bit unrealistic, doesn't it?"

He arched an eyebrow, waiting for me to elaborate.

I sighed and flopped down next to Totle. "Lewis's dad called me a gold digger and offered to pay me off to get out of his life."

Penn sighed. "He's done that before."

"So I've been told. Doesn't make it any less humiliating."

"I imagine not," he said. "Especially with your experience with my mother."

"Yeah. That didn't help. But...it was Lewis. He...fuck." I didn't know why I couldn't say it. It felt as if I was proving Penn right by admitting what Lewis had done.

"You can talk to me, Natalie. I'm sure anything Lewis has done, I've heard worse."

I sat back up, took a deep breath, and then let it out. "When my book went to auction, it sold for seven figures to Warren. They weren't the first publisher to try to buy it, so I thought that all of this had happened on my own merit."

"But?" he urged.

"But Lewis interfered and drove the price up to get me more money."

"Ah. And now, you feel like you didn't earn any of that. Like you got preferential treatment, but not because of your work."

"Exactly!" I snapped. "It feels like the success of the book was because of Warren flexing its muscles and not anything to do with the book."

"Well, for one thing, the book is incredibly well written, so don't discount your talent."

"Fine, talent, whatever. But, fuck, I feel so...duped. Like, I thought that Lewis might have been involved, but I didn't ask him. I should have asked him, and now, I feel stupid. Like, his dad now thinks I'm a gold digger because of this, and I didn't even know."

Penn waited until I'd finished my rant. Finishing his bourbon, he settled back into the armchair. "What are you going to do about it?"

"What do you mean?"

"Besides come here and rant to me about something I already guessed. What are you going to do about him withholding information from you? I hate to be the bearer of bad news, but it's never just *one* thing." Penn sighed. "The stupid fucking bet should have taught you that."

My anger sliced through me as hot as a poker. The bet had that reaction. But also, he wasn't wrong. It hadn't just been Emily or Katherine or his mom...there had been something else, and he hadn't told me what it was. He'd held it back, even as I'd asked him. Everyone had. Lewis had lied. Penn had lied. Katherine had told me about it, but I'd thought she was lying.

"You think there's something else he's hiding," I said.

"You're the one who came back to the Upper East Side, Natalie."

The words stung. Yes, I had. I'd said I hadn't wanted this life, and then I had somehow gotten embroiled in it again. So, the question was...did Lewis have another secret? And could I trust him after this?

"Why are you being so nice to me?" I asked, suddenly cautious. "You don't want me with Lewis."

"No, I don't," he confirmed. "But I do want you happy. Seeing you in my apartment with red-rimmed eyes, here as a desperate measure, is not the way I wanted you to come to me, Nat. So, right now, this isn't about me and you. This is just about you. And I've played this game way longer than you have. I'll help you play it if I have to."

"I don't want to play games," I whispered.

"I know." He shrugged helplessly. "Neither do I. But, if you don't, you won't survive the Upper East Side."

His final word was punctuated with his phone buzzing noisily on the table, drawing both of our attention. He stepped forward and flipped it over to see who was calling so late at night. His eyebrows rose, and he chuckled.

"Didn't see that coming," he muttered under his breath.

"What?"

My eyes moved to the screen, and there, in bold white letters, read *Lewis*.

"This should be good," Penn said and then put the call on speaker.

"*L*ewis," he said, "it's been a while, man. What's up?"

"Is she there?"

Penn glanced up at me. "Is who where?"

Lewis huffed out angrily. "Natalie. We got into a... disagreement, and she ran out. She's not at her apartment. She's not with Jane."

I could tell that he was frustrated and likely pissed off. I couldn't imagine what he must have gone through to get to the point where he would call Penn to try to find me. He must have gone to my apartment, and when he'd found that I wasn't there, he'd panicked and called people who knew me. Luckily, or perhaps unluckily, that list was pretty small in the city. Jane and Penn.

"Really? A disagreement? About what?"

"Penn, is she with you?" Lewis growled low.

His eyes cut to mine, and a silent conversation passed between us. He wanted to know if he should tell him that I was here. Or if he should leave him to fret longer.

I nodded. I couldn't hide here forever anyway.

"She is," Penn finally said.

A string of curses followed softly. As if he'd jerked the phone away from his face so that he could scream them into the night. I winced.

"She's here, and she's fine. She just needed to calm down. I think you should give her some space."

"I don't give a damn what you think, Penn," Lewis snapped. "If you lay a hand on her, I will destroy you."

And then he promptly hung up. The silence was a living thing between us. My hand half-reached toward the phone as if to comfort Lewis. To reassure him that nothing had happened here. But he was gone. Leaving me more on edge than ever.

"Well," Penn said, dropping the phone back on the table, "that went about as well as expected."

"He's probably on his way here."

"Probably."

"I guess that's my cue." I set the drink down, kissed Totle's head, and stood.

"You don't have to go just because he's coming here, Natalie."

He stepped toward me, bridging the distance we'd had between us all night. I looked up into those blue eyes, lost to them for a moment. He stroked back the silver hair from my face.

"You're safe here."

"I know," I whispered. "But I highly doubt he's going to leave this alone."

"I can refuse him access to the elevator. You don't have to face him yet. Not until you're ready. On your terms. Not his."

"I still should go."

But he didn't move. And I didn't move. We just stood together. Trapped perpetually in this inescapable vortex. A whirlwind of passion and pain. Of all the unspoken reasons that I'd shown up at his place. And all the unspoken reasons he'd allowed it.

His hand still held that stray hair. His fingers slipped up into the tresses. An intimacy that should have never been allowed. The mingled heat that couldn't be cooled. The desire that raged like a tempest, no matter how we tried to push it aside.

"I want to kiss you," he told me. His voice strained. His breath heavy and tortured.

"I know," I breathed.

"I've pushed you, and it didn't work, Nat." His lips dipped lower, lower, lower. Hovering, inching, waiting. "It's hard to have you here now. All I want is to pick you up and carry you into my bedroom."

"We can't."

His nose touched mine. Brushed against it once, gentle and somehow intoxicating. The tension taut. I arched toward him. Not quite touching. Not giving in. But not quite turning away either.

"I have to go," I reminded him.

"I'm fighting for you." He threaded his other hand up into my hair. "I didn't say I'd fight fair."

His lips skated against mine as he held my face in place. His tongue darted out and licked across my bottom lip. I shivered all over at the tease of it all.

"Penn," I murmured. My brain going fuzzy. "He's going to kill you."

He smirked. "Then I might as well make it worth it, huh?"

I pressed my hand to his chest and tilted my forehead against his before he could make good on his promise. "Please don't put me in this position."

"You know that I want you."

"I do."

"You knew that coming here."

"I did," I whispered weakly.

"And you want this."

"If I kiss you, then I have to tell him." I pulled back enough to look in his eyes. "And then our argument is about you. Not what happened. I don't want that. I need to talk to him and find out the truth. This...this just complicates things."

He sighed as if he hated to see my reason. My rather valid reason.

"I will rain check that kiss," he said, dropping his hands to my sides and pulling me in for a hug instead.

I slipped my hands around his neck and breathed him in. "Thank you for being there for me when I needed you. I'm sorry it's...about this."

"Yeah." He abruptly broke away and turned back to the kitchen.

"Penn..."

"Good luck," he ground out and then headed for the liquor cabinet.

I swallowed hard. This wasn't what I'd wanted. Fuck. All I did was fuck it all up. And now, I had to go face Lewis when I wasn't ready.

I ruffled Totle's head and then left Penn's apartment without another word. He was probably going to drink himself into a stupor. I wouldn't mind doing the same right about now.

Especially when I stepped off the elevator and found Lewis walking into the building.

"Natalie," he said in relief. "I've been all over the city, looking for you."

"I know."

"Why didn't you answer your phone?"

"I needed time to think."

"With him?" he all but snarled.

I gave him a flat, level look. "Nothing happened with Penn. He just listened to me and let me draw my own conclusions."

"Oh, I bet he did."

"Let's not do this right now."

"I just need to know if, every time we have an argument, you're going to go run to him," Lewis said.

"Are we planning to have a lot more arguments?" I asked, my anger trying to slip its leash once more.

"You know what I mean."

"I don't think that I do," I said sharply. "I have been nothing but honest with you, Lewis. *Nothing* but honest. I even told you when he kissed me at Harmony's party. I told you when I had to tell him to leave us alone. You watched me do so. I don't see *any* reason that you wouldn't trust me when I said that nothing happened right now. Unless perhaps your guilty conscience is speaking."

"I don't have a guilty conscience," he said.

"Then what is this?"

"It's more like, I yelled at my own father for what he did to you. Then, when I went looking for you to apologize, you were nowhere. When I finally worked up the nerve to call Penn—fuck, can you imagine how that felt?—you were actually there. So, I'm on edge. Sue me."

I narrowed my eyes at the tone of his voice. "It was wrong of me to go to Penn's. Especially when you didn't know where I was. But I cannot believe that you are actually using this outrageous tone with me right now when *you're* the one who has been keeping secrets and *lying* to me again. Again." I shook my head as my anger spilled into my words. "After you lied to me about the bet, I wouldn't think you'd be stupid enough to do that again."

"It wasn't a lie."

"A lie of omission is *still* a lie!" I yelled.

"Okay. Okay." He held his hands up. "Can I just take you home, and we can talk about this there?"

"No. We can talk about it right now."

"You're still mad."

"You fucking think so?"

"I'm sorry, okay? I'll say it as many times as you need to hear it. I'm sorry that I didn't tell you about the money. Or the deal with the publishing company. I'm sorry that I couldn't save you from what my father did. I should have seen what was coming when he was acting so nice. It was a ploy, and I fell into it. And I hate it. I'd take it all back if I could."

"Fine. I just need to know what else there is."

"What do you mean?" he asked, suddenly on guard.

"There's something else you aren't telling me, and I want it out in the open."

"Why would you think there's something else?"

I narrowed my eyes. "Because this is the Upper East Side. I've been fucked over by this world before. I saw warning signs and ignored them. And I won't do that this time."

"Are you comparing me to Penn?" he demanded.

"I'm speaking from experience. Not drawing a comparison," I told him. "You pushed the company to give me more money. If you'd do that and not tell me, what else would you keep from me?"

His eyes moved back and forth over my face, as if he were debating what the hell to say next. And I could see it then. See it all over his pretty face that there was more. He was deciding whether or not he would lie to me.

"Tell me right now," I said, low and brutal, "or I walk."

"I was going to see you on your signing tour. They're standard for an author in your position. But I hadn't factored in the fact that you'd refuse a tour," he said carefully. "So, when I heard from a contact at the company that they were thinking of bringing you into the city anyway, I told them to pull the trigger."

My mouth went dry. "You…orchestrated my appearance in New York."

"It was already in the works. I just…told them to make it happen."

"Did Gillian know?" I asked, remembering that moment of surprise on her face when he'd shown up.

"No. She didn't know about any of my involvement. Her work with you was all her."

"And you did it…so that you could see me."

"I'll admit to wanting to see you again. That was why I was so nervous when I saw you at the publishing house that day. But…I wanted you to have everything and more. I still do."

I didn't know what to think about that. On one hand, he'd done it all to see me. Which was charming, but also…it felt like I was a marionette on strings. He was the puppeteer, scheming to put things into place for me to be here with him.

On the other hand, his affection was genuine. And he'd been honest. He hadn't lied and tried to hide behind what he'd done this time.

"And that's…that's it? There's nothing else?"

He shook his head. "Just that. And I'll have nothing to do with the new book. I swear."

I nodded. My mind was abuzz with all of this new information. I didn't know how I felt about it. Or what I should do with it. Whether I should be flattered or angry. All I knew for sure was that his heart was in the right place. He was a hundred percent earnest, standing there on the footsteps of Penn's apartment. So, maybe he'd done the wrong thing for the right reasons.

"I think I need to go home," I finally said.

"Let me take you." He gestured to the door. "You shouldn't walk through the park this late, alone."

I sighed and took that first step. "Okay."

I followed him out to his car and let him drive me back to my apartment. We were silent on the way there. I didn't know what he was thinking. And I couldn't process my night. I wanted to hold on to my fury for his lies. But he *had* come clean. I'd asked him to, and he'd admitted it.

The whole thing left me feeling triggered. After what had happened with the bet last year, I kept waiting for the other shoe to drop. And now, it had.

"I know that you're still mad," Lewis said once the car finally rolled to a stop, "but I swear, I did it all for you. I didn't intend to hurt you. But, of course, my intentions don't really matter when it comes down to it, and I see how this hurt you." He reached for my hand, linking our fingers together. "Please, just give me the chance to prove to you that it won't happen again."

I stared into that face. That beautiful face. One that had lied to me. One that was trying to right the wrongs. One that had hurt me. One that had thought he was helping me. I saw the two sides. The dual nature of this hurt.

It would be easy to only see the negative. To think that he'd done this selfishly. To think he was a sickly and purely Upper East Side schemer. But that was my fear talking. That was the fear that I was being played all over again. That I was about to get screwed over spectacularly, and it was better to run from this than to stick it out. Than to give him another chance.

And I was so tired of living with that fear. What he'd done wasn't like the bet. It hadn't been to hurt me. It had been to help me. If in a roundabout way.

Finally, slowly, I nodded. "Okay."

He brought my fingers to his lips and kissed each of them. "Thank you. You won't regret it."

"Good," I whispered. I slipped my hand out from his. "I'm going to go up now."

"Care for some company?" he offered.

"I think...tonight, I should just be alone."

"I could walk you up."

"I'll be fine," I told him. When he looked unconvinced, I said, "We'll be fine, too." Then I stepped out of his car and walked into my building, more than ready to leave the entire night behind.

*L*ewis was a fucking idiot. Had he not learned a goddamn thing from my mistakes? Was he desperate to repeat them, just to prove that he could fuck up as monumentally as I had? Another thing he wanted to take the trophy for?

I couldn't get the image of Natalie's tear-splotched face from my mind. The broken way she'd caved in on herself at the realization that she'd been lied to again. The trap she'd fallen in so easily.

And I hadn't even been able to be blunt about it. Either she wouldn't have heard me or it would have hurt her more. I'd given her enough to figure it out on her own.

Lewis was as goddamn Upper East Side as the rest of us. He might want to play the white knight, but that wasn't his true identity. He was smooth and could lie his way around a viper. I'd know. I'd seen him do it more times than I could count.

And I didn't want to continue to watch him do it with Natalie.

I was going to do what I probably should have done that

first day I'd seen the picture of them at Rockefeller. I was going to fucking find out what his angle was. And Lewis was going to tell me himself.

"Hello, Lewis Warren's office. Hold, please," the secretary said into the phone. "Yes, Lewis Warren's office. I understand. Thank you. Hold, please." She clicked the button again and repeated her mantra.

I waited for her to fully notice me.

She glanced up in surprise. "Hello. How can I help you?"

"I'm here for Lewis."

She scanned her computer. "And your name is?"

"I don't have an appointment."

"Oh, sorry, you need to schedule all appointments in advance."

"We're old friends. Penn Kensington," I said, easily dropping my name.

Her eyes widened. Yep, she knew who I was. Sometimes, I hated this world.

"Oh, Mr. Kensington. Let me see if he's free."

"Don't worry about it"—I checked her nameplate—"Brandi. I'm here to surprise him." I winked at her.

She laughed, her face flushing at my attention. She leaned on her elbow and gazed up at me. "Okay, go on. Be quick. He has a conference call soon."

"Will do. Thanks so much, Brandi. I'll let you get back to work."

"Of course." She waved at me and then went back to her headset.

I bypassed my first obstacle with a smile and mindless flirting and reached for Lewis's office door. His face was priceless when I stepped inside. Shock, then anger, and then empty nothingness. That blank mask we'd all developed young.

"Penn," Lewis said. "This is unexpected."

"I'd say it's long overdue," I said.

I strode confidently across his massive office and sank casually into the chair in front of his desk. I kicked my feet up, planting them on the top of his desk. He narrowed his eyes in annoyance. It was delicious.

"If you're here about Natalie, I really don't have anything to say to you."

"We've known each other a long time."

Lewis shrugged. "So?"

"So, I think we can cut the bullshit," I said evenly, even pleasantly.

"There's no bullshit between us."

Lewis shot me a smug look as he leaned back in his chair. Looked about as happy to be in this position as his piece-of-shit father. Mine had been an alcoholic and a whoring idiot. But Lewis's dad had just beaten him down with expectations. Nothing was good enough. No one was good enough for him.

"That, I do disagree with."

"Disagree all you like outside of my office. I'm busy. Don't you have to teach or something?"

"I don't teach on Wednesdays. And, anyway, this felt more pertinent."

"You know, we *have* known each other a long time. So, I already know what you're going to say. And you can leave your self-righteous bullshit at the door. Your morality and happiness and philosophy shit. I don't need or want to hear it."

"Then, we're on the same page. Since we both know that you have no qualms with ambiguous morals," I said evenly.

Lewis narrowed his eyes in distaste.

"After all, you're only after Natalie because I had her first."

He laughed. "So, that's what you think?"

"You've been doing this shit since we were kids. I think I can recognize it when I see it. You always want what I have. And now, you think you've won."

"I have," he drawled with satisfaction.

"Except that she came to me last night," I reminded him. I set my feet down and leaned forward toward his desk. "What happens next time you show your hand?"

"There is no hand," Lewis ground out.

"Please," I said with a laugh, "you're talking to me. It's always a game with you."

"Not with Natalie."

"Sure thing." My tone dripped sarcasm. "And you didn't orchestrate her book to end up with Warren. And you didn't post her picture on Crew so that I would see it, and you didn't bring her places to show her off. You didn't purposely kiss her in front of me at Harmony's. Same old games, Lewis. I know how you play them."

Lewis shook his head at me. Then he pulled open a drawer in his desk and removed a box from the top. He set it onto the desk between us. I stared at it. Shock rippled through me. My eyes were wide in alarm. My cool gone.

"Is that what I think it is?" I asked.

"I told you that it wasn't a game."

He left the box sitting between us. I couldn't bring myself to open it. A diamond that would fucking ruin everything.

There was ringing in my ears. My hands balled into fists. This could not be happening. It didn't even make any fucking sense.

"Are you crazy?" I blurted.

He arched an eyebrow. "Not in the slightest."

"She is never going to say yes to that." I threw my hand at the offending box. "It's been a *month*."

"I'm prepared to wait to ask her when she's ready, Penn. I already am."

"You've lost it."

I couldn't even fathom how this had all taken such a turn. Lewis could not propose to Natalie. Not in any world. This was a game. This was a piece I hadn't seen coming. A rogue piece that was smashing across the board that I'd thought I was navigating with ease.

"Maybe you'll stop bothering us now. You know it's serious. You know I intend to be with her forever. Walk away," Lewis said, dark and menacing.

There was no getting through to him. No way for him to see how utterly crazy it was to purchase a ring for someone after only a month of dating. After they'd just had a blowup argument the night before.

This was still a game. And he thought that ring was a checkmate. But I'd find out the truth. I needed him to think that he'd won. Think that I was bowing out.

"Well, fuck," I said, running a hand back through my hair. I had to be fucking convincing. He knew me as well as I knew him. "I thought you were just fucking with her. I didn't realize you were actually serious."

"I am." He picked up the box and set it back into his desk. "Took you long enough to notice."

"Jesus." I shook my head. "I just want what's best for Natalie."

"That is what I want as well."

"So, if that's you, then I'll...do what's best for her."

I swallowed my pride and held my hand out. Lewis looked at it skeptically and then stood and shook.

"Thanks, man," Lewis said. He still looked suspicious but also...smug as shit. Like he actually thought he was winning.

I had every intention of doing what was best for Natalie. I just suspected that Lewis and I differed on what that meant.

PART V
SURPRISE, SURPRISE

NATALIE

32

*S*now was falling lazily onto the Manhattan streets. A thick blanket of white was covering the roof of St. Patrick's Cathedral. The tourists wore heavy coats, hats, and gloves. They peered up at the beautiful neo-Gothic–style landmark with awe, stopped to take pictures, and gawked at the stream of wedding attendees as they stepped out of limos and traipsed up the stairs like it was a red carpet.

I shivered under my coat that wasn't quite appropriate for a New York winter but had been fine back home in Charleston. Lewis stepped out of his Mercedes behind me. He radiantly smiled down at me. I knew he was pleased that I'd decided to come with him. It had seemed doubtful up until the point where my feet had carried me out of my apartment building and into his car.

Now, I was here, and I was frozen in place.

Entering that building would make a statement as much as leaving did. If I left, then Katherine would win this round. And she'd use her advantage for everything in the future. Leaving didn't mean freedom from the Upper East Side. It meant surrender.

And I refused to stand down in this battle.

Which meant I needed to walk inside. To proclaim that I wouldn't be bullied by Katherine. But it might mean this battle would turn into a war.

"Are you ready?" Lewis asked.

I couldn't tear my eyes away from the church. This wasn't just about Katherine either. This was about my relationship with Lewis. I'd told him we'd be fine, and he'd been nothing short of incredible since then. Under normal circumstances, being a plus-one at a wedding wasn't a declaration of intentions, but it was today. And I still hadn't forgiven him for what he'd done to get me here. Good intentions or not.

"Natalie?" he asked, cautious and patient.

I took a calming breath and then nodded. "I'm ready."

We stepped forward into the throng of guests and up the stairs, and then we entered the enormous church, already half-filled with wedding attendees. It was a stunning building with pews for hundreds of people. High-vaulted ceilings were held up by enormous columns. The walls were interspersed with elaborate stained glass art and sculptures to the saints. At the front was a raised dais for the priest to perform the ceremony.

I shed my jacket as we walked down the aisle toward our seats.

Lewis's eyes slipped to me. "Is that the dress Jane got you?"

"Yeah."

"I thought you were going to have Elizabeth give you a dress."

I shook my head. "I decided to just wear this one. Felt more...me."

Sort of. Not bohemian enough, but at least I'd picked the thing out.

"You look beautiful." He kissed the top of my head.

Etta and Charlotte saw us first.

"Natalie, you look great," Etta crooned.

"That's not an Elizabeth dress," Charlotte noted.

I laughed softly at their attention. "Nope, just one from Bergdorf."

"But it was such a good opportunity," Etta said.

"Maybe another time," I told them.

"Give her some space, girls," Nina said, ushering them away from me.

My eyes slipped up to Lewis's mother's, and I froze at the sympathy there. She knew. She knew about what Edward had done. She knew about my humiliation. I was instantly uncomfortable. I didn't want to be pitied.

"Natalie, such a pleasure to see you." She pulled me into a hug as Lewis slid into the booth next to his sisters. Her voice lowered significantly. "I heard about what happened with my husband. I am sorry about that. It will never, ever happen again. It should have never happened in the first place, and I'm horribly embarrassed that he said those things to you. To be clear, I do not think that at all. You're a beautiful, dedicated, charming young woman, and I'm thrilled that you're dating my son."

"Thank you," I whispered. My voice was choked. I didn't realize until she'd said it how much that actually meant to me.

I darted away from her before she could say anything else and make me relive that horrible moment. Especially since Edward was standing at the other end of the pew, speaking with a man in the row behind us, who I didn't know. I hoped he didn't try to say anything to me.

Lewis slid his arm around me. "I'm glad that you're here with me."

"The survey is still out," I said softly.

He frowned. "Regretting coming?"

"No, but this isn't easy for me either."

He pressed a kiss to my knuckles. "It'll get easier."

"People keep saying that, and it hasn't proven true yet."

"It will," he assured me.

I shrugged indifferently and turned to survey the scant pews in front of us. We were right at the front of the church in reserved seating for friends of the bride, which was really debatable.

Addie and Rowe were seated right before us along with two sets of parents and a slew of other young siblings I didn't recognize. I had to gather that their parents were divorced and remarried with step- or half-children. Addie and Rowe were the oldest.

Penn was seated in the row in front of them with his mother, Mayor Leslie Kensington. Just seeing her set my teeth on edge. She'd been the one to throw me out of my job at Katherine's request, and I still hated the way she had treated Penn in all of it. Next to them was Jane, who caught my eye and fluttered her fingers at me and then gestured for me to come to her pew.

My eyes darted to Penn's mother and then back to Jane. This was going to be fun.

"I'm going to go talk to Jane," I told Lewis.

He frowned when he saw who Jane was seated next to. His jaw clenched, but he just said, "All right."

I stepped out of my pew and slid into the seat next to Jane. "Natalie, oh wow, look at that dress! I am so glad that you wore it here."

"Well, thank you for getting it for me. It's good to see you."

"Girl, I have been so busy. I thought the soft opening would be the hard part. It's the New Year's opening that's going to be *insane*. It's a masquerade, and the lineup is already out of this world."

"I'm sure it will be sensational," I assured her.

"Worth the work."

I glanced down the rest of the pew, looking for the missing Kensington. "Where's Court?"

"Oh, he's the best man," Jane said with a grin. "Those boys have been drinking all morning. The texts I've gotten." She laughed. "You wouldn't even want to know."

"Jane, who is your friend?" Leslie asked, turning toward us.

Our eyes locked together. The last time we'd seen each other, she had fired me. It gave me a small bit of pleasure when her eyes widened with recognition.

"Oh, Leslie, this is Natalie. She's a *New York Times* best-selling novelist. And she's hard at work on the next one."

I loved how smoothly Jane had said that all. She had to know that Leslie and I were connected prior to this, but she had given me a blank slate.

"And, of course, Leslie is the mayor of New York City."

"Natalie," Leslie said in surprise. She offered me her hand. "It's good to see that you're doing well for yourself."

No thanks to you, was what I wanted to spit at her.

But, instead, I played nice. I took her hand, and we shook amicably. I saw Penn's eyes dart to that handshake and then away. Part of me knew that most of Leslie's ire that day had been focused on her son, and I was the unfortunate person who had gotten in the middle of it. It didn't make it hurt any less.

"Thank you. It wasn't an easy journey," I said pointedly.

"I bet not." Then, she nodded her head at me. "All the sweeter then."

She smiled once in acknowledgment of her part in what had happened. I figured it was as close as I'd ever get to an apology. Better than I'd thought it would have gone.

"Next week," Jane said, "I am bringing you into the club to get your opinion on the New Year's party."

"Sounds good. Pencil me in."

I slipped out of the pew, prepared to return to my seat with Lewis when I glanced up and saw Penn. He was speaking to the couple who had been sitting in the space reserved for Katherine's family.

Penn's voice cut through my exit. "Natalie, have you met Katherine's brother?"

I shifted back toward him, unsure of how to proceed. I knew that Lewis must be watching us. That he wasn't comfortable with me being around Penn. But it would look rude to just completely ignore him.

"I didn't know Katherine had a brother."

"It's a common misconception." The brother, tall and handsome with an easy smile, held his hand out, which I shook. "I'm David, and this is my wife, Sutton Wright."

His petite wife beamed back at me. She had dark hair that fanned out to blonde at the ends. She was stunning in an unassuming way, and when she spoke, I heard a trace of a Southern accent. "Pleasure to meet you."

"Your accent is adorable," I said before I could stop myself.

Sutton covered her mouth and looked up at David with a glare when he started laughing. "Is it that noticeable?"

"It reminds me a bit of being back in Charleston."

"Oh! You're one of us!" Sutton said. "I'm from Lubbock, Texas. Middle-of-nowhere West Texas, but these Northerners act like it's another planet."

I laughed and decided instantly that I liked this Wright girl. "Oh, trust me, I know."

"How's Jensen?" Penn asked. "I haven't seen him in the city much."

"Trying to knock up his girl," Sutton said with a laugh.

"So...busy," Penn offered.

"Who is Jensen?" I asked, wondering how they all knew each other.

"My oldest brother," Sutton explained.

"We met when he was here, getting a degree in architecture," Penn explained. "The Wrights run a construction empire."

I raised my eyebrows at Sutton in surprise. She didn't seem like the kind of person who fit in around here, running an empire.

But she held her hands up. "I just run a bakery. I leave the business to my siblings and David."

"Wow. Well, it was great meeting you," I told Sutton honestly.

I couldn't even believe that David was related to Katherine. He looked like he'd gotten out of the Upper East Side, too. Completely out. How had he done it?

"You, too! Us Southern girls have to stick together."

Penn stepped toward me before I could walk away. "Can we talk later?"

I bit my lip. "I don't think that's a good idea."

"It wasn't a good idea to come talk to me the other night, and you did it anyway. How is this any different?"

"Live and learn," I muttered and then made the mistake of looking up into his baby blues.

"Natalie, please, five minutes at the reception."

"What do you have to say to me then that you can't say to me now?"

"I don't want an audience," he said and then nodded toward Lewis, who was staring unflinchingly at us close together.

I took a step back from him. "No," I whispered. "I can't."

"Nat, this is important." And he sounded like it really was. Though I had no clue what he could possibly need to tell me.

"I'm sorry," I said with a shake of my head. Then, I turned and walked back to where Lewis was seated.

"Have a good chat?" he asked in a clipped tone.

"He was introducing me to Katherine's brother."

He slipped an arm across my shoulders. "I don't like him that close to you."

"He's part of this world too, Lewis. I don't think he's going to go away," I grumbled. Stupid Upper East Side.

"I know. Just old rivalries rear their head."

"It was literally nothing."

"Number one rule of the Upper East Side, Natalie: it is never nothing."

I turned to look at him in surprise. Uncertain of how to respond to that. But then the wedding music began, and I didn't have to.

33

"*Y*ou can still get out of this," Lark said anxiously.

I was standing on the raised platform before the enormous trifold mirror my hair and makeup team had brought in for the occasion. I'd kicked everyone out of the room, except Lark, a half hour ago. I knew that the five other bridesmaids—who I'd picked seemingly at random, but primarily because they had the most number of Crew connections—hadn't been happy by the arrangement.

But they weren't my friends.

I didn't have friends.

The crew I'd grown up with my entire life was family. Lark, Penn, Lewis, and Rowe. I would have had them all back here with me. But instead, it was just Lark, trying to talk me over the cliff. Not off it.

"Okay, this is what we'll do." Lark immediately went into planning mode. Her work as a campaign manager shone through as she saw me as just another project she had to fix. A fire she had to put out. "I'll distract everyone by sending them for alcohol. We'll scamper to the back door and grab a cab back to my apartment. Poof, runaway bride."

I ran my hands down the front of the one-of-a-kind Elizabeth Cunningham designer wedding dress. The bodice was strapless with a sweetheart neck. Made out of the softest, most delicate white lace with dozens of tiny white buttons running up the back. It swept down to my feet with an impressive train that would flow out behind me as I walked down the aisle. A twenty-foot empire veil would be affixed to the intricate braided design at the top of my head. White. Perfect virginal white.

"No wedding. No Camden," Lark continued.

My eyes found her in the mirror. "I can't."

"Physically, you are able."

"I can't," I repeated.

"But you don't love him!" Lark gasped. "How can you do this when you don't even *like* him? It can't just be the money. We all have money. The crew has money. You can have mine. I don't need it."

"Lark," I said, shaking my head.

"Is it the bet?"

I frowned. My dark red lips turning down at the corners. The bet. What a stupid fucking idea. The fucking bet that had ruined everything. Taken Penn from me. Forced me into actually going through with this arrangement. Even wrecked our tried-and-true crew. Little holes splintered in our unflappable love and loyalty.

"No. I just have to do this."

"I don't want to see you unhappy," Lark told me.

I almost laughed. But I couldn't even manage it. Unhappy. I'd been unhappy for years. What even was real happiness? It didn't belong to a girl whose father had lied, cheated, and stolen everything from her. Who ended up in prison, destroying my mother, who hadn't even been able to look at me for years. It certainly didn't belong to a girl whose brother had abandoned them all at the first sign of trouble.

I wanted my old life back. The one before the fraud. The one when I'd had everything. When I had been on top of the world. And I hadn't had to love or even like Camden Percy to build that future for myself.

It wasn't as if Penn was going to suddenly change his mind. To go back to the boy I'd known who worshipped at my feet. I'd been so naive then. Thinking he'd always come when I called. And now, he wasn't here to save me. But to feed me to the wolves.

"I'll manage," I finally got out.

"You're miserable. Camden makes you miserable. He's abusive. Katherine, please listen to me. We've all been saying it from the beginning. We *know* the kind of person that Camden is. You do, too. You shouldn't subject yourself to his whims."

She was right.

Camden was abusive.

Not physically. He'd never hit me. But he didn't have to, in order to land blows.

Emotionally, he twisted me around his little finger. Mentally, he fucked with the way I thought. And, when we fucked...well, it wasn't just fucking. There was passion, fueled by anger and dominance. His need for submission from me. Another game he played. At least the sex was good. That was about all he had going for him other than the string of Percy hotels he owned.

"Why are you so set on this?" Lark asked.

I didn't even know how to explain it to myself. It wasn't just about security. I had the penthouse overlooking Central Park. I still had a dwindling trust fund that I could probably stretch if I had to. It was more than that. It was an arrangement. Something Camden and I had crafted together for our mutual benefit. I was getting the better end of the deal, as he now knew exactly how little money I owned. We'd had to fork over tax and bank account information before signing prenups. It worked. We worked somehow...even when we hated each other.

"Maybe I don't want to fail at one more thing."

Lark sighed. "It wouldn't be a failure. You deserve better."

A knock sounded on the door, and the wedding planner, Virginia, burst in. "Time to go, Katherine. Are you ready?"

Lark shot big, round eyes at me, silently begging me to change my mind. But I couldn't.

"Yes," I told Virginia.

"Great. I have the veil. Let's get you both in position."

Lark and Virginia helped me down from my pedestal and picked up the long train of my dress. We marched down the hallway and into position at the back of the church. Virginia tucked my veil into my hair and then moved to cover my face.

I held my hand up. "Leave it."

She shrugged and left my face uncovered. I wanted to face this down with clear eyes. Alone. As always.

The music started. Virginia hurried bridesmaids out on cue. Lark shot me one more look of despair before stepping into the church in her dark red dress with a bouquet of white flowers.

"Okay, let them get all the way down, and then it's your turn." Virginia beamed at me. "Don't forget to breathe."

"It's just another runway," I muttered as she turned back to face the entrance.

"Canon in D" filtered through the church as it moved from the strings of the quartet I had chosen. The sound bloomed and magnified. The doors opened before me. I stood, silhouetted in the atrium, as the hundreds of guests rose to their feet to face me.

For a split second, I faltered. Debated. Wondered if Lark

was right. If I should turn around and run. But it was a moment, and then it was gone.

I stepped forward. Virginia straightened out my train and then the never-ending veil as I walked past row after row of guests. Their faces were a blur. I kept my eyes focused forward as the altar came into focus. The priest in his ceremonial attire. A line of bridesmaids and groomsmen. Everyone identical. Then, Camden standing in a tuxedo that had been handcrafted by a designer in London. I wasn't close enough yet to discern his expression. That was probably for the better.

As I got closer to the front, I began to recognize more faces. My crew taking up the front rows. My mother seated so regally beside David and his little Texas bride. Camden's father, Carlyle, seated next to Elizabeth Cunningham. They'd eloped and somehow kept it from the press. They'd have a big wedding sometime next year. Next to Carlyle was Camden's heinous sister, Candice, and then Elizabeth's daughter, Harmony, the whore who hated me. My new "family."

I skipped back to my side of the aisle and nearly froze in place. Natalie. Our eyes snagged, and for a split second, we stared daggers at each other. Then, she tilted her chin up. A stand of defiance. The bitch had the audacity to show her face and at my wedding nonetheless. I'd give her points for having balls, but she clearly had not taken my statement at Trinity seriously.

I passed Natalie, my blood boiling. And then I landed on Penn. My Penn. I just wanted him to look at me. To object. To *do* something.

But he just made eye contact with me. Looked sad for me. Pity.

Penn Kensington pitied me.

I'd told Lark that I wouldn't run. But I hadn't known until

that moment that I'd been hoping it was Penn who would talk me out of it. Not just stand there as I went through with it. He really wasn't going to stop it.

I swallowed and turned back to the man I was marrying. I was finally close enough to see the smirk on his strong features. A beautiful exterior hiding a dark interior. His look said only one thing—*mine*.

After tonight, I would belong to him.

He'd own me.

And no one was even going to object.

Not even me.

NATALIE

34

*K*atherine and Camden said I do.

They kissed before the huge crowd.

Sealed their union.

It took a solid hour with mass, and when the wedding party finally filed out, it felt too loud for what had just happened. I knew it wasn't just me that thought whatever we had witnessed was...wrong.

I had no affection for Katherine. And I liked Camden even less. They probably deserved each other. And yet, I'd seen something in Katherine's eyes when she walked down the aisle. Fear.

Then, she'd found my face in the crowd and glared at me. As if, of all the attendees, I was the only one who didn't belong. I probably should be reveling in the fact that she was getting what was coming to her after the shit she'd put me through. But that wasn't me.

Lewis directed me out of the pew and down the aisle. His mom and sisters were clustered around us, discussing how beautiful and over the top and amazing the wedding had been. It felt like we'd been at two different weddings.

I glanced up at Lewis. "That was painful."

He frowned. "Yeah."

"I don't think anyone else noticed."

"Well, no one else knows that it's arranged."

I hadn't thought about that. "I almost feel bad for her."

"She could have gotten out of it."

"Then, why didn't she?"

He shrugged. "I really have no clue."

But I had a hunch, and he was walking right past me. Careful not to touch me or even really look my way. Penn Kensington. Katherine must have thought he'd save her. Her knight in shining armor. But no one was there to save her. She'd had to save herself, and for some reason, she'd thought this was how she did it.

I shook my head as I ducked into the back of the car with Lewis. It was only a half-mile walk between St. Patrick's Cathedral and the reception at The Plaza. But the snow was coming down even harder than it had when the ceremony first started. No one was going to make that walk when most of the attendees had drivers or had hired someone for the occasion.

We were whisked the scant blocks up to The Plaza, and Lewis helped me out into the cold. We rushed across the snowy sidewalk and up the steps that led into the historic twenty-story building that occupied the prestigious space on the corner of Fifth and Central Park South.

Lewis dusted snow out of my hair and off my coat. "It's practically a New York City blizzard out there."

"I am not fully equipped for it."

He drew me in for a quick kiss and then walked through the lobby and into the foyer that led into the Grand Ballroom. The interior of the ballroom was decorated with thousands of red and white flowers. The classical style of the ballroom was highlighted with the intimate chandelier and flickering candlelight. The entire effect was effervescent and utterly romantic. I had to hold my breath to capture the entire image in my head.

Lewis put his hand on my arm to hold me from walking out of the foyer. I glanced up at him in question.

"I have a surprise for you."

"A surprise?"

"Well, more for us tonight."

He removed a small plastic card from his pocket. He passed me the card with The Plaza logo stamped onto it. And, suddenly, I understood.

"You got us a hotel room?"

He shrugged. "I thought it would be romantic. A way to reset."

Reset was an interesting word choice. I knew why he'd done this, of course. I had been more cautious about our relationship since all of that had come out. I hadn't been staying at his apartment like I had before. I was the kind of person who lived by the motto, *If someone shows you who they are, believe them.*

It was why I still didn't trust Penn. Why I detested Katherine. I couldn't stomach Camden. And now, I'd never be able to look Edward Warren in the face.

But Lewis...I just felt unease about his actions. I wanted to move on from them. Reset, as he'd said. Maybe this would be the way to do it.

I pocketed the key and smiled up at him. "It's a good idea."

He grinned from ear to ear, wrapped his arm around me, and directed me through the doors to the reception. We gave a host Lewis's name and were immediately directed to our table. As we got closer through the maze of tables, it became quite clear who was also seated at our table.

"Shit," Lewis muttered.

Neither of us had considered it.

Katherine had put the crew together.

Penn and Rowe were already seated at the table along with a model, who appeared to be Rowe's date, and four other people I didn't recognize. There were three vacant seats. One between Penn and Rowe. One for Lewis. And one...for me.

Katherine must not have even looked at the guest list. Or the seating chart. Because my name was even printed on the card in sweeping gold letters. Right between Penn and Lewis.

I hesitated before stepping forward. I swallowed back my rising unease about coming here. It'd be so easy to turn around and walk out the door. Instead, I pulled my chair out and took a seat.

The table was silent. Everyone waiting for someone else to make a move. The other five people were oblivious to what was going on. Though I had no idea how they couldn't feel the tension in the moment.

"Uh," Rowe said, leaning forward on an elbow, "this is awkward, right? I'm not making this up?"

Lewis snorted. "Social cues."

I cracked a smile. Rowe sure knew how to cut the tension even if he was just pointing out the obvious.

"Where's your date?" I asked, gesturing to the empty seat at Penn's side.

His blue eyes gazed back into mine, as if to say, *That would be you.* Instead, he said, "I never RSVP'd. Katherine just assumed."

"Oh."

"And you couldn't ask one of the many beautiful women you've been seen with?" Lewis asked, leaning forward. "Who was that one brunette you were with all the time? Shelly?"

"Chelle is my teaching assistant," Penn ground out.

"Yeah. Nothing going on with her?"

"That would be unethical." His response was dead and flat.

Lewis shrugged. "Never stopped you before."

"So," I interjected at that. I shot Lewis a look of distress. "How about this place? Really something."

"You've seen one wedding in the Grand Ballroom, you've seen them all," the woman to Rowe's left said to me. She was a standard unit of buxom blonde model. The kind Rowe tended to favor. "But your dress is gorgeous. I saw that at Bergdorf and am kicking myself for not trying it on."

"Seconded," said one of the other women at the table. "So jealous."

I blinked, surprised by the attention. I'd loved the purple off-the-shoulder dress with its old Hollywood feel. The way it'd hugged everything while still looking classy and sophisticated. I hadn't expected people to be jealous of it.

"Thank you," I said.

Luckily, the rest of the table kept a steady stream of conversation while the crew sat around, silent. It was almost sad, considering how I'd seen them the first time. How well they knew each other. But also, how easy the banter had been between them. I hadn't known then that it was bred from lies and secrets and loyalty, not just love. But to see that kind of friendship splintered was upsetting.

Even if it was their own fault. With the stupid bet. It was still sad. A bit like seeing a family fall apart.

Thankfully, we didn't have to wait too long for Katherine and Camden to show up. They walked gracefully into the room together as they were announced as Mr. and Mrs. Camden Percy. From the look on Katherine's face, that must have stung. The wedding party took up their seats at the front of the room, and then dinner was served.

I was damn well ready to leave as soon as we possibly could at this point. Being seated between Penn and Lewis was bad enough. But the anger that they kept venting at each other was something else entirely. I'd seen them together any number of times…even since Lewis and I'd started dating, and they hadn't been like this. Something must have happened, but I didn't know what.

I was digging into my dessert when I heard Rowe's date talking to the other woman who had complimented my dress. My head tilted up, and I strained to see if what I'd thought I'd heard was true.

"And this is a book?" the second woman asked.

Rowe's date nodded. "It's *insane*. Told like a total insider, Jana."

"Seriously, Michelle? You think someone from the Upper East wrote it?"

"Has to be. No other explanation."

"I've never even heard of it. Tell me the name again."

"Oh, let me pull it up on my phone."

My mouth went dry as I waited…and waited.

"Here it is. BET ON IT by Olivia Davies." Michelle pushed the phone in front of Jana's face.

Which was good because mine had gone pale as a ghost. They were talking about my book. Holy fuck! They were talking about *my* book on the Upper East Side. Trying to figure out who in the inside circle had written it. Oh god. I'd never imagined.

"It's so juicy, Jana. And I have thoughts on who I think the characters are based on."

"You've convinced me. I'm going to go get my copy now." She'd already pulled up her phone to purchase it.

"I need to know who you think Emerson is. She's a real heinous bitch. I can think of a dozen of us without a blink," she said with a laugh.

"Heinous bitch is like Upper East Side MO."

"Totally. I bet it's Candice. No one is as nasty as her.

You're going to have to tell me who you think it is when you read it."

"Oh, I will."

"But Luke." Jana fanned herself. Unknowingly getting hot and bothered at the thought of *Penn* sitting only three seats down from her. "He's so fucking sexy. Don't blame any of them for fighting for that man."

"Fictional men are just so much better."

I couldn't take it anymore. I needed to get out of there. Away from this conversation. When I'd written that book, I hadn't thought about the Upper East Side reading it and speculating. But I should have.

I pulled out my own phone and texted Amy our signal on shaky hands.

Okay???

Lewis put his hand on mine. "Don't worry about it. They're not going to put it together," he whispered.

"Let's hope not."

Thankfully, with dessert over, the rest of the plates were cleared, and the party began. Penn immediately disappeared from our table, as if standing in our presence for that long had been real torture.

I grabbed my small bag and followed Lewis toward the dance floor, carefully avoiding both Michelle and Jana. Katherine and Camden were waltzing to their first dance and were soon joined by the rest of the party. I swayed with Lewis, resting my head on his shoulder.

"What if they figure it out?" I asked.

"They won't. It's fine. I read it. It could be any number of people. It wasn't like you made the main characters the mayor's son and a girl whose dad is in prison for securities

287

fraud. You fictionalized it. Unless they were there, they're not going to know."

He was right. I'd made it unrecognizable from what had really happened and who the people were. But still...

A few dances in, my phone started ringing. I glanced down at it and saw Amy's number appear.

"I have to take this," I said with faux concern. "Amy knows I'm here. She wouldn't call if it wasn't important."

"Yeah, of course. Go ahead. I'm going to get another drink."

I nodded at him and then beelined for the exit. I felt a twinge of regret at the slight deception as I answered the phone.

"Hey, Amy."

"Phew, I haven't done that in so long. Wedding not so great after all?" Amy drawled into the phone.

"It's been horrible, honestly. I'm so ready to leave."

"Well, you must be if you're on the phone with me after you signaled the *save me from my date* message."

I laughed. "It was the only way I could think to get away from these two women who were discussing who they thought wrote BET ON IT and were the main characters in my book."

Amy gasped. "So cool!"

"Not exactly. I don't want them to know!"

Amy laughed as I eased into an empty alcove near the entrance to the party. It felt like I could finally breathe again, away from the limelight.

"What did you decide to do about your boy?"

"Well, I'm here with him," I said.

"Real convincing, Nat. You're not naive. Are you going to be able to forgive him for what he did?"

I sighed and tilted my head back. "I'm trying. It's still soon after what he did. Let me get through this wedding and then Christmas. I'll be better when I come back for New Year's."

"I cannot fucking wait for you to get here for Christmas. We are going to do all the things. All of them."

I laughed. "Well, thank god."

Amy continued rambling about all the things she had planned for us for Christmas, but my eyes locked on a figure moving toward me. Penn stopped a foot away, and I cleared my throat to interrupt Amy.

"Hey, Ames. I have to get back."

"Right. Right. Okay. Text if you need another excuse to get away."

"Thanks. Love you."

"You, too. Bye, babe."

I hung up the phone and met Penn's penetrating gaze.

"We need to talk," he said.

I sighed. "Why? Why do we always have to talk? Can't we get through an evening without talking?"

He just smirked, as if imagining all the evenings we'd done just that. But he was smirking into his cell phone and then handed it to me. I took it in surprise.

"What's this?"

"Just look."

My eyes skimmed the page, and suddenly, I pushed off of the wall, straightening in shock. My stomach plummeting. My hands shaking. I was going to be sick. I was staring at the first page of my new manuscript, IT'S A MATTER OF OPINION. The manuscript no one had seen but me, Caroline, and Gillian.

"How the *fuck* do you have this?" I hissed.

"That's what we need to talk about," he said calmly.

"Tell me right the fuck now, Penn. This isn't a joke."

"I know it's not. Let's go somewhere private. I don't think

we should do this where people can see us. They might…notice."

My hand clenched on his phone. I needed answers. I needed answers right the fuck now. And if that meant five minutes alone with Penn Kensington, then fuck it.

"I don't know how we're supposed to get alone."

"We could go outside."

I shook my head. "It's too cold."

A devilish grin spread across his face. "I have an idea."

"What?" I snapped.

"You're not going to like it."

"I don't like that you have that fucking manuscript on your phone either, but here we are. Tell me."

"You have a hotel room?"

I sighed and then withdrew the small plastic key from the purse at my hip.

He plucked it from my hand. "That'll do."

"I don't even know what room it is," I objected.

He laughed. "Lewis always gets the same room."

"This had better not be a fucking trick," I snapped at him.

He sobered immediately. That laugh disappearing, only to be replaced with regret. "It's not a trick. Honestly, I wish it were. It'd be easier than this explanation."

His words washed over me. This wasn't a joke with him. It wasn't some deception to get me into a hotel room. Good. Because I didn't find any of this particularly funny. And going up to the room with Penn was pretty stupid. But the only thing on my mind was that goddamn manuscript.

So, I finally nodded. "Five minutes, Penn."

NATALIE

35

*P*ure, unfiltered adrenaline pushed me into the elevator. Penn didn't even hesitate when he strode out onto the fourth floor. He'd clearly been here before. More than once. But I could hardly concentrate on that fact. There was a roaring in my ears that wouldn't abate. And a sinking pit in my stomach, saying that whatever he was about to tell me would wreck me.

Still, I went.

I followed him down the hallway to a doorway. He pressed the key to the lock, and I waited. Hoped for a minute that he was wrong. That Lewis had never had *this* room before. But then the lock clicked, and Penn pushed the door open. My heart sank even further.

"How did you know it would work?"

"We used to come here for parties in high school. Get trashed and then stay here instead of at our parents' respective houses. They used to keep this room on standby for us."

"Oh," I whispered.

Penn pushed the door open, stepped inside, and whistled low. I followed him inside to see why he'd done it. The room was pure romance. Hundreds of unlit candles covered nearly every flat surface. A bottle of expensive champagne chilled in a bucket near the balcony, next to a bouquet of red roses. Rose petals trailed off and out of sight.

I set my purse down on the chair before following the petals around the corner. They revealed the bedroom with its own elaborate decorations, including a king-size bed covered in deep red rose petals.

He'd thought *this* was our reset? He'd thought romancing me would make me feel better that he'd lied to me?

I shook my head at the ostentatious display. This might have been romantic in another scenario, if he'd done it just because instead of to make up for what he'd done wrong. But all I saw was him throwing money at a problem.

"Well, well, well, how romantic," Penn droned sarcastically.

I tore myself away from the sight before me. We weren't up here to look at the room. We were up here because I wanted to know how the fuck Penn had my manuscript on his phone.

"Tell me."

Penn handed the phone back to me. It was open to a different page. I didn't know what I was looking at. It looked like a file with a bunch of documents. I scrolled, seeing all three of my unfinished manuscripts.

"My books! What the fuck?"

"Keep scrolling. It gets worse."

I narrowed my eyes and then kept looking. I found a slew of emails, a press release, some business documents for property, some videos, and pictures. *A lot* of pictures.

"Oh my god, these are pictures of me in Charleston," I whispered. "When I was out at the beach with Amy. What the hell?" My eyes jumped to Penn's in distress. "Where did you get all of this?"

"That's Lewis's file on you."

My eyebrows rose sharply. "His *file* on me? What the hell does that mean?"

"As long as I've known Lewis, he has kept a file on his obsessions, especially of the female variety. I've seen them in the past. A list of his...accomplishments of sorts."

"And this is *mine?*" I shook my head in shock. I was seriously disturbed. Some of this information was private, some was creepy to the max, and some I didn't even fully grasp what it was. "What the hell is all of this?"

"It has the manuscripts he lifted from the publishing company."

"Excuse me?" I hissed.

"Yep. Looks like he took them from your submission. Plus, the emails to Warren about the money increase, emails forcing them to bring you out, and getting Club 360 on board for your party."

I hissed through my teeth. "He didn't."

"That's not all." He snatched the phone back, scrolling through the file he must have already gone through. "This is a deed to your building. He bought it around the time that you decided to move here."

My eyes widened in shock. I didn't even know what to say.

"This is the video footage from the surveillance cameras in your building. Oh, and all the pictures from Charleston that he probably had a private eye collect for him. Among other miscellaneous things, like a few receipts from various boutiques and—oh, yeah, this Harry Winston receipt for half a million dollars."

I was speechless. Utterly speechless. I didn't even know where to begin.

"Half a million dollars," I gasped. "What the hell is he buying for half a million dollars?"

Penn's gaze swept to mine. Anger—blistering, hot anger—seeped from them. "You can't guess?"

My hand went to my mouth. "He didn't."

"Oh, I saw it."

I blinked and then blinked again. I didn't even know how to process all this information. The lies. The betrayal. The... stalking. He hadn't just orchestrated a way for us to be together. He had done things I would have never been able to think of.

Buying my building? Why?

Video surveillance and a private eye? What the actual fuck?

"This is...insane," I gasped. "I mean, I asked him point-blank if there was anything else, and he owned up to the emails to bring me out. He said that was it."

Penn frowned. "He gave you one truth to keep you from looking for the rest."

"You told me," I muttered, realization washing over me. "You said there's always more. You were right."

His hand softly came down onto my arm. Comforting. Just a light touch to say he was here. "I really hoped that I wouldn't find it. To spare you."

"How exactly *did* you get this?" I asked.

"Well," he said, scratching the back of his head, "I kind of broke into his apartment."

"You did what?" I gasped. I stumbled back a step.

"Okay, look, it isn't as bad as it sounds." He held his hands up as if he was worried that he'd scare me away. "I went to see him after you came to my apartment this week. I thought it was all a fucking game with him, and then he told me he was actually serious. Showed me the fucking ring. I wanted to believe him, Nat. But I just...didn't. I've known him too fucking long."

"So, you thought breaking into his apartment was the right move?" I asked hysterically.

"No. Of course not. I told myself that, if he loved you and wanted to do right by you...if you weren't another one of his fascinations, then he wouldn't have a file. He'd treat you like the incredible woman that you are. I told myself I would go to his apartment and see if he had one, and if he didn't, I'd bow out. I'd fucking get a job somewhere else and leave you two to the Upper East Side."

My heart stopped at those words. "You would have left?"

"For you to be happy?" he asked softly. "Yes. And also because I couldn't have endured watching it."

"So...you went looking for the file."

"Yep, and that motherfucker had this fucking thing on his computer. The manuscript you'd just told me about. All the footage and pictures. I flipped my shit and downloaded the whole thing, and then I knew I had to tell you."

"And you had to tell me here?" I asked softly. "At the reception? You couldn't have...called me?"

"Would you have met up with me?"

"I don't know, Penn!"

"Lewis was acting crazy. He had a ring. I didn't know if he was going to propose tonight or not," he said, clearing the distance between us. "I wasn't going to fucking let you marry him. No fucking way. Not knowing what he'd done. The game he had played to win you."

"It's all just a fucking game," I spat. "Another fucking game."

My anger burst. Everything I'd been holding in unloaded at once. I pushed against his chest. But he stayed firm, enduring that anger as if he were weathering a storm.

"Natalie," he said, reaching out to stop me.

But I couldn't be contained. "How? How could he do this to me? How could he lie? Just *fucking* lie to my face. I don't understand." My voice broke. "I asked for the truth. Is the truth that fucking hard?"

"No," he said.

"Don't fucking talk to me about that," I yelled at him. "You lied, too. You held everything back. This is your fault, too."

"I lied. I'm sorry. I was wrong. But I wasn't fucking stalking you, Natalie. I didn't plan a way for us to be together. We just *were*. Let out your anger about Lewis, but don't confuse the two."

"Fine. No anger for you, just him. Seems fair," I said sarcastically. I pushed away from him again, deaf to his reasoning. My world had tipped upside down again. I'd had that caution about Lewis, but I'd just told Amy that it was going to be fine. I needed time to process. And now, *this*?

How did I even move on from this?

This wasn't a stupid bet that had gotten me fired. This was my boyfriend actually creepily stalking me. Not just arranging for us to meet, but going behind my back and forcing us together. Taking pictures and videos of me without my knowledge.

If that wasn't bad enough…all three of my manuscripts I'd submitted to Warren were there. He knew how I felt about him reading my work. He knew. I'd told him time and time again. It was the only thing I'd never given up on. So, he'd gone behind my back and stolen the books.

"I've taken a year of your anger. Fuck, seven years of your anger, Natalie. But I did this for you. I didn't want you to find out another way or years down the line when you were fucking married, okay?"

I beat against Penn's chest, letting out all my frustration and grief. "How could he do this to me?"

"Natalie, stop. Just stop."

When it was clear that I wasn't going to be consolable, Penn reached forward and grabbed both of my wrists. I struggled against him, and he pulled them over my head, backing me into the wall and bracing me against it with his body.

"Breathe," he said soothingly. "Breathe, Natalie."

I took a deep inhalation and slowly released it. I'd been near hyperventilating. And I hadn't even known it. Just panic coursing through me. Taking over. My whole body was shaking. The knowledge that I'd fallen into this trap again—only worse—had shattered something vital within me. I couldn't seem to find that string to pull me back to myself.

"He read my manuscripts," I whispered, my bottom lip trembling. I bit down into it, hard enough to keep me in the here and now. My blue eyes were clear as I looked up into his face. "He fucking read them."

"I know." He sounded pained. "I'm sorry. I wish I could save you from this."

He'd tried. He'd told me. Addie had told me. But I hadn't listened. I'd been so fucking stupid. And now, where was I?

I shook my head and suddenly felt exactly how we were positioned against the wall. Penn's hips pressed into my own. His hands securing my wrists over my head. His lips mere inches from mine.

It hadn't been sexual until that moment. Until the only thing that I could see was his mouth and feel was his cock and want was him.

I jerked forward against his bindings and pressed my mouth against his.

He pulled back sharply. "Natalie, stop. I'm not going to kiss you because you're mad at him."

"Okay," I said and tried to reach him again.

"I'm serious."

"I've wanted this since I saw you again," I told him. "And now, there's no reason to say no."

He faltered for a moment. Struck by my words. Contemplating them. "I…"

"Penn," I said with fire in my eyes and heart, "shut up and kiss me."

And he did.

NATALIE

36

*A*bandon. That was what his lips tasted like.
Bliss. That was what his hands felt like.
Reverence. That was what his body sang to me.

Our lips crushed against one another, vying for authority. We demanded more and more from each other. Wanted to give in completely to this feeling. To the knowledge that we both wanted it and nothing stood in our way.

My fingers fumbled with buttons. Each one making me curse his damn suit. I needed skin. I wanted his heat. I pushed his jacket off of his shoulders and let it drop to the floor, forgotten. He removed his tie and then yanked his own shirt off, heedless of the crumpled mess it now made at our feet. He reached for the buckle of his suit pants, but he was already sliding the zipper down my dress. A thousand-dollar dress, wasted on the hotel room floor.

"Fuck," he breathed when he saw me standing there in nothing but a lace thong and high heels.

"Yes, please," I responded.

His grip on my thong tightened, and suddenly, I heard a tearing sound. I gasped as the material ripped away.

"Oh my god."

"Guess you don't need those anymore." He laughed softly at my exclamation and then captured my lips with his again.

I'd managed to undo his belt buckle, but he brushed my hands aside and forced them back over my head.

"Don't move those," he instructed.

My body was humming with desire as I watched what I couldn't touch. He unbuttoned his pants and slid down the zipper. His pants pooled around his ankles, revealing his cock to me. My mouth watered, and I almost moved my hands to stroke him. But his gaze held me in place.

He slipped his hands on the outside of my thighs and hoisted me into the air. My hands dropped down onto his shoulders in shock as he braced my body back against the wall.

And neither of us had a moment to think before he thrust into me, filling me to the hilt. I groaned, leaning forward to kiss him again.

"God, yes," I muttered incoherently.

This wasn't steady, sweet seduction. This was Penn taking back what was his. What had always been his. Since that first night in Paris. Up until the moment he had fucked it all up. And even then, I'd wanted him.

I'd tried to deny it. I'd told myself I couldn't want someone that I didn't trust. That I wouldn't give in. But, now, with all the barriers down, I knew that I'd been lying to myself.

Lying so hard.

Penn Kensington knew me inside and out. He'd fucked with my head and my heart. He'd tried to make it better. And he'd damn well been repentant about it. I knew that I held grudges, but it wasn't until that moment—the very moment where we were joined together as one—that I saw how much damage they had done here.

Would I ever forget the damage he had inflicted? No. But right now, it didn't matter. I could forgive him his stupidity here and now. I could move away from that anger and resentment of him using me. Manipulating me. Because it was obvious, so obvious, that this was real.

So real. More real than anything else.

And, while I was boiling over with rage, none was directed at him. Not the one who had been trying to warn me and now seemed to want to put me back together.

My head cracked against the wall as he drove up into me again. Our bodies smacking together. Our chests heaving. My breasts bouncing with the rhythm as he pounded into me.

This wasn't gentle or coaxing. It wasn't discovering my body. Because he already knew every damn inch of it.

This was taking, owning, claiming me in the most basic sense.

It was hedonistic.

Self-indulgent.

Wild.

We were wild with no boundaries. Nothing between us anymore. No secrets. No plans. No games.

The heat built. It consumed. My body shuddered from the waves of pleasure that coursed through me as he rocked into me.

"Oh fuck. Oh, Penn," I called out into the hotel room.

I let it go. All the pain and hurt. I channeled my very being into that moment.

Then, I broke apart.

Into a million little pieces.

I yelled, "Fuck," about a thousand times into the silent room as he slowed his pace to match my orgasm.

I was still seeing stars as he kicked out of his pants, carried me across the room, and gently laid me down on the bed. My hair fanned out all across the bed, getting tangled in the rose petals. He stared down at me as if I were the most beautiful thing he had ever seen in his life. That look in his eyes…I had seen it before. An emotion that I couldn't name in that moment, but, with my whole being, I knew what he was saying with those baby blues.

We'd separated after he lay me down, but he easily slid back into me. I inhaled sharply, still sensitive from the last orgasm. He grinned at that. A cocky smile that said he knew what he was doing to me. And fuck, he did.

"I have wanted this for so long," he said as he started up a rhythm again.

"For a year," I murmured.

"Every day for a year." He pumped into me harder. "Just like this."

I didn't deny it. My body had ached for him. More of him. All of him.

And, when we were like this, everything else disappeared. I knew it would all come back later, but I didn't want it between us right now. I didn't want anything between us right now.

"More," I begged.

He pressed my knee up, giving himself a deep angle into me. "See? You do beg," he said with a smile.

"I'll beg all you want if you fuck me right now."

He leaned forward until our lips were almost touching. "Ask me again, love."

My body pulsed as he kept a slow, steady pace. I wanted more. I wanted the force he'd used against the wall.

"Fuck me, Penn. God, just fuck me."

His smile grew, and then he kissed me, hard. Restraint fled him. He slammed into me to the point of pain, but it only brought more pleasure. More, more, more. I didn't want him to stop. Not as he fucked me until I was incoherent again.

Until both our bodies seized up, and we hit our climax together. Him not able to hold out any longer as I clamped around him with the strength of my own orgasm.

I rode the wave of pleasure until I thought I was going to pass out. Then, I finally stilled, my breathing ragged. My voice raw from screaming. A fine sheen of sweat coating our naked bodies. I stroked his hair and gently kissed his shoulder.

"Fuck, I missed you," he murmured against my chest as he slowly eased back up to his elbow. "Nothing compares to you, Nat."

My fingers ran along his jawline. I was lost to the euphoria of our coupling. "You're the best I've ever had."

He nodded. "Always."

He began to pull back, but I stopped him in his place.

"Let's not go back to reality yet."

His lips captured mine once more. "No reality until you're ready. Right now, it's just us. Nothing else exists."

I bit my lip and then agreed. He slid off of me and went to clean up. I stretched out on the bed like a cat and yawned. I felt like I'd just run a marathon. I could sleep for a week.

Penn came back out, and I switched places with him, taking care of my needs before returning to the bedroom, naked. He'd slung on his boxers and suit pants, though they remained undone.

"What are you doing?" I asked.

He popped the cork on the champagne and laughed. "For you?"

"Oh my god, Penn, you can't open that."

Penn grinned. "Didn't want it to go to waste."

He poured us each a glass and passed one to me.

"I cannot believe you just did that. We're never going to get this room to look right again."

"Who cares?" he said, dragging my naked form against him again. "I don't care who knows what we did tonight."

I sighed and took a sip of my champagne. I felt shockingly levelheaded, considering the fit I'd been in only a half hour ago. "I should probably go downstairs. There's a conversation I need to have. And it's not going to be pleasant."

"Hey." He tilted my chin up to look at him. "What happened to nothing else exists but us here?"

I downed the last of the champagne. "I shouldn't ignore it. It's better to rip off the Band-Aid."

I could see that Penn wanted to say more. That he had questions about where this left us. But I didn't have answers for him right now.

What we'd done was...wonderful. Beyond wonderful. It had been perfection. Things were just complicated. I needed to get everything else in order before I could even think about us. It was better to leave us here, where we were both blissful, than to make decisions under the influence of sex.

I pressed one more kiss to his lips and then went to grab my dress. He went back to the champagne bottle, lifting it to pour us each another glass. I could tell that he had hoped for more from me by the tilt of his shoulders. But he wouldn't push me. Not after what had happened tonight.

"Can you help with the zipper?" I asked, turning my back to him.

His finger hit the bottom of the zipper when I heard a click.

My eyes went to the door in confusion. And then dread.

As Lewis Warren walked into the room.

PENN

37

"*F*uck," Natalie breathed next to me.

My eyes followed hers to find Lewis standing in the doorway.

He stopped with the door ajar as he took in the scene before him. The disturbed rose petals. Me zipping up Natalie's dress. The fact that I was shirtless with my pants still undone. The open bottle of champagne. The room *he'd* purchased for *their* romantic evening. Which we'd used for our own escapade.

His jaw set. His hands balled into fists. His eyes turned murderous.

"What the fuck is this?" Lewis demanded.

He glanced between us, waiting for one of us to explain, to give some rational explanation for what he was witnessing, but I sure as fuck didn't have one.

I calmly slid on my shirt and jacket and turned to him. "This is exactly what this looks like."

"Penn," Natalie hissed.

He took one more glance at us. At our state of dress and the way I stood just a bit in front of her. His eyes caught on

Natalie's discarded underwear. He lost whatever semblance of calm he'd had before he barged into the room. It shattered from his cool exterior. The mask slipped finally. Finally. And the real Lewis surfaced.

He barged across the room, clearing the distance in three quick strides. Then, he swung on me. I had seen it coming and dodged the first swing, but Lewis wasn't holding back and landed the second one in my gut. I wheezed as the hit knocked the breath out of me.

Distantly, I heard Natalie yelling. Telling Lewis to stop. But it was just me and him now.

My fist connected with his face. Pain seared through my knuckles as I cracked his jaw sideways. But adrenaline pushed me forward, and I'd deal with that later.

He hit me again—in my ribs this time—and I gasped at the pain. But I didn't care. I rushed him, knocking him backward off of his feet and throwing him to the ground. I landed on top of him and threw another fist into his face.

He swung his body to get momentum and jabbed his elbow into my face as he rolled me off of him. My lip split on contact, and blood dribbled down my chin.

Then, suddenly, Natalie was between us. Screaming in our faces. And her voice broke through.

"Stop! What the fuck is wrong with you two? This isn't how we handle this. Stop it! Stop it!" she shrieked.

She was standing between us with her arms spread wide. Her blue eyes manic and afraid. My eyes drifted back to Lewis, who looked as if he was about to launch himself at me again. But he wouldn't go through Natalie.

I slowly got to my feet again. My chest was heaving, and I brushed at my split lip with the back of my hand, wiping the blood away.

"Can we act civilized instead of like fucking animals?" she yelled at the both of us.

Personally, I had no idea how she wasn't pummeling Lewis herself. She had gone from hysterics and hyperventilating to this in a pretty quick span. I knew that she wasn't okay. That all of this would hit her like a freight train once she was alone, but damn, she was fierce.

"Sure," I spat out.

Lewis held his hand up. "You call fucking him behind my back civilized?"

"Don't fucking talk to her like that," I snarled. She might be cool, but I wasn't.

Her eyes narrowed at Lewis's condescending tone. "You have no idea what this is about."

But Lewis was already looking at me again. "This is a new low for you."

I stepped forward, drifting into Natalie's personal space. I wanted to get her away from him. His anger was directed at me, but it could shift in a split second. And it'd burn white hot before she'd even get a chance to call him out on his bullshit.

"Is it really though?" I asked with a laugh. I put my arm around Natalie, sliding her out from between us and to my side. "I told you that I'd do what was best for her. You just didn't realize that we differed in what that meant."

"Penn, stop it," Natalie growled. She shook me off. "This is my fight."

I didn't listen to her. This had been a long time coming. A long fucking time. Longer than she probably even realized.

My friendship with Lewis had always been a tenuous thing. It had been built on secrets and competition. Loyalty born of the fact that we both knew enough to bury the other, but the fight would be to the death if either of us ever tried. It wasn't a real friendship. And I'd known that the minute he went after Natalie.

"Lewis knows that the fault belongs with me," I said.

Lewis's eyes swept to hers. I could read the desperation there. And he didn't even know what she knew yet. "He used you again, Natalie. Manipulated you into this."

Natalie huffed when I cut off her response, "It's too hard to recognize that she wants me and not you? You didn't see that all along?"

Lewis's voice dropped low, full of venom. He pointed his finger at me. "I will fucking kill you for this."

"We both know you won't do it. I have enough on you, too."

"Would you both shut up?" Natalie finally cried. "This isn't about your little friend feud. This shit is about the fact that you lied to me," she accused Lewis.

"Natalie, I haven't lied to you," Lewis said in the most obnoxiously placating tone.

I snorted. "Like hell you haven't."

"Shut your fucking mouth, Kensington, before I fucking throw you out of this room."

Natalie ignored us both. "You lied to me. You didn't just get me the money and arrange for me to come to New York. You kept a fucking file on me, Lewis!"

Lewis stilled. His eyes widened in shock. "How?"

"And you don't even deny it."

Check-and-mate.

"*N*atalie, I...I don't even know where you heard that."

"Heard it?" I snarled. "Oh no, I didn't hear it, Lewis. I saw it. I saw the whole goddamn thing. You bought my building. And took pictures of me. You *spied* on me." I glared at him with all my pent-up fury. "And then you read my books. The one thing I told you that you could never do, you went behind my back and did anyway."

"There's a perfectly reasonable explanation for that file," he said calmly.

He stepped forward as if he was going to reach out for me, but I drew back. Closer to Penn, but not touching him. Far enough back to draw a line of demarcation.

His eyes narrowed at that step. "But you would have heard that if you'd talked to me. If you'd just come to me with these concerns. But no, you ran to him."

"I didn't *run* to anyone. I was presented with facts," I spat. "And was able to interpret that you did all of these things and lied about them. There's nothing for you to explain."

I still couldn't even believe how this day had shifted. Seeing that file had broken me. Taken the last innocent piece of my soul and crushed it under the weight of the Upper East Side. Because there were no depths that these people wouldn't stoop to. There was nothing they wouldn't do to get what they wanted. They would lie, cheat, and steal for what they thought belonged to them.

And when it had hit me, I'd fallen apart.

I wasn't back together yet. I was still scattered on the floor. But I would not stand here and allow these men to fight over me. I would not allow them to mock and goad each other for another chance at drawing blood. Not when the real culprit hadn't owned up to his faults. When he didn't even know what had happened that pushed me straight into Penn's arms.

While I knew that I probably shouldn't have done that, I didn't regret it. I couldn't regret it.

"I can't believe that you just cheated on me, and you have the audacity to call *me* a liar," Lewis said. He stood taller, indignant.

"You are a liar," Penn spat.

"Don't," I warned him.

"Natalie," Lewis said with a shake of his head, "I loved you. I *love* you. I just…can't even believe that you would do this to me. After everything I've done for you. Everything was for your benefit."

"You keep saying that, but I don't think it means what you think it does," I said.

His eyes narrowed. What did he think, that I'd hear him say he loved me and cower and beg forgiveness? I didn't need forgiveness for what I'd done.

"And I didn't cheat on you," I told him plainly. "We were over the minute I found out about that fucking file."

Lewis shook his head. All high and mighty. "This is disgusting."

"You can't even talk about it, can you? You haven't given me your supposed reasonable explanation because there is no explanation for your behavior. You can blame me for what happened with Penn, but at least I own up to it. We were together because there's no possible way that I would ever be with someone who did what you did to me."

"I'm the one who has been there for you and helped you. I've done everything I can for you to be happy."

I almost laughed at how pathetic it sounded. But I could see his anger burning hot again, and the last thing I wanted was for another fight to break out. "Don't try to spin this shit. That's what you always do. I gave you the opportunity to come clean, and you held back *everything*. Everything!"

"You heard what you wanted to hear," he finally snapped. It was as if he'd lost his cool, and he didn't even fucking care anymore. "You didn't want to know the lengths that I had gone for you. You think that you would have gotten where you were without me? I got your book published. I convinced you to move here, so you could write. I got you a reasonable apartment in Manhattan. And suddenly, you think I'm the bad guy here?"

I shook my head in disgust. "You are totally delusional."

"Natalie, we should just go," Penn said. Whatever he must have heard in Lewis's voice made him nervous.

"You're not going anywhere with him," Lewis said. "I've given you everything. And now, you're listening to his bull-shit. He's turned you against me."

"He really didn't."

"How did you get the file then?" Lewis asked.

I glanced over at Penn, and Lewis just laughed. "That's what I thought. And you don't think he manipulated it in any way? You think he told you the complete truth? Not to fool you in getting you back? Did you even fucking consider that maybe *he* was the one who was lying?"

I hadn't. Not once.

Lewis choked on a laugh. "Of course not. Because Penn Kensington is a fucking saint. He didn't put a fucking bet on you to screw with your head. He didn't have sex with random women constantly just to toy with Katherine. No, he's perfect. And you believed his lies without even a thought."

"Lewis, drop the charade," Penn said. "You know that I didn't lie about this shit."

"I'll admit it. Yes, I have a file on you, Natalie. I keep a file on everything. It's how I organize my life. It's not a secret to anyone who knows me. Which is why Penn obviously knew there would be one," Lewis said calmly. "But I'm a thousand percent certain that whatever file you were shown isn't the real one. That it was manufactured against me."

I shook my head. I hadn't considered that. I hadn't considered it…because the evidence was right in front of my face. How would Penn have gotten access to my manuscripts? Lewis had an obvious way to get them. A way I had never thought of until I'd seen them there.

"Stop twisting shit around," Penn said. "You told me last year that you liked Natalie, and you'd fallen in love with her words. But I know for a fact that she had never let you read them. She didn't even let *me* read them."

"You can't lie your way out of this," I told Lewis.

"You have no proof that any of that is even mine. You *want* to believe the worst of me," Lewis said, taking a step forward. Penn stepped between us. "I don't even know why you were with me if you wanted to fuck him instead."

"That's *not* what this is about," I spat. "This is about you *stalking* me, Lewis. For a year before we dated and then *while* we were dating. You didn't need to do any of this. You didn't need to take pictures of me or have video surveillance of my building. You could have waited for me to give you my manuscripts. But you don't respect me. You think that I'm a game piece that you can move around."

"Natalie, I don't…" His voice was strained.

I held my hand up. "I've made up my mind. It's over. Stop what you've been doing. Stop following me around and trying to supposedly help me. I don't need your help anymore."

"Please, we can work this out. It's him that's the problem." He pointed at Penn.

"If you continue this behavior, I'll file a restraining order," I said breathlessly. The threat hung between us.

Lewis clenched his hands into fists. "You wouldn't."

"I don't want to. I didn't want any of this." My voice wavered on the last line. My strength was ebbing.

I was mad at Lewis, but I had cared for him. The time we'd been together hadn't been a lie for me. He'd just lied to me through it all. And now, that was all I saw.

"Just…let me go."

"I can't," he said, his eyes wide.

I shook my head. And I knew that he meant it. That he wasn't going to let it go if I didn't stop this.

"I'm sorry," I finally said. "Sorry that you felt you had to lie to get me, to keep me. Sorry that you're still doing it now, even when all the evidence is in front of us. But I'm not sorry about Penn. And I'm not sorry about leaving."

I stalked across the room, stepped into my heels, and snatched up my purse.

When I turned back toward the door, Lewis lunged for me. He grabbed my elbow, preventing me from leaving. "Don't."

"Let me go," I said, calm but firm.

"Lewis," Penn growled. He was there in a second, ready to stop it if anything happened.

But Lewis just looked dejected. Like my words had finally sank in. "Don't go like this. We can try again."

"No"—I extracted my arm from him—"we can't."

My heart constricted as I eased past him and out the door. I hated what had just happened. How it had all gone down. The fact that Lewis had seen what we'd done, so he now clearly blamed Penn for our breakup. When it was all his lies. And secrets. And obsession.

I was nearly to the elevator when I felt Penn catch up with me. Our eyes met for a minute, and then I turned away. He knew me well enough not to say anything.

His shirt was still undone. His tie had vanished, likely never to be seen again. He hastened to right himself. Though it was obvious that we were both more rumpled than we'd been earlier.

I'd come to Katherine's wedding to prove a point. That I wouldn't back down from a challenge. It had all unraveled from there, and now, there was no reason to be in attendance.

But when we bypassed the entrance to the Grand Ballroom, there was a crowd of people standing around, reading on their phones. Not what I would have expected of a reception party. Then, Jane appeared. Her eyes rounded when she saw me, and she darted toward me.

"Oh my god, Natalie, there you are. I've been looking all over for you," she gushed.

"Why?" I asked warily.

"Your pen name," she said. "Someone found out you're Olivia."

"What? How?" I gasped frantically.

"I don't know. But someone leaked it to the press."

I took the phone she offered me and read the headline of the article she had up, suddenly feeling faint.

New York Times Bestselling Novel *Bet on It* Author Olivia Davies Reportedly a Pen Name for Former Temp Worker. Not the Insider You Expected!

NATALIE

39

"No," I breathed. "No, no, no, no, no."

I skimmed through the article with my heart in my throat. This couldn't be happening. This…this couldn't be real.

And yet, it was.

The article was a tell-all in its reveal of me. Slamming me for writing a fucking *fictional* account. As if it didn't say *based on* on the fucking cover. It painted me as a jilted ex. Someone who had lost in all of this and was desperate for revenge. As if I'd written it for that and not to expunge the contents of my soul onto the page.

It claimed that I'd painted the picture to appear like I was an Upper East Sider who had fallen into this group. When, in fact, I was just the help. A washed-up temp worker who was watching a home in the Hamptons last fall. That the book wasn't some insider information that was worth reading; it was just a boring outside perspective of someone who wished they could live in this world.

And since the article was an editorial from someone in the know, it was clear that they didn't think that my information was important enough to come from 'the help.' I effectively had no voice in this. And would be given no response. Just a salacious headline that tore me from my apparent pedestal.

Basically, I was no one important. The book sucked. And I was kind of a whore.

"Holy fuck. I don't…" My hands were shaking as I all but threw the phone back at Jane.

"How the hell did someone get this information?" Penn demanded. "Does the author list a source?"

I shook my head.

"This is slander. We could go after them."

"I don't know what to say," Jane said. "How many other people knew about this?"

"Hardly anyone. Maybe a half dozen people."

"None of us would have leaked this," Penn said.

Jane agreed. "Someone else had to know. Someone out to get you."

"Shit, I don't even know what this means for the book. I have to call my agent," I gasped. "Fuck, it's Saturday. She's not going to answer. I'll have to email her. I hope she doesn't see the article before she gets my email."

I fished into my purse and pulled out my phone. My brain was running a million miles a second. There had to be some kind of damage control that Caroline could do. Or Gillian. This was…beyond words.

I'd thought that finding out about Lewis and the subsequent breakup would be the death of me, but…my career was hanging in the balance. The only thing that I'd ever wanted to do with my life. The thing I'd finally secured happily. And now…I didn't know where I stood.

"Natalie," Penn murmured softly.

"What?" I asked, glancing up at him.

But he was looking elsewhere. I followed his line of

vision and found the dark-haired beauty clothed in white, walking toward us.

"Katherine," I muttered. I wasn't ready for this confrontation. Not after Lewis. Not after this debacle with my pen name.

Her smug smirk was relentless. "Hello, Natalie."

"Look, I'm leaving now anyway, so you can save your speech for someone else."

"Speech?" Katherine asked. "No, I don't have anything planned. I'm actually glad that you're here now that I think about it."

I narrowed my eyes. Not good. "Why?"

"Because now, I get to see your reaction. See the dread in your eyes instead of imagining what it looked like back in your sad apartment."

"*You* did this," I realized.

"How did you find out?" Penn demanded.

Her eyes flicked to his. Something like pain flashed across her face but was replaced with that blank stare she'd walked down the aisle with.

"Did you honestly think that you could keep secrets in this town?" Katherine asked.

"That's rich, coming from you," Penn quipped.

"Who told you?" I demanded.

"I have eyes and ears everywhere."

I shook my head in disgust. "You are a disturbed woman."

Katherine laughed. "Sure, Natalie. Whatever you have to tell yourself. You should have listened to me," Katherine told me. "You thought that you could come to my city and threaten me. I told you that I own this city. And I do. You don't belong in it. Let this be a lesson for how miserable I can make your life."

"Make *my* life miserable?" I asked with a slow blink. "Why would you even care? Oh wait, we know the answer to that,

Katherine. Because you are miserable, and you want everyone to join you. You want to bring people down onto your level, which happens to be at the bottom of the ocean where you're drowning. That's what you want in life. Misery. That's why you had this sham of a wedding today."

"You know nothing about my life, Natalie. Keep lashing out. It's not going to help you."

"I don't know or care why you did it. Either way, it's a petty, baseless move. And you're going to fucking pay for what you did."

Katherine pressed a hand to her stomach and chuckled. "Oh, honey, please."

"I'm going to make you regret this," I said seriously.

"Sure you are, kitty cat," Katherine said with another laugh. As if I'd made the joke of the season. "I'm so scared."

I didn't care how she'd found out. Or what her utter damage was. I just knew that she had come after me because I was the only person who had ever stood up to her. I was the only one who had told her no and not backed down. And I didn't want to back down here.

Even as that string I'd been holding on to snapped. Even as I felt myself descend down, down, down into the darkest place of my being. Even as I held on to the dark and decided to call it home.

I knew with every fiber of my being that I would not let Katherine Van Pelt do this to me. How many other women had she beaten down for having strength? She'd always gotten away with it. And I wouldn't let her do it to me.

My stomach might be in knots. I might want to throw up. Fear might be the only lifeline I had. Knowing I'd have to wade through the social humiliation of this revelation. Figure out how to still live my life after the death of Olivia Davies. And still, I would not break before her.

"Go back to the hole you crawled out of," Katherine spat at me.

"I don't even recognize you anymore," Penn said with a shake of his head.

"Same, love," she said. "Same." Then, she flicked her dark hair off her shoulder. "Now, you'll have to excuse me. I have a reception to finish."

With that, she turned and strode back into her own party. The devil in virginal white.

My hands were shaking, and the last shred of control I had been clinging to in Katherine's presence was collapsing.

"I can't believe she did this," Penn said. "It's vindictive, even for Katherine."

"I just...don't know how she even fucking found out," I gasped.

"Someone must have told her. I don't think she would have cared to figure it out on her own."

Tears welled in my eyes. Ones I'd held back all night. But I didn't want to shed them. Not here. Not at all.

"God, you were right," I said. I balled my hands into fists. "This world chewed me up and spit me out. And they just keep fucking winning. Even when they're wrong, they always win."

Penn sighed. "I did want you to get out. They've been playing the game a lot longer. The board wasn't even."

I brushed at the tears, determined not to let them fall. I wouldn't allow it. Katherine would never get my tears.

"I need...I need to get out of here."

"Of course," he said. "I can take you home."

"I bet this will all blow over," Jane said softly.

I looked over at her. "I find that doubtful."

"I believe it. Get away for Christmas, and when you come back for my New Year's Eve party, it'll be like nothing ever happened."

"My pen name was revealed. Katherine humiliated me in front of the entire world. I don't think a week is going to change anyone's mind."

Jane frowned. "I'm so sorry, Natalie. I hate that this happened to you. Let me know if I can do anything. Anything at all. My connections are at your disposal."

"Thanks," I muttered and then continued toward the exit. I was almost out into the freak blizzard when I realized, "Fuck, I don't have my coat."

"Do you want me to go back in and get it?"

I shook my head. I couldn't bear the thought of it. "I have another at home. I'll just…consider it another casualty to the evening."

Penn slid his jacket off and wrapped it around my shoulders. We were silent as we took a cab back to my apartment. He'd never been inside my apartment. Never even been to the building. And I found that I didn't want his first time to be seeing me pack and break down.

I turned my back to the door when we got upstairs. "This is me."

"Can I come in?"

I debated on whether or not I was making the right move and then shook my head.

"No?"

"Not right now," I amended.

"Natalie, let me take care of you."

"I think…I need to take care of myself in this one."

"You don't have to do this alone," he told me.

"I know. But I'm going to go inside and pack and leave the city. And I don't want that to be the first time you come inside." I shed his jacket and passed it back to him to prove my point.

"You're just going to leave?"

"I'm a mess. I need to go home and regroup. Think this all

through. Process. I don't even know what my agent is going to say. What my editor is going to say. I was already going home for Christmas. I'm going to buy a ticket for tonight and get there early."

Penn slipped his hands into his pockets. "I hate to bring one more thing into your headspace right now, Nat, but... where does this leave us?"

"I don't know," I whispered honestly. "I don't know anything right now."

"Let me rephrase that," he said. He brought his hands up to my jaw and stared deep into my blue eyes. "This is what I want, Natalie. You. Just you. All of you. You exactly as you are."

"Penn," I whispered, "I don't know if I'm ready."

He pressed a kiss to my lips and then stepped back. "That's okay. I'm not going anywhere. I'll be here when you are."

Then, I watched him walk away with all the promise of a better tomorrow for us. And I stepped inside to face the bitter reality of today.

EPILOGUE

NATALIE — SIX DAYS LATER

*A*my held her hand out for the tub of icing. "I want the chocolate."

I handed it to her and scooped up the half-finished container of rainbow chip. "This is the best therapy."

"My mom sure does know best in this regard."

"She sure does."

Another tub of icing. Another broken dream. Another shattered reality.

I'd flown home on the first flight out of New York City. Amy had met me at the airport, and I'd confessed everything that had happened in minute detail on the car ride home. We were still eating icing over it six days later.

"I still can't believe that bitch had someone write that article on you."

Amy had read them all. All the outlets that were reporting on it. And then the comments of people who had read it. She hadn't let me do it, but she'd recapped it. And it hadn't been pretty.

I'd heard back from Caroline after I emailed her. She'd said to keep my head down for now. That it would probably only help book sales with the added drama. Which was morbidly comforting.

"I know," I agreed. "Katherine Van Pelt, the insecure bitch."

"Just imagine how many other people she's hurt like this, Nat."

I nodded. Oh, I'd thought about it. All the people who she'd ruined before me. Who weren't strong enough to endure her. It had to be a long-ass list.

"I wonder how many there are," I said. "And how they live now. Do they all have to stay on their knees, cut off because she said so? Why exactly does Katherine Van Pelt get to decide?"

"Because she's made everyone else afraid of her. She's ruthless. And she's a fucking cat with nine lives. She always lands on her feet."

"Yep. That's exactly it. It's because she's never had consequences to her actions. She's never had anyone make her pay for what she's done. The worst thing she's ever gone through is losing part of her trust fund. Boohoo."

Amy scooped out another huge bite of chocolate icing. "So, are you going to go back into the city after this?"

I flopped back on the couch and stared at the ceiling. "I don't know. I guess so. I have to clear out my apartment at least. I can't stay there with fucking Lewis having surveillance footage of the building."

"Yeah, creepy as fuck. Which is just so weird. I normally pick up on the creep vibe. And he really didn't have it."

I closed my eyes against that pain. "No, no, he didn't."

"I'm sorry. Let's go back to cutting up Katherine. She's easier to deal with than Lewis."

"Maybe we should move to something stronger," I suggested, setting my container of icing down.

"I'm down," Amy said. "Let me see what I have."

I reached for my phone, which I'd been mostly avoiding since everything had blown up. I'd only been checking to see if there was news from Caroline or Gillian. I'd had to suspend my Crew account because of the surge in activity. And the number of comments calling me a liar, fake, whore, bitch and every other imaginable dirty name.

I had a few texts from Melanie checking in, which I ignored. I'd invite her for a drink if she wasn't attached at the hip to Michael. I scrolled to the next one from Jane.

Thinking about you! Please, please, please come back. New Year's won't be the same without you.

I sighed. Another thing to decide.

I'd clicked off the message, deciding not to answer, when my phone rang. I saw that it was Caroline and sat up straight before answering.

"Hey, Caroline," I said. I hadn't expected this.

"Natalie, I'm glad that you answered."

"I'm surprised to hear from you. I thought you were in San Francisco with your son."

"I am. But I just heard from Gillian."

"You did?" I asked with dread at the way she'd said that. "I thought Warren was out until after the New Year."

"Normally, yes, but she came back early. And I'm sorry, Natalie, it looks like she's going to pass on the literary novel."

My stomach sank. "She is?"

"Yeah, I didn't want you to find out in an email. I know what you've been going through and thought it'd be better to hear it from me."

"That's...wow. She made it seem like she'd take anything I gave her."

"I don't think it had anything to do with what she wanted."

I frowned. "What do you mean?"

"Well, after your pen name was announced, it seems that the company doesn't think that someone who writes...mainstream tell-alls can produce the kind of literary novels they're looking for."

"Wait," I said, standing abruptly. "You're saying that... because I wrote BET ON IT, which is still selling like crazy, I somehow can't write any other kind of book?"

"That is how it was presented to me."

"That's bullshit," I spat.

Caroline cleared her throat. "Between you and me, Natalie?"

"Yeah," I muttered. Fury coursing through me at the ridiculous explanation.

"Gillian hinted that the rejection came from above her."

"Okay..."

"All the way from the top."

My heart stopped beating. "Lewis."

"She didn't say that outright, but that was my first guess, considering you told me about your unfortunate breakup."

I blinked. I couldn't believe this. Lewis had...blocked my book from publication. He had stripped me of the thing he knew that I loved most. The books he'd claimed to love as much as I did.

No.

No, he couldn't do that.

But, of course, he could.

His family owned the fucking company. He could do whatever he pleased. Just like every other Upper East Sider. They had all the control, all the money, all the power. They were untouchable. And they could destroy my world in the blink of an eye.

Caroline was still rattling on. Telling me that she still planned to submit the book to other publishers. How it might be a good idea to choose another pen name for the literary novel if I still wanted to write it. Or maybe it was better to go back to Olivia and own that brand.

I nodded and said all the right things at the right times, but I wasn't really listening. When I hung up, I stared blankly forward. Not with shock. No, something darker. Something that crawled out of that deep, dark place that I'd succumbed to six days ago. A place I hadn't known existed, and I didn't know who I would become if I unleashed it.

But I did know that I was done playing by my own moral code.

Done playing by the rules.

They were not going to get away with what they had done to me. They were not going to walk free and clean just because they had money and power. I had told Katherine I would make her pay for what she had done, and I had meant it. But it wasn't until this moment that I knew that I would not stop until I got my revenge.

Until they all burned.

To Be Continued

Read the epic conclusion to Penn & Natalie's story in *USA Today* bestselling author K.A. Linde's new billionaire romance...

CRUEL LEGACY
(Cruel, #3)

Darkness swept in.

Smothering everything in its inky black.

I have turned into their worst nightmares.

And I will not rest until they pay.

For everything.

Coming July 16th!
Preorder everywhere now!

ACKNOWLEDGMENTS

This was the hardest book I have ever written. That might change in the future, but it took everything out of me to write this, and I'm so proud of how far I came to get to this point. But I would not have been able to get through this at all without the people behind me. Especially my husband Joel who put up with me working eighteen hour days for weeks on end while I recrafted the fifty thousand words that I deleted from the original manuscript and started over.

Most importantly Diana Peterfreund and Mari Mancusi, who finally saw the problem that we were all incapable of seeing, and helped me figure out how to navigate a major rewrite. You made the book so much stronger. I'll never forget our walks through Dog Island in Austin as I was trying not to have a panic attack.

To all the other players who helped me structure and restructure this story until I was pleased. Since we all know that it took a lot to get me to that point. Rebecca Kimmerling for reading and rereading and plotting and replotting for all of eternity. Staci Hart for talking me through it for hours and making me laugh. Anjee Sapp for pushing me to go farther each time, to not tip toe around the issue and just dive right in. I need that. And for running everything for me when I had my freak out. Rebecca Gibson for telling me it didn't suck, even when you were lying. Katie Miller, Polly Matthews, and Lori Francis who read the clean version and thought it was everything I wanted it to be.

Danielle Sanchez who loves this series and promotes the fuck out of it. You were there for me during release week panics, and I loved how much we stepped up and became a team! Jovana Shirley for awesome postpartum edits and always working me into the schedule. Sarah Hansen for this stunning cover. The green really pops! Lauren Perry for the photography. You always know the most beautiful people! Alyssa Garcia for all my hundreds of graphics that I request of you last minute...every time. Ashley Lindemann for her help with my newsletter, without you I would be a mess. Linde Squad for your tireless efforts and incredible energy around these books!

All the bloggers and readers who took the time to buy, read, review, promote, and gush about this book. I am so humbled by your love of my motley crew and their dark side. Penn and Natalie have been marinating for a long time. It brings me such joy to see that you love them as much as I do.

I can't wait to bring you all more in this series, and I'm freaking out about that it will be over. But stay tuned for the finale Cruel Legacy coming July 16th (the day after my birthday!).

ABOUT THE AUTHOR

K.A. Linde is the *USA Today* bestselling author of the Avoiding Series, Wrights, and more than thirty other novels. She has a Masters degree in political science from the University of Georgia, was the head campaign worker for the 2012 presidential campaign at the University of North Carolina at Chapel Hill, and served as the head coach of the Duke University dance team. She loves reading fantasy novels, binge-watching Supernatural, traveling, and dancing in her spare time.

She currently lives in Lubbock, Texas, with her husband and two super-adorable puppies.

Visit her website
www.kalinde.com

For exclusive content, free books,
and giveaways every month.
www.kalinde.com/subscribe